One WEDDING
Two BRIDES

Fairy Tale Brides

One WEDDING Two BRIDES

Fairy Tale Brides

HEIDI BETTS

Entangled Publishing, LLC
2614 South Timberline Road
Suite 105, PMB 159
Fort Collins, CO 80525
rights@entangledpublishing.com

Amara is an imprint of Entangled Publishing, LLC.

Edited by Alycia Tornetta
Cover design by Fiona Jayde
Cover photography by Juliya Shangarey/Shutterstock

Manufactured in the United States of America

First Edition July 2018

There's no escaping this one... This book absolutely must be dedicated to my brother, Toby—computer genius extraordinaire, who rushed to the aid of this Damsel in Distress like a true Prince Charming. This book literally would not have been possible without the time and effort you put into recovering it after that little disaster with the disk. I won't even hold it against you that you read the first chapter out loud to a crowd of friends in your dorm room. (I just hope you didn't read them any of the "good parts." ;))

Chapter One

Before you get serious about a cowboy, make sure he values
you more than his truck.

Monica Blair stumbled into the reception hall, clutching the
doorframe for balance. Tugging the train of her beaded gown
behind her, she made her way unsteadily past milling guests
and tables covered with smooth white linens. The band's
pathetic, slightly off-key version of "Endless Love" drifted
over the sea of people, each note cutting into her brain like a
chainsaw. When an empty chair came into view, she lurched
toward it and fell onto the hard seat.

She shouldn't have come. Before getting on the plane,
she'd had a plan. A good one, too. At the moment, however,
even the smallest detail of that strategy escaped her.

She'd also had a bottle of champagne with her. Looking
around, lifting both hands and seeing them empty, she
wondered where the expensive wine could have gone.

Probably left it in the cab.

She waved a hand in front of her, making an unconcerned

gesture. This was a wedding reception; they were sure to have champagne. Suddenly thirsty, she glanced at the table in front of her and spotted several half-empty glasses. Grabbing the nearest one, she downed the now-warm liquid, then moved on to the next.

An elderly gentleman appeared at her elbow, and she blinked several times to clear her vision.

"Can I help you with something, young lady?"

His voice was polite, but his eyes looked suspicious. Or maybe it was her imagination. She was feeling a little tipsy at the moment.

"Are you in the right place?" he asked, touching her arm.

"This is a wedding, right?"

"Yes."

"Well, then, I'm in the right place," she said. "I'm the bride."

He gave her an odd look.

"The *other* bride," she explained.

"The other bride?"

"The second one. The first one. The real one." She launched to her feet, then clutched the corner of the table to steady herself.

"See my dress." She shook the hem in front of him. "I bought this to marry that swine. That pig. That…that *groom*."

She pointed in the pig's direction and then glanced down at her gown. Why was she wearing it? She remembered carrying it with her to the airport but didn't recall putting it on.

"I'm sorry, but…"

A clinking sound broke through the chatter of the room, quieting the band, the older gentleman, and the other guests. A penguin at the head table stood, one side of his mouth cocked in a grin.

Monica couldn't quite put her thoughts together, but

he looked slightly out of place. Like he was uncomfortable being so dressed up. Of course, she could be wrong. At the moment, she'd consider herself lucky to be able to put her finger on her nose.

"I'd like to propose a toast to the newlyweds," the penguin said into the small black microphone in his hand, giving the tight black tie of his tuxedo an unconscious tug. "To my sister and new brother-in-law. May you forever be as happy as you are at this moment."

Monica's eyes flooded with tears as he smiled down at the newly married couple. That should have been her toast. Even if she'd never seen the man before in her life, he should have been talking about *her* happiness, not theirs.

Everyone clapped, sipped briefly from their own champagne flutes, then went on with their conversations and revelry.

Grabbing another glass of room temperature bubbly from the table beside her, Monica made her way to the front of the room. No one paid her any attention. Even the older man who'd seemed genuinely concerned about her had forgotten she existed.

The wedding party's table sat on a raised platform that came to Monica's waist. Setting her glass aside, she tried hefting herself up butt first. When that didn't work, she threw her stomach forward and climbed the rest of the way up with her knees. Quite an accomplishment, considering she was wearing a full-length wedding gown.

Once on her feet, she bent over to retrieve her champagne and nearly fell but managed to keep her balance by clutching at the edge of the table. Her hand came away covered with frosting, which she tasted before lifting her glass.

"I have a toast to make, too. Mmm, good cake," she said to no one in particular and took another lick.

The bride and groom began muttering, but no one else

seemed to be paying attention. Spotting a black cord stretched across the tabletop, Monica gave it a tug. The microphone the best man had used earlier slithered forward, making a horrendous, high-pitched shriek. It fell to the floor with a clunk and bounced across the platform as she pulled the wire closer. Once she had the mike in her hand, she blew into the black, foam-covered tip and pounded on the tabletop until heads began to turn.

She lifted the glass of champagne to her mouth and the microphone over her head.

"That's better." When the words came out no louder than her normal voice, she crossed her eyes and switched the position of her hands.

"There," she said, pleased when her voice boomed from the surrounding speakers. "I have to make toast. A make to toast." She waved her free hand, sloshing wine on her sleeve. "Whatever."

Matt leaned across the table and grabbed her arm, trying to lower it. "Monica, what are you doing here?" he asked, recognition and shock etching his face.

She jerked away from him, spilling even more bubbly over the back of her hand and the cuff of his tuxedo jacket. "Don't touch me, you rat." Shaking a finger at him over the rim of the champagne flute and trying to keep his face in focus, she said, "You have some 'splaining to do, Matt the Rat."

"Sit down, Monica," he whispered harshly. His eyes drilled into hers, telling her not to make a fool of herself... or of him.

"Not until I toast you and your lovely new bitch. I mean, bride." She turned back to the crowd and spoke loudly enough for everyone to hear. "I have a toast to propose to Matthew Castor and his new bride, what's-her-name."

A loud murmur broke across the room, stealing Monica's concentration. "*Shhhhhh*. Shut up! I have something to say, and I'm going to say it before anyone else has the chance to get married."

She teetered a bit but remained standing. "To the gride and broom...bride and groom: I hope you're both very happy with yourselves."

She downed the wine in her hand, then slammed the glass onto the tabletop, surprised when the delicate crystal didn't shatter from the impact.

"No, that's not true," she said, turning to face them with the microphone practically pressed to her lips. "I hope you're both miserable. I hope you spend your honeymoon in Pago Pago during a monsoon and both come back with a social disease. I hope you go bald," she cursed Matt, sparing a derisive glance for the head of thick, well-groomed hair he was so very proud of.

"And you"—she gestured to the flushed, embarrassed bride—"I hope you get fat and he leaves you for his secretary."

The bride clutched the sleeve of the man beside her, the handsome one who'd made the first toast. "Ryder, please," she begged frantically. "Do something."

The man stood and made his way along the length of the dais. Monica watched him moving behind the others at the bridal table for a moment, then turned back to the horrified onlookers.

"This man..." Monica waved behind her. "This man was supposed to marry me. I devoted four years of my life to him. I bought this dress because he said he wanted to marry me. *Me!*" she said, thumping her chest. "And then he goes and marries this harlot. This...this...*homewrecker.*"

A unified gasp filled the room.

"I don't even know who she is. She might be a very nice person, but she's not *me*, which means she's not supposed to be the bride. *I'm* supposed to be the bride."

A hand reached out to her, and she looked down to see

the somewhat fuzzy face of the toast man.

"Let me help you down," he offered.

"I don't want down," she said loudly, stepping back to avoid his grasp. "I want these people to know what a rat Matt is. Matt the Rat. Matt, the man who proposes to you, takes your money, then marries another woman behind your back."

Her arms fell to her sides, the microphone hanging limply by its cord as she clutched large handfuls of her gown. "What am I supposed to do now?" she asked, speaking solely to the man in front of her. "What am I supposed to do with the rest of my life now that the man I thought I loved is married to someone else?"

"For starters, you can give me your hand."

He sounded so calm, so rational, when she felt as though her head was about to explode. She wanted to scream her betrayal for all the world to hear. She wanted to pound the table until she wasn't furious, and then pound it some more.

"This really sucks, you know that?" she said, but made no move to accept his assistance.

"Sometimes life sucks, sugar." And before she had time to gasp, he moved forward, stuck a shoulder beneath her midsection and pulled her off the platform.

She hung over his back like dry cleaning. The microphone slipped from her fingers and hit the floor with another amplified *clunk*.

For a moment, stunned into silence—and just a little afraid she'd toss her cookies—Monica did nothing. Hanging upside down and bouncing methodically as the man moved through the reception hall did nothing to settle her queasy stomach or throbbing head.

Matt quickly grabbed the abandoned mike and began making excuses to the confused, mumbling guests. "Sorry for the interruption, folks. Just a lost bride at the wrong reception." He laughed nervously. "Is everyone ready to do the hokey-pokey?"

Hokey-pokey? I'll give you hokey-pokey, Monica thought angrily as the startled band took their cue and began tapping out the first chords of the song.

"Put me down!" she ordered the man beneath her, giving his back a thump for good measure. Then she grabbed the sides of his tux jacket as she slipped, afraid she would fall from her precarious perch.

The man held her loosely with one arm across the backs of her knees, letting the bulk of her body dangle over his shoulder toward the ground.

She heard the sounds of female giggles and male guffaws as they passed through the crowd. "Put me down," she repeated tightly.

"In a minute," he said, still calm and assured. He pushed open one of the double doors leading outside and carried her into the bright sunlight.

Without giving a thought to where her teeth might land, she opened her mouth and bit down as hard as she could.

"Oow!" he bellowed and stopped in his tracks. His free hand curved behind his back to rub the opposite butt cheek.

She expected him to drop her. When he did, she'd run back to the reception and give the guests—and Matt—another piece of her mind. Instead, her self-appointed keeper simply shifted her from his shoulder to the crook of his arm, like a football player carries the ball down center field.

She hung at thigh level now and could easily have bitten him again, but the solid grip of his arm around her waist only made her more aware of her nausea.

"If you don't put me down, I'm going to puke."

"So puke," he said, continuing his long, even stride.

She opened her mouth, intending to do just that on as much of his leg as she could hit, when he suddenly stopped, set her feet on the ground, and straightened her upper body for her.

She groaned, wishing he hadn't done that. Now she was sure to lose her lunch.

He brushed the chin-length curtain of hair out of her face and hunched down a bit to fix her with a steady, blue-eyed gaze. "Okay?"

"I don't think so," she answered honestly.

He opened the door of a sparkling clean but well-dented and slightly rusty black pickup truck, swept a pile of papers and what looked like unopened mail out of the way, and lifted her onto the bench seat. Leaving her sideways, he tucked the hem of her dress around her legs and pulled her head forward.

"If you're going to throw up, do it outside my truck."

Letting her upper body fall between her knees, she gulped in huge breaths of air, waiting for the sick feeling to pass. Her gaze fell to the ground at his feet and then...

Is he wearing cowboy boots? With a tux?

She lifted her head a fraction to see if she'd accidentally fallen into the hands of the Lone Ranger.

"Better?" he asked when he saw her studying him.

No mask. No Tonto. She glanced at the black vinyl seat of the truck, dirty white padding sticking out of several rips and tears. Definitely no Silver.

She watched him leaning against the bed of the truck, broad shoulders, narrow hips, and all. His sandy blond hair fell across the side of his forehead, nearly covering one of those beautiful, ocean-blue eyes.

If he wasn't the Lone Ranger, he could definitely double for Clint Eastwood's character in that old TV western she used to love watching with her grandfather. What was his name again?

"Good," he said, taking her silence for assent. He swung her legs into the cab, moved the folds of her dress out of the way, and slammed the door.

Head 'em up, move 'em out.

Now that stupid theme song was rumbling through her brain. As if she didn't have enough useless information wrestling for attention up there. She pulled the plug on the soundtrack in her head and tried to focus on her present predicament.

The Rawhide Man rounded the truck and climbed in the driver's side as though she weren't even there. The only thing missing from his ensemble was a dusty old cowboy hat. *Correction*, she thought, as she noticed a well-worn Stetson on the dashboard. There was nothing missing.

"Where are we going?" she asked.

"Away from the party, darlin'. Where you can't make any more trouble."

He started the engine and a roar of throbbingly loud honky-tonk music blasted from the speakers. Her eyes nearly bugged out of her head, and she knew her already quivering gray matter was close behind.

She caught something about thanking Mama for the cookin' and Daddy for the whuppin' just before the Lone Ranger leaned forward to flip off the volume. The song's rhythm echoed through her mind for several more seconds.

He checked for traffic and pulled onto the narrow, practically deserted asphalt road. "Where do you live?"

"Chicago," she answered automatically. "And I wouldn't have made trouble if Matt hadn't gone and married that floozy in there."

"That 'floozy' happens to be my sister." He didn't sound angry, but his voice held an edge she hadn't noticed before.

"Oh, no," she groaned, resting the side of her face against the sun-hot window.

"What?" He took his foot off the gas, tossing her a panicked glance. "Are you going to be sick?"

"I'm already sick. Do you have any idea how it feels to

be traded in for a newer model? I didn't even get left at the altar—I got left at home."

"Look, I don't know what Matt told you, but I'm sure he didn't marry Josie after leading you to believe he'd marry you."

She sat up like a shot. "He didn't *lead* me to believe anything! He *asked* me to marry him. He told me we should plan a fall wedding. And then he just up and marries her."

"Josie."

"Whatever."

Her head fell to the side again, and she closed her eyes against the pain in both her head and her heart.

"So you came all the way from Chicago to stop the wedding," he said.

She started to shake her head, then thought better of it when the black behind her eyes began to swirl. "I knew I'd be too late for the wedding, but I had to let Matt know I knew."

"Knew what?"

"That he was getting married without me." Her companion didn't respond to that, and she didn't have the strength to look at him. "I was going to confront him. Throw my wedding gown in his face and conk him over the head with a nice, cold bottle of bubbly. But I must have drunk all the champagne and put the dress on in the airport restroom."

Or on the plane, she thought, as the image of struggling with thick folds of fabric in a bathroom the size of a high school gym locker sprang to mind.

Her companion looked at her like she'd just lost her mind while he watched it fly out the window. Then he turned away and asked, "Is there somewhere I can take you? The airport? A hotel?"

She ignored his suggestions, focusing on her own thoughts. "I have to do something to get back at Matt."

"Haven't you done enough already?"

"No. He has to know how much he hurt me. He has to know he made a mistake and regret it for the rest of his life." Matt had betrayed her. He'd ruined everything, and he couldn't be allowed to get away with it. She wasn't just going to make him pay her back for the money he'd stolen; she was going to *make...him...pay.* Then she'd make sure the entire world knew what a rat he truly was.

She opened her eyes then and turned to face the man who had prematurely ended her revenge. "You have to help me."

He spared her a glance before turning back to the road. "Help you get back at my sister's new husband?" he asked with a chuckle. "You're two balls short of a bull if you think I'll go along with something like that, darlin'."

"We can do it." She sat up excitedly, struggling to fold her legs beneath her with six yards of satin and taffeta fighting her every inch of the way. "We just have to think of something that will infuriate Matt. He hates being bested, you know."

"No, I didn't know that."

And he didn't sound like he cared.

"Chess, racquetball, everything. He can't even stand for me to finish reading the paper before he does. It drives him nuts. So we just have to come up with something that will really tick him off."

"Such as?"

His fingers flexed and tightened on the steering wheel, and the movement of those long, tawny digits almost made her lose her train of thought.

"I don't know." She gave a huff because he didn't seem to be trying. Didn't he understand how important this was? "Maybe we could steal his car. Or his plane tickets. Where are they going on their honeymoon?"

Not giving him a chance to answer, she went on. "Never mind, it has to be better than that. I need to make him sorry.

Show him he made a mistake, that he married the wrong woman." Her eyes widened as an idea came to her, and she began to grin. "That's it! I'll make him jealous."

"How are you going to do that?"

"By being the perfect wife."

"He's already married," the Lone Ranger reminded her, as if she didn't know. "To someone else."

"I'm not going to marry *him*," she said, the solution patently obvious to her. "I'm going to marry you."

Chapter Two

The best way to get married is with ignorance and confidence.

Ryder Nash almost slammed on the brakes at her announcement. Instead, he took a moment to gather his wits, knuckles tightening on the steering wheel.

She was drunk, he knew that much. But now he was beginning to wonder if she might not be clinically insane, as well.

He turned his head, letting his eyes bore into her. "Are you crazy?"

"Probably," she admitted, absently rolling one of the thousand pearl-like beads of her dress between a thumb and forefinger.

Even for a crazy person, he had to admit she looked mighty fine in that form-fitting, snow-white gown. Soft, flyaway hair framed her porcelain features—a pert little nose, high-arched dark brows, and satin bow lips licked to a moist, kissable shine.

Kissable? What was he thinking? He didn't even know

this woman and yet here he sat, contemplating how soft and pliable her lips might be if he leaned over and touched them. Right…about…there.

"But it will work," she continued, her words energized by alcohol and a loss of inhibitions. "If we get married, we can show him what a happy couple we are. How happy *I* am. He'll be totally jealous and realize he married the wrong woman. Then he'll leave her, but I won't take him back. He'll have nothing."

"But you'll be married to me," he reminded her, even though he had no intention of going through with her hare-brained idea. He was going to get her to a hotel where she could sleep it off and then go home to do the same.

She shrugged both shoulders, losing her balance and grasping for the door handle. The silky, beaded fabric of her wedding gown started to slide off one shoulder, then slipped even more when she reached into her cleavage and came out with a cell phone.

Ryder stared for a split second at the slight jut of her now bare collarbone before returning his gaze to the road. He wanted to chastise himself for entertaining any thoughts at all about her body, but—considering she'd just announced her intentions to marry him—he figured *looking* was the least of his problems. Besides, she had a body like Venus de Milo with arms and didn't seem the least self-conscious about the bits and pieces that were showing. He wasn't made of wood.

Just then, a certain part of his anatomy stirred with interest, reminding him that at times he most certainly *was* made of wood.

"So we'll get an nulliment. An annalment." She gave a frustrated huff, still poking at her phone. "A divorce. People do it all the time. For lesser reasons than this, too," she said with a carefree wave of her hand.

"You don't even know me," he pointed out, his chest

feeling suddenly tight. "I'm just some guy who dragged you out of a wedding reception before you could make an even bigger fool of yourself." And he was beginning to regret it.

"I know you." She leaned across the seat to lay a hand on his arm. "You're my hair climber."

Her fingers dug into the material of his tuxedo jacket as she weaved a bit to one side.

His brows knit. "Your what?"

"Hair climber." She straightened and moved back toward the passenger side of the cab, nearly overcorrecting and smacking against the other door as she returned her attention to her phone. "You know, the prince guy who climbed up Rapanetzel's—I mean Rapanunzel's..."

"Rapunzel?"

"Yeah, you're the guy who would climb up my hair to rescue me from the tower if I needed it."

"You'd need to grow it out a couple more inches before I could hitch my boot in that 'do, sweetheart," he told her, casting a glance at her dark, shoulder-length hair.

Her brow creased. "Don't try to confuse me with irrelevant fats...facts."

He shook his head and bit back a grin. "Do you need rescuing from a tower?" he asked, almost afraid of her answer.

She nodded, her head wobbling a bit, as though she couldn't stop it once the motion began. "Definitely."

Yeah, like I'm hero material.

His conversation at the reception with his fortunately *former* girlfriend came back to him in a wave of agitation. Stephanie had sauntered up, bold as you please, to give him one of those "poor baby" pouts. And then she'd said something about how sad it was when a young girl like Josie got married before her perfectly eligible, *much* older brother.

He wasn't *much* older. Only twelve years.

Of course, if Stephanie knew how bad things were at the

ranch right now, she wouldn't have bothered with even that much of a dig at their failed relationship. She was all about keeping up appearances with regular hair appointments and manicures, while he was currently all about keeping the wolves from the door. He was in debt up to his eyeballs, and just yesterday on the way in to his sister's rehearsal dinner the bank had sent an email saying he'd been turned down for the loan he needed to make Rolling Rock the only ranch in two hundred miles that offered equine therapy.

That plan had been in place long before the tornado that had torn through and ruined the main barn...not to mention about a hundred thousand dollars' worth of other stuff he had yet to repair. Ever since Xander O'Neill's boy had been diagnosed with cerebral palsy and he'd been forced to drive Tommy halfway across the state twice a week for the treatment that seemed to work best, Ryder had gotten it into his head that equine-assisted therapy would be the perfect addition to what he was already doing.

He loved raising cattle and working with horses, but how great would it be if one of those things could also help people? Especially kids with special needs.

Then Xander had gone and married that physical therapist from the place he was taking Tommy, and she was bussing tables in town, just waiting for Ryder to get his shit together so she could start working with Tommy and bunches of other kids—as well as adults, he supposed—on the Rolling Rock.

He had the space and was training the horses himself, but all the special equipment he needed wasn't cheap. Once they had the program off the ground, Ryder had no doubt it would shoot them into the black. Hell, not only would it be a godsend for a lot of folks in the area, but insurance paid through the nose for stuff like that. But he hadn't exactly been rolling in dough before the tornado, and without another loan, there was no way he could work his way out of the rut he was in.

Ryder couldn't believe he was even entertaining this woman's bizarre proposal. (Pun intended.) He'd never pictured himself married. He'd chalked Stephanie's remarks at the wedding up to bitterness. To the fact that no matter how hard she tried—and, boy, had she tried!—she'd failed to drag him down the aisle.

But now, with her words well sunken in and spinning around in his head like a cyclone, he began to wonder if she wasn't right. Maybe he was hanging on to his bachelorhood a little too tightly.

Do the words "death grip" mean anything to you? a voice in his head asked caustically.

Even if he did soon give up the single life, it wouldn't be with a gal like his ex. Stephanie might be pretty on the outside and a wildcat in the sack, but beneath the surface was a nasty streak she wouldn't hesitate to make known the minute she didn't get her way. He'd learned that the hard way. And it wouldn't be with this woman, either—a virtual stranger who seemed bent on breaking up his sister's marriage. What kind of man did this damsel-in-distress think he was?

Not that anyone other than a half-baked stranger would even consider hitching up with him...at least not once she knew what kind of hole she'd be getting herself into.

"We're not that far from Las Vegas," this particular stranger continued, in an attempt to persuade him to her way of thinking. "It says here we can pick up a license at the county clerk's office and get married at the chapel across the street, if we want. I just need to fill out the online apprication... applitation..." She gave a heavy sigh. "*Form* ahead of time."

For being drunk and possibly a few ribs short of a barbecue, she sure seemed to be figuring things out at a record pace.

"I assume we'd need photo IDs, maybe blood tests," he

tossed out, thinking it would throw a nail under her tire.

But she just kept right on trotting along.

"No blood tests. Just personal info on the form, then IDs when we get there."

Well, he had her there, didn't he? She'd shown up to his sister's wedding reception in a pretty enough gown but otherwise empty-handed. Pulling a cell phone out of from between her boobs was a nice trick, but he doubted she'd managed to hang on to anything else on her drunken bob-and-weave through the airport. He was surprised she'd been lucid enough to get through airport security, frankly.

And thank you very much for doing such a great job, TSA. If they'd stopped her at the gate, Josie's reception might've gone off without a hitch, and he wouldn't be stuck having this inane conversation with Little Miss Party Crasher.

But since he was, he had to figure out some other way to put a pin in her plans.

"Do you *have* a photo ID?" Ryder asked.

"Of course," she answered much too quickly and cheerily for Ryder's peace of mind. Then she dug into the bodice of her dress again, hand coming out with what he assumed was her driver's license between two fingers.

Damn and double damn.

The first damn was for the ID, which he'd have laid odds she couldn't produce. The second was for her propensity to reach into that lovely bit of cleavage and bring out random items like a master illusionist. He was starting to think of the front of that dress—and her boobs—as a very seductive version of a magic hat.

"That's all well and good, darlin'," he told her, determined to come up with another reason he was not going to drive to Las Vegas and leg-shackle himself to a complete stranger. "But you still haven't convinced me to kiss my bachelor days goodbye and let you use me to get back at my sister's new husband. You heard that part, right?" he asked.

When she didn't respond and continued to peck at the screen of her phone, he repeated the vital portions, slower and with more emphasis. "My *sister* and her new husband."

"Uh-huh. Uh-huh." Another pause. More tapping. "I'll pay you," she offered out of the blue.

His heart took one powerful jolt against his rib cage as he watched the woman beside him as long as he dared before turning back to the road. There were three magic words with the potential to make everything else go away. Too bad he was a half-decent guy and not some schmuck who'd take advantage of a woman, drunk or not.

"Yeah, right. I'm not taking your money," he replied firmly, as much to stop himself from even wanting to as to put an end to her sales pitch.

"No, really—I'll pay you," she said again.

He didn't want to ask, didn't want to play into her possible delusions or devious plans, but no matter how tightly he clenched his jaw, he couldn't seem to help himself. "How much?"

"How much do you want?" she retorted, still engrossed in her phone.

He wanted enough to pay off his debts, which were growing larger with each passing day. Enough to keep the bank from repossessing his ranch, which they were threatening to do, and make the necessary repairs after last summer's tornado. Enough to open Rolling Rock for equine therapy and get his life back on track. Enough that he wouldn't have to ask his parents for help when they'd done too much for him already these past few years.

"How much do you have?" he asked cautiously, telling himself he was just humoring her.

"Fifty thousand dollars."

His eyes rounded and the air whistled out between his

teeth. Holy hell. He only needed half that much to not only keep his ranch but fix it up and move toward modernizing the entire operation.

"You don't have fifty thousand dollars," he said, thinking she must be pulling numbers out of the air just to convince him to help her.

"Do, too," she insisted, her words clipped. "My savings."

Affronted, she finally lifted her gaze from that blasted phone and raised herself a little higher on the seat. She spread her arms between the dashboard and the back of the seat to keep her balance as she turned in his direction. Her gown had slipped even farther down her shoulder and came dangerously close to revealing another shade of skin altogether at the center of her breast.

Doesn't she have anything on under that damn dress? He shifted uncomfortably. She'd managed to stuff a phone and ID and God knew what else down there, but apparently a bra had been one item too many.

When he didn't say anything for a few minutes—mostly because any blood in his brain had abandoned ship and headed south the minute his eyes had locked on her increasingly impressive rack—she slid sideways on the seat, close enough for her cloth-covered breasts to rub delicately against his cloth-covered arm. What he wouldn't give for a truckload of moths right about now.

"If you marry me and help me get even with Matt, I'll give you all the money I have."

He wanted to say yes. He really needed that money, and this would be an easy way to get it. But she was drunk, he reminded himself. Possibly not even mentally stable. What kind of man would take advantage of a drunk—albeit attractive—loony bin patient?

"I don't think that's such a good idea," he forced past his dust-dry throat, nobility winning out over gut-wrenching instinct and desperate need.

"Please," she begged in a soft, cajoling voice. Then she tilted her head, batted her lashes, and stuck out her bottom lip. A posture she'd seen too many times on TV, he suspected. She didn't quite pull it off. It looked more like she'd been punched in the mouth and had sand thrown in her eyes both at the same time.

"I'm not taking money from a woman."

"Well, that's kind of sexist. You won't take money from a woman, but you would from a man?"

"That's not what I meant," he nearly growled. "I'm not *taking* money from anybody."

And wasn't that a wallop of a little white lie? He'd already borrowed from Peter to pay Paul, and he sure as blazes wouldn't turn down a winning lottery ticket or a nice, fat inheritance from some unknown relative twice removed.

She breathed out a disgruntled sigh. "Don't be so darn literal," she informed him. "If you won't *take* the money, we'll call it a loan. You can pay me back after our annulliment."

He gave a snort by way of reply. Right. What would he pay her back with—sawdust and broken dreams?

Slowing down, he swerved to avoid a pothole, and her butt hit the seat with a plop.

Not that it deterred her one little bit.

"Okay, how about we call it a business deal, then? What kind of business are you in? I'll be your partner!"

That gave Ryder pause. A business agreement wouldn't be charity, and it wouldn't be a loan he could never pay back; it would be an investment. Equine-assisted therapy had the potential to start bringing in money almost as soon as they began taking on clients, which meant she would see a return on her backing before too long.

Even if she was a few checkers short, it was something they could put in writing, make legally binding. She'd get what she wanted from the deal, and he wouldn't be taking her money…he'd be borrowing it for a while until he could make sure she got it back—with interest.

With every nerve of his body screaming for him to marry the damn woman and take the money she was freely offering, the gentleman in him still tried to change her mind.

"You don't want to marry me." He kept his tone stern. More to stiffen his resolve than to quell hers.

"Yes, I do. I really, really do!" she responded so quickly, she couldn't possibly have thought it through.

"I'm a rancher, darlin'. I spend all my time with cattle and horses," he said. "At the end of most days, I smell worse than they do."

"I don't care. I like horses. Maybe you can even teach me to ride." She shrugged again as she slipped down on the seat, into a slouched position.

He took head-to-toe inventory of her, from the soft, porcelain flesh of her fingers to the tips of her stylish, white satin heels. She didn't look like she'd ever seen a horse in her life, but he sure as hell could imagine teaching her to ride. Reverse cowgirl was a personal favorite.

"I've been a bachelor all my life," he added. "I wouldn't know the first thing about living with a woman. I leave wet towels on the bathroom floor, dirty dishes in the sink. I'm a slob."

"'S'okay with me," she slurred. "I don't care how untrained you are."

As hard as he tried not to, he had to chuckle at the idea of a man needing to be "trained." It was probably true. There were times—like now—when the horse stalls were cleaner than parts of his house.

"What do you say?" she asked, making a great—and apparently difficult—effort to pull her legs up by the three-inch heels of her shoes and prop her feet on the dashboard.

The action caused the pile of unpaid bills he'd moved earlier to slide back across the seat. One stamped with FINAL NOTICE in bold red lettering jumped into his vision like a coiled rattlesnake, and the humiliation gave him pretty much the same sick feeling in the bottom of his gut as a deadly sidewinder would have.

A thousand arguments raced through his mind. He wasn't ready to be tied down and certainly wasn't in the market for a business partner. He didn't need a woman underfoot, getting in his way, throwing tantrums, and telling him what to do. When he did decide to marry, it would be to a woman who knew what running a ranch was all about. She'd ride and rope, be tough enough to get thrown, but climb right back in the saddle. She'd cook and clean and all-in-all make his life easier.

One look at the woman next to him and he knew she would only make his life more difficult. Hell, she'd already made his life more difficult, and he'd known her for less than an hour.

So why wasn't he trying harder to dissuade her from both her goofy marital plan and her apparent eagerness to ply him with cash? Why didn't he put his foot down and say, "No way in hell, woman!"?

Something about her made it impossible for Ryder to say no to her. It wasn't that she was beautiful—though she absolutely was. Maybe it was her determination. He didn't want to crush her spirit more than it already had been. And who knew what guy she'd proposition next if Ryder didn't keep an eye on her.

She was offering the money he needed to finally turn the Rolling Rock profitable, for chrissake. It wasn't a personal decision but a business deal. And wouldn't it burn Stephanie's britches if he took off from his sister's wedding only to attend one of his own!

A small smile tugged at his lips. His ex would be furious. She'd probably try to scratch his eyes out next time she saw him. Which was about what he'd wanted to do when she'd sidled up to him at the reception with that new lap dog boyfriend, young enough to be his son, at her side. It would serve Stephanie right if he got married—and not to her.

Not that he'd set out to intentionally upset Stephanie. They were better off without each other, and he suspected she knew it. But it sure would be nice to see her face the next time they ran into each other if he had a lovely new bride on his arm.

He shot a glance at the woman beside him. A stranger. A drunken stranger. A drunken stranger out of her mind with grief.

A stranger dressed for a wedding. Hell, they were both dressed for it. What more of a sign could he ask for? Maybe Fate had dropped this woman—strange as she was—in his lap for a reason.

The hem of her gown slipped just then, catching his eye and slowly revealing the turn of her ankle, smooth calves, the delicate bend of a knee, and two very slim thighs. The kind that went all the way up.

Damn! He was going to do it.

One glimpse of that smooth skin and the thought of what it would be like to get her all the way out of that dress, and the rest of his argument died in his throat. Fifty thousand dollars and a chance—just a chance—to get between those silky thighs. It was more than some men could hope for.

And it wasn't like it would be a real marriage. Something in name only. Maybe with a few fringe benefits.

It had been a while since he'd been with a woman, so he certainly wouldn't turn her away from his bed if that's where she wanted to be. And he could be mighty persuasive when he tried; he'd do his damnedest to make sure that's *exactly* where she wanted to be.

But in the end, no matter what passed between them, they could both get out of it. Annulment, divorce, whatever it took. They'd just play at being husband and wife for a while. Until Stephanie's eyes bugged out of her head and the bank stopped breathing down his neck. Until this woman saw that Matt and Josie belonged together.

What better way to make sure she didn't tarnish his baby sister's happiness than to keep an eye on her? Like the saying went, *Keep your friends close and your enemies closer.*

"You're sure?" he asked, half hoping she'd change her mind before he did something stupid. "About the money *and* the husband/wife thing."

She blinked several times, and he realized she'd nearly fallen asleep. He might have been better off not disturbing her.

Too late now.

When her vision cleared, she gave a determined nod. "I'm sure."

"It's gotta be in writing," he told her. "All of it."

"Fine with me," she said with a shrug, then went back to what he assumed was the online marriage license application she seemed so intent on filling out on her phone.

He almost smiled as he turned the wheel of the truck a fraction, heading for Route 93. Toward Vegas. "Well, then, I guess you do know me."

"I do." Then she rested her head against the window and let out a yawn. "So what's your name, anyway?"

• • •

Ryder stood in front of a black-clad minister who looked like he'd done this at least a thousand times already today. The tiny chapel, adequately named Chapel o' Love, sat on the very outskirts of Las Vegas and was the last place Ryder thought they could get this thing done before heading home. They'd already driven into the heart of Vegas, where he'd stirred his bride-to-be enough to wobble her way into the county clerk's office and pick up the marriage license. She'd fallen asleep again almost as soon as he'd lifted her into the truck, and he'd had to shake her awake again to make their way inside the chapel, sternly reminding her that this entire fiasco had been *her* idea.

Finally, as he'd talked to a woman in a skin-tight, zebra-striped jumpsuit about setting up the ceremony, she'd sobered herself enough to pull the newly minted marriage certificate from her endless cleavage, give her full name—it appeared he was marrying a Monica Elizabeth Blair—and walk herself down the aisle, which was all of six feet long.

He signed the necessary papers and paid what he considered an exorbitant amount for rings that probably weren't worth spit, just so his bride would have something on her finger. He also had her sign the most basic agreement he'd been able to fit on the back of that damn FINAL NOTICE, stating she'd invest fifty thousand dollars into the equine therapy plans for the ranch now that he'd gone through with his part of the bargain. To be paid back at a fifty-fifty split from equine-assisted therapy profits as soon as the enterprise began making money, with a reasonable amount of interest tacked on, to be fair.

She stood beside him now, her arm linked with his, trying not to drift back into la-la land. Her head rested on his shoulder, and Ryder hoped the preacher took it as a sign of a bride-to-be's adoration rather than what it really was— alcohol-induced exhaustion.

As the minister droned on about love and commitment, Ryder gave himself a mental pat on the back for *not* making a run for it. In the past, any time he'd contemplated marriage in any way, shape, or form, it had caused him to break out in a cold sweat. Maybe because marriage signaled an end to his self-reliant, carefree lifestyle. Or maybe because the idea of being responsible for another person shook him all the way to the soles of his boots.

Sure, he'd been responsible for Josie for most of her life, but only in a big brother capacity. Mom and Pop had always been there to provide the main instruction. Ryder only had to tell her silly stories, kiss her skinned knees once in a while, and scowl at any boy who dared to even look at his little sister cross-eyed. Other than that, he'd been footloose and fancy free, responsible for no one, answering to no one, pleasing only himself. It was a good life. He didn't want to see it end.

From the corner of his eye, he caught Monica stifling a yawn and wondered why he was willing to stand at the altar now, after avoiding it so well all these years. It certainly wasn't because he thought this woman would make him a good wife.

Ha! He barely managed to bite down on a scoff. If anything, she'd bring him more trouble than he could handle. She was a woman scorned, a woman with pain in her heart and vengeance on her mind. A woman with a plan.

God help them all.

Yet here he stood, in front of what he hoped was a bona fide Man of God—in Las Vegas, you never could tell—binding them together as husband and wife, till death or divorce did they part.

Ryder nodded at all the proper increments, said "I do" when the time came, and prompted Monica to do the same. No second thoughts, no cold feet, no last-minute escape route popping into his head. He simply stood there and got married.

And the only reasoning he could come up with—other than the promise of being able to pay off his debts—was that he knew this wasn't a real marriage. It didn't matter if he wasn't husband material because Monica didn't want a real husband. She only wanted someone to be her husband long enough to try to make Matthew Castor jealous. It didn't matter if Ryder could care for her or make her happy, because Monica wasn't marrying him to be taken care of. And the only thing that would make her happy, apparently, was revenge.

So he just had to sit back, say "I do," and sign the annulment papers when the time came. He could do that.

When the preacher said he could kiss the bride, Ryder took Monica's chin between his fingers, lifted her face, and placed a soft kiss on her lips.

"Well, Rapunzel, you're out of the tower. Now what?"

Without opening her eyes, she smiled and snuggled back into the crook of his shoulder. "My prince," she murmured.

So much for a delighted bride, he thought as he scooped her into his arms and carried her back out to the truck.

Chapter Three

Don't worry about biting off more than you can chew—your mouth is probably a whole lot bigger than you think.

Monica stretched, yawned, and then rolled out of bed, heeding the pressure on her bladder over the pounding in her head that urged her to go back to sleep.

Stumbling across the carpeted floor, she walked into the bathroom and was suddenly surrounded by a jungle of hanging vines, grabbing at her arms and face. She swatted them away, opening her eyes enough to see that it wasn't vines but long-sleeve shirts accosting her. Thank God. For a second there, she thought she'd stumbled onto the set of a new Tarzan movie. And she just was not in the mood to deal with any Ape Men this morning, especially if it meant living in a tree house and peeing in the bushes.

Backing out of the closet, she tried another doorway, paying more attention this time to furnishings. She traveled a lot for her job and was used to waking up in strange places. From luxury hotels to dingy motels, and even the occasional cabin in the woods, where she bunked with a dozen other crew members. Sometimes she even had trouble navigating her own apartment when she was first home after a trip, so not finding the bathroom on the first try wasn't exactly unusual. The second attempt, though, was a win.

After going to the bathroom, brushing her teeth to get rid of the terrible exhaust-pipe flavor every time she swallowed, and running a hand through the tangle of her hair, she went back into the bedroom, hoping to catch a few more hours of sleep before being forced to face reality.

She must have downed a gallon of egg drop soup and shrimp lo mein with extra MSG, then vegged out in front of the TV half the night to feel so sluggish this morning. Of course, considering Matt's betrayal, she thought she'd handled herself pretty well. At least she hadn't thrown herself off the Sears Tower or cried herself to sleep. Or, worse yet, crashed his wedding like she'd momentarily considered.

Crawling back into bed, she pulled the sheet up to her chin, then wrapped her arm around the extra pillow. So warm and soft and...*moving?* With a stifled scream, she threw off the covers and jumped out of bed. A sandy-haired head rested near the edge of the mattress, connected to bronzed shoulders and a smooth, equally tan back.

Her gaze darted around the room, looking for some weapon to defend herself as she considered calling 911. But this wasn't her bedroom, she realized, or even an on-location hotel room, which meant the man in the bed most likely belonged here...and she didn't.

She covered her eyes, wondering where she had picked him up and why she would suddenly have a one-night stand when she'd never been promiscuous a day in her life.

Oh, lord, he was moving. She raced back into the bathroom and slammed the door, resting her head against the hard wood until she could calm her frantic nerves.

What have I done? Who is this guy? What if he won't let me leave?

A knock on the other side of the door scared her senseless and caused her to yip before she had a chance to slap a hand over her mouth.

"Excuse me," a deep, muffled male voice uttered. "But, um…do you know you're in the bathroom?"

She opened her mouth to reply, but only a small squeak came out.

"Are you okay in there?"

"Who are you?" she managed, glad her voice sounded only half as panicked as she felt.

"The name's Ryder Nash, ma'am," he said, a note of amusement evident in his tone. "I'm surprised you don't remember me."

I don't remember anything, she thought, but refrained from telling him that. After all, she may need to make up some kind of story later on to escape.

"Look at your left hand," he told her.

Confused, she glanced down.

This time, a full-lung scream did escape her lips. She didn't even bother to clamp a hand over her mouth or try to stifle the noise. She just screamed and screamed until there was no air left to breathe.

"Oh my God," she muttered. "What have I done?"

"Excuse me, Rapunzel," the masculine voice said again, in the most annoyingly calm voice. "But if you're done screaming, I'd kind of like to use the privy."

Privy? Dueling banjos started playing in her head. Oh, man, what kind of local yokel had she hooked up with?

And then her mind fixed on the first thing he'd said. *Rapunzel*. He'd called her Rapunzel.

Had she actually told this total stranger one of her repressed fairy tale fantasies? Worse yet, had they acted it out?

Her mind boggled. Her eyes crossed and she slid down the length of the door to the cold tile floor. She heard him knocking, but none of his words registered.

There was a ring on her finger. A diamond ring. But worse than that, there was also a small gold band.

If this meant what she thought it meant, she was in deep trouble.

She was in a strange man's house...in a strange man's bathroom. And, apparently, she was *married* to that strange man.

Good heavens—what had she done?

His knocking continued, and finally she snapped, "*What?*"

"If you don't mind, I have to piss like a racehorse," he said in a frustrated, brook-no-arguments voice. "Let me in."

She rolled to her knees, then used the rim of the bathtub for support as she raised herself to her feet.

"All right," she said, her hand on the knob. "I'm going to open the door, but I want you to stand back and let me pass before trying to come in."

He didn't respond, but she thought she heard him utter a muffled expletive beneath his breath.

"I mean it," she said, forcing a bravado into her words that she definitely did not feel.

After a moment, she heard a gritted, "Fine."

Opening the door a crack, she peeked out and saw him standing at the far side of the door, arms at his sides. As her gaze moved up his body, she spotted strong, hairy legs, a pair of hunter green and white wide-striped boxer shorts, and a swath of dark, suntanned skin surrounding his navel and moving upward.

When her hazy brain began to notice things like a washboard stomach and strong, smooth pectorals, she closed her eyes to hold back a tide of panic. A near-naked man was waiting to use the bathroom while she waited for the earth to open up and swallow her whole.

A tall, lithe, drop-dead gorgeous, half-nude man, she corrected. And she hadn't even gotten above the neck.

Considering his state of undress, she suddenly realized she had no idea what *she* was wearing. For the life of her, she couldn't recall from her earlier trip to the bathroom, and the thought that she might be more naked than he was kept her from glancing down. Instead, she used her hand to feel across her chest and hips.

Releasing a relieved breath, she lowered her eyes and saw that she was wearing her *Snow White and the Seven Dwarfs* bra and panties. Not what she usually wore to bed, and it wasn't much, but at least it was something. She grabbed a towel from the shelf behind the commode and covered what she could of her all-too-bare body.

"Could you move back, please," she asked. "Just a few steps."

The man swore under his breath—though she heard the expletives clearly enough this time—but he did as she requested. She threw the door open, launched herself across the room, and thanked him all in one swift motion.

Still bouncing on the king-size mattress, she turned just in time to see the bathroom door slam shut. Knowing she might not have much time, she dropped the towel, jumped off the bed, and threw back the covers, searching for anything that might belong to her.

She didn't know what she was looking for exactly, but was sort of hoping she'd find her clothes. Instead, all she found on the wrinkled sheets were small, round pieces of multi-colored confetti.

Dear God, what had they done that required confetti? She'd been with a few men in her time, but never once had she impressed one so much that he felt the need to throw a parade in her honor.

When nothing more turned up in the bed, she began scouring the rest of the room. Draped over a sturdy oak rocking chair in the far corner, nearly hidden behind the long dresser, was a full-length, beaded wedding gown. She picked it up, held it to her body, and almost cried.

It was her wedding gown. The one she'd bought to marry Matt.

So what was it doing here? The hem was smudged brown with dust and dirt, and a light, yellowish stain marred the edge of one sleeve. She sniffed the spot and decided it must be champagne or some other form of alcohol.

How had her dress gotten in such bad shape? She'd never even had it out of the bag.

Unless…

A sudden memory tugged its way through her muddled brain. Rushing through a busy airport with a huge garment bag, little bottles of assorted airplane liqueurs, struggling to fit down the aisle of a plane, people gasping and staring…

Oh, no.

She glanced at her finger, then the dress, then the bathroom door. All thoughts of escape drifted away as her knees gave out and she fell into the rocking chair, clutching the gown to her breasts.

In the back of her mind, she heard the bathroom door unlatch, heard the soft pad of feet crossing the floor. And then a tall, male shape loomed over her for a moment before hunching down in front of her.

He didn't touch her, merely rested a hand on the arm of the rocker. "Are you okay?" he asked softly.

"I'm not sure," she said, then raised her eyes to meet his. Cobalt blue. *Intense*, she thought. But kind. Kind and concerned. "I guess that depends on who you are."

One side of his mouth lifted in a weak smile. "I think you've figured that one out for yourself. I take it you're not happy about it."

"If this is a dream, I'm happy. You can wake me up now." She tried for a light, joking tone, but failed. Her gaze fell back to her lap. "If it's not, you can just shoot me and put me out of my misery."

"Being married to me isn't going to be a fairy tale, I know, but I don't think it's cause for *hara-kiri*, either."

She groaned, her head falling back against the hard wood of the chair. "We really are married, then. This isn't a joke?"

"No joke," he said, rising and moving about the room. "I've got the ring and papers to prove it."

She opened her eyes to watch as he found a pair of jeans crumpled on the floor and tugged them over his lean hips.

As husbands went, she supposed she should be grateful she'd gotten a handsome one. He was easy to look at, with brownish-blond hair and bright blue eyes. A small scar cut through his right eyebrow, but other than that, his face was flawless. With those cheekbones and that straight nose—not to mention bronze skin usually found only in tanning salons—he could easily be on the cover of *GQ*.

"You shouldn't be so surprised," he said, digging in his closet for a clean shirt. "After all, this whole thing was your idea."

Her eyes widened. "*My* idea?"

He turned, a devilish glint shading his expression. "Yours, darlin'. Lock, stock, and barrel."

He finished buttoning the red, blue, and white long-sleeve shirt he'd pulled from the closet and tucked the tail into his trousers.

"I've got livestock to take care of," he told her. "Make yourself at home. I'll be back around lunchtime."

Grabbing a beat-up cowboy hat off the dresser, he opened the bedroom door and disappeared from view.

Great. Left alone the morning after her wedding. And the *wrong* wedding, at that! What had she gotten herself into?

Chapter Four

When you're tryin' somethin' new, the fewer people who know about it, the better.

While the stranger who called himself her husband was out with the livestock—dear God, *livestock*—Monica decided to get dressed and see just what kind of disaster she'd created of her life.

The only thing in Ryder's bedroom resembling female clothing was the bra and panties she'd woken up in and the wedding gown draped across the rocking chair. Digging through drawers, she found a pair of new-looking blue jeans and grabbed one of the many long-sleeved shirts hanging in the closet.

In the bathroom, she paused for a moment in front of the sink, leaning heavily on its edge. Ignoring the tiny flecks of whiskers dotting the porcelain—and every other sign of male occupancy in the room—she stared at her reflection in the spotty, streaked mirror. She looked tired. More than that, she looked stunned. And she couldn't imagine that feeling fading any time soon.

She didn't want to touch his things, didn't want to be naked in his shower or dry off with one of his towels. But unless she washed away the hazy effects of sleep, she'd be a zombie all day. And she'd already used his toothbrush—a shudder ran through her at the thought—so what was the difference?

After a long, somewhat abrasive shower with a soap that smelled like Mr. Clean, she dressed in her confiscated clothes, foregoing a bra and underwear, considering she'd been wearing her only set since…well, she hoped yesterday, but couldn't really be sure. She washed them out in the sink and draped them over the shower rod to dry. If she was lucky, maybe they'd be ready by the time she caught a flight back to Chicago.

Her hair hung straight as straw, still wet from her shower. The light blue cambric shirt she'd nabbed from the closet billowed about her shoulders, knotted at her waist. She couldn't see the rest of her appearance in the small mirror, but looking down, she noted the bagginess of the jeans and how they barely managed to catch on her hips. She had to hold on to at least one belt loop at all times to keep them from falling straight to the floor and leaving her naked from the waist down. With her luck, there would be a witness to the zenith of that humiliation, and she'd end up on the internet in some viral video, the butt of the world's joke in perpetuity. Pun intended.

Apparently, her new husband didn't own a single tie or extra belt that she could use to hold them up. And because the pants were so long, she'd cuffed the legs several times, almost turning them into clamdiggers.

She moaned aloud. Bleach her hair blonde, give her a rope belt and quirky Southern accent, and she could be a dead ringer for Ellie May Clampett. The thought made her laugh, even as the agony of the moment hit her in the solar plexus. With her lifelong love of classic movies and black-and-white television, she'd often wished she could be more like Ellie May. Now here she was, one wild "critter" away from fulfilling a childhood dream.

Finally understanding what people meant when they said "Be careful what you wish for," she took a deep, stabilizing breath and decided to venture outside the bedroom to see what the rest of her new residence looked like.

For a man, he kept a fairly nice house. It was a ranch-style home with only one level, most of the walls done in a muted eggshell. The place could use a woman's touch, she noted, but the southwestern motif was actually kind of pleasant. A variety of blues, oranges, and browns brightened the rooms and brought it a step above what she might term "plain."

Framed photographs hung here and there on the walls, rested on top of an occasional dresser or bookshelf. She assumed most of the people in the pictures were family members or close friends of Ryder's. They looked happy enough, and he looked happy with them. They weren't professional photographs, but they captured the moment and the emotions of their subjects, which was what photography was really about, anyway.

Having been in the fashion business for the past few years, she'd almost forgotten that people were supposed to smile while having their pictures taken. Most of the models she shot had clips and pins digging into their flesh from ill-fitting clothes or were on the verge of passing out from lack of food.

If the bedroom and living room looked decent, then the kitchen was a disaster area. Empty food and drink containers cluttered the counters, dirty dishes filled the sink and spilled over onto every available surface, and dirty footprints tracked across the linoleum floor. She opened the cupboard doors beneath the sink only to see that the garbage was overflowing. No wonder he'd thrown the rest of his trash on the counter.

In the ugly, avocado green refrigerator, she found a half-empty jug of whole milk, a six-pack of beer, and about two swallows of orange juice at the bottom of a plastic bottle.

Why am I not surprised?

Finding a clean glass, she poured herself some milk. Though she much preferred skim, she decided to chance the fat content and just hoped Ryder wasn't the type of guy who drank straight from the container.

With a little something in her stomach, she pulled a stool over to the wall phone and tried to think of the best person to alert about her current situation. It had been ages since she'd had to bother with a landline, and all of her contacts were saved on her cell phone. But *that*—which she'd been so delighted to find during her search of the bedroom—was in the back pocket of her oversize pants, as dead as peep-toe cork wedges, with no charger in sight to bring it back to life.

There weren't many numbers anymore that she knew by heart, so she had to wrack her brain for who to contact. And since she wasn't even sure what state she was in at this point, Monica had a sinking suspicion she'd have to use a one and the area code to reach anyone she knew. After punching a long string of numbers, she waited for someone at the other end to answer.

Two rings later, she heard a voice she recognized. "Brooke, it's Monica. You're not going to believe this."

"Monica? Where are you? I've been trying to reach you for the past two days." Her friend's words all but reached hysterical level. "I thought you were dead or kidnapped or—"

"Two days?" Monica covered her eyes and tried not to think of how many states a body could cross in two days' time.

"Yeah. I haven't talked to you since Thursday night." Brooke paused for a moment, then added quietly, "When you found out about Matt."

She remembered that. She remembered seeing the announcement in the *Chicago Tribune*, reading that her fiancé was getting married Saturday morning—but not to her. She'd called Brooke, frantic, crying her eyes out. And then…

Well, the rest was a bit of a blur.

"Listen," Monica said. "My phone is dead, so I can't access my calendar. Can you tell me what I've got scheduled for the next couple days?"

"Sure."

Monica heard keys tapping and pages fluttering in the background. Leave it to Brooke to have all the details right at her fingertips. Monica's best friend and also her agent/manager, Brooke was a big believer in backing up her backups. She would have everything saved on her phone and laptop, as well as written down in her day planner.

"Monday you're going over your shots for the *Charlotte Russe* winter collection and you have a six p.m. on-site for *Young Miss* at Grant Park. Then you're in New York until Friday for a meeting with the *Marie Claire* folks."

Monica groaned. This was going to ruin her career. She'd been doing so well, really beginning to establish herself as an up-and-coming photographer in the world of fashion. Designers, well-known magazines, and even a couple of reality shows had started asking for her by name. But until she figured out what was going on and how to deal with her—she swallowed hard—*husband*, she couldn't see any way to get back home right now.

"I need you to either reschedule that *YM* shoot and the meeting in New York, or send another photographer, Brooke. And you can pick which photos to send to the *Charlotte Russe* people. I trust you. I just can't make it."

"Are you joking? Do you know what it means to shoot a cover for *Marie Claire*?"

"I do. And I'll be there for the actual shoot, whenever it is, honestly I will. But believe it or not, I have bigger problems right now."

"Impossible. How could anything be more important than setting up a job with *Marie Claire*?"

Monica grimaced. "Try the fact that I have no idea where I am, and I woke up married."

"You *what*?"

She tried to laugh, but the sound came out as more of a strangled gasp. "My sentiments exactly."

"Monica," her friend whispered. "What did you do?"

Lunchtime to Ryder, Monica learned, was closer to 3:00 p.m. than noon. She'd been alone in the house since 6:00 a.m. and hadn't seen a soul.

After convincing Brooke that she would be all right, and to either cancel or reschedule all of her appointments until further notice, Monica spent her time wandering around the house. She peeked where she probably shouldn't have, but since she *was* the man's wife, she figured that gave her some sort of legal-ish right to snoop.

Thankfully, she was back in the kitchen, scrounging around for something to eat when she heard the front door open and heavy footsteps moving in her direction. Panic skittered down her spine a moment before she straightened and took a deep, calming breath.

"Hey," Ryder said, sounding tired and slightly out of breath.

She turned, planning to offer a similar greeting. Instead, the word stuck in her throat, and her eyes all but bulged out at his appearance.

He'd left the house in fairly good condition, but he

returned now looking like he'd been dragged behind a truck for fifty miles.

"What happened to you?" she asked, concern overriding her initial anxiety about facing him once again.

He glanced down at himself, then back at her. "Nothing, why?" He slapped a pair of thick, leather gloves on the counter, then set his dusty brown cowboy hat on top of them.

"You look terrible," she told him. Normally, she might have struggled to be polite or just kept her mouth shut, but in this case, she was too shocked to recall manners.

He looked bad, like really awful. His shirt and pants were covered with dirt. Not just a sprinkling of dust, but full-fledged dirt, some spots on the verge of being caked with mud. Even his face was streaked brown and dotted with sweat. A spot of red lined one side of his jaw, as if it had been rubbed raw.

Ryder chuckled. "Welcome to my world, honey."

The endearment caused her stomach to lurch, reminding her that they weren't just casual acquaintances. Small talk seemed ridiculous in her current situation, especially since she had no idea how she'd gotten into it.

She tried not to flinch when his arm brushed her chest as he reached in front of her to open the refrigerator door. He grabbed the orange juice, twisted off the cap, and drank the few drops that remained at the bottom of the bottle. He replaced the lid, then turned slightly and tossed the empty container over his shoulder. It clattered into the rest of the mess on the counter, sending several empty containers spinning. Amazingly, nothing fell to the floor.

"Sorry the place is such a mess," he mumbled. "My housekeeper quit last month, and I haven't had a chance to clean or really shop for food since."

She'd noticed. Other than a box of saltines and a couple cans of soup, the cupboards were bare.

Next, Ryder reached for the milk and chugged several

long gulps straight from the jug.

Monica groaned and moved to a stool on the other side of the countertop.

"What's wrong?" he asked, wiping his mouth on his sleeve.

"Nothing," she said, resting her head in her hands. She felt a dull throb begin at her temples. "It's just that I drank some of that milk this morning."

"That's okay. There's plenty here."

She laughed weakly and muttered half to herself, "Yeah, that was my main concern."

He put the cap back on the jug and returned it to the shelf. "What was your main concern, then?"

"It's too late now," she said, shaking her head. "It doesn't matter. I'd just been hoping I was pouring milk from a container that your lips hadn't been in direct contact with." From the corner of her eye, she saw one side of his mouth quirk up in a grin.

"Considering where my lips were last night, you shouldn't be too worried, darlin'."

She groaned aloud this time, not even attempting to hide her feelings. "Don't say things like that. At least not until I have some idea of what happened."

"You still don't remember?"

When she lifted her head, she saw him leaning against the refrigerator, arms crossed over his chest. She gave herself a mental shake to keep from recollecting what that chest looked like under his shirt. All smooth and tan.

She forced her lungs to inhale. "I recall a few things, early on. But I don't remember you," she told him honestly.

He came across the kitchen, pulling an empty stool from her side of the counter to his and straddling the cushioned seat, hitching his boot heels on the wooden rungs.

"I came home from work Thursday night, started reading

the *Tribune*, and saw my fiancé's picture in the wedding announcements. Except that I wasn't with him. I wasn't even mentioned in the article." She pulled a face.

"How did an announcement get in a Chicago paper when the wedding was being held here in Nevada?"

"Nevada," Monica repeated in awe. At least she knew where she was. She also now knew that she'd only traveled to the state where Matt's wedding was being held, not beyond. *Whew!*

That sexy mouth of his lifted in another half-smile. "Where did you think you were?"

"I didn't have a clue," she told him. "And don't think that didn't freak me out for most of the morning."

He smirked. "So you saw the announcement...then what?"

"Well..." She ran a finger over the bridge of her nose, toward her forehead, racking her brain for details of the past few days. "Matt's parents live in the Chicago area, I guess. I've never actually met them, but I assume that's why the announcement was in the *Tribune*. I was fairly upset when I saw it, as you can imagine. I called my best friend and cried for a while, then sulked around the house the rest of the night, and by morning I guess I sort of decided to do something about it. I don't recall much of what I had in mind now, I only remember running through the airport carrying my wedding dress. And maybe changing into the gown at some point...possibly on the plane." She grimaced. Which meant she probably left her other clothes on the floor of the airplane restroom. God knew where they'd ended up, but even if the airline found them and stuck them in Lost and Found, there was no way she'd reclaim them now.

"That explains that, then," he said, his face showing no sign of what he was thinking.

"Explains what?"

"You showing up at the reception in a wedding gown." He paused, letting the image sink in, then added, "It doesn't explain why you were so drunk, though."

Monica gasped. "Drunk? How could I have been drunk?" And then she groaned. She and alcohol did not mix well. Oh, she liked it—sometimes a little too well. But more than a drink or two and she started to lose track of her thoughts... not to mention her inhibitions. "Oh, no. I didn't get another tattoo, did I?"

His brows raised with interest. "*Another* tattoo?"

Her cheeks warmed. "The last time I was out with friends and drank too much, I ended up with this ugly frog on my..."

"Butt?" he offered with a grin. Or was it a leer?

She inhaled deeply and refused to look him in the eye. "No," she said slowly. "Not my butt."

Definitely a leer. And his gaze began to wander just a little too far south for her peace of mind.

But he'd already spotted her navel ring between the sagging waistband of her borrowed jeans and the knot she'd made of his oversize shirt and seemed completely captivated by it. His eyes rounded and his tongue all but fell from his mouth.

It was just a belly button ring, for heaven's sake; she'd had it for years—and gotten it while she was stone-cold sober, thank you very much. But from the expression on his face, she expected to look down and find herself naked.

"Eyes front, cowboy," she warned, scooting her stool even farther beneath the counter.

He stared at the region of her hidden midriff a moment longer. He also swallowed, she noticed. Hard. She bit her lip to keep from smiling. No wonder some women could get a man to do anything for them. Show a little skin—and perhaps a bit of jewelry in seldom-seen places—and they became mesmerized. She tucked that piece of information away and tilted her head, waiting for him to continue.

His eyes darted back to the counter below her breasts, searching. Then he seemed to shrug off his fascination with her body piercing altogether. "All I know is that you showed up three sheets to the wind. Made a complete fool of yourself in front of about two hundred people," he added brusquely.

"I showed up drunk?" she asked, confused. And then understanding dawned. "Oh, no. The little bottles of booze on the plane. And the champagne," she added with a groan. His eyes locked with hers, silently questioning. "I bought a bottle of champagne at the airport before I caught a taxi to the reception. I was going to give it to Matt as a wedding gift. Or crack him over the head with it, I'm not sure which." She twisted her fingers together to keep from fidgeting. "But it was a long ride, and I was upset. I must have gotten thirsty."

She saw his mouth pull together as he fought a laugh. "You opened a bottle of champagne in a cab?"

"The driver might have helped. I think he was hoping it would calm me down."

"It didn't calm you down," he said.

She wished she could curl up on the floor and slip into a coma so she wouldn't have to face any further humiliation. "You'd be a better judge of that than I would. I don't really remember much after that."

"Would you like me to fill in the rest?" he asked charitably.

She groaned. "All right," she said slowly, reluctantly. "As long as you promise to bury my body afterward. Somewhere no one will find it. Maybe then the humiliation will die with me."

He chuckled again, shifting on the stool. "It wasn't as bad as all that," he assured her. "The talk will die down in ten or twenty years."

Chapter Five

Good judgment comes from experience, and a lot of that comes from bad judgment.

Monica let her head fall to the counter again, hoping the impact would knock her unconscious.

"Matt's new wife is my sister, you know."

She sat up so fast, the bones in her spine snapped. Her eyes rounded.

"You don't remember that part, huh?" he asked with a smug smile.

"No." She looked skyward, praying for divine intervention. "Oh, lord, what did I do?" Her gaze swung back to him. "If she's your sister, and I ruined her wedding reception, then how did you and I... How did we..."

"End up in bed together?" His grin widened and a devilish glint sparkled in his eyes.

She wanted to slap that look off his face, but was too busy trying not to burst into flames of embarrassment. Her face flushed sixteen shades of red. She felt it. At the speed of light, heat rushed from the bottom of her neck to the top of her head, coloring every inch of skin in between.

He was joking. He *had* to be joking. She knew they'd *technically* been in bed together, but she'd been passed out and he'd only been sleeping. Right? She'd know if they'd done more than that.

"That's a long but very amusing story," he said, either ignoring or not noticing her abject horror and disgrace.

She waited for the rest, not wanting to hear, but knowing she had to if she was ever to make sense of the day she'd woken up to.

"You created quite a stir at the reception, I'll give you that. Came in drunk off your ass, climbed onto the platform in front of the bridal party, and made a long speech about how you were supposed to be the one married to Matt. You called him 'Matt the Rat.'"

She snorted. That description was still accurate, in her opinion.

"Matt tried to quiet you down. Josie was frantic."

"Who's Josie?"

"My sister."

She blushed again. "Oh."

"Josie asked me to do something about you, so I did."

Monica raised her eyes, meeting his gaze. "How?"

"Threw you over my shoulder and carried you out like a sack of grain, that's how."

She nodded. "That must have been very humiliating." For both of them. "Thank you, I guess."

Smiling, he said, "You didn't seem too grateful at the time. More green around the gills. You threatened to vomit on me."

Could this day get any worse? Could he possibly reveal anything more embarrassing than what he'd told her already? Unless...

"Did I?" she asked weakly.

"Nah. You were too busy hatching your plan."

"My...plan?" she choked out.

His smile grew wider. "To get even with Matt. You figured that if we tied the knot, you could make him jealous so he'd leave Josie and come back to you."

"And you went along with it?" she asked, shocked. "Against your sister?"

He shrugged a shoulder. "Not really against my sister. I figure, if Matt is a big enough jerk to mess around on Josie, then she's better off without him. If he's an okay guy and you're just overreacting..."

He paused as if he expected her to refute his words. But how could she? If putting on a wedding dress and crashing someone else's reception wasn't an overreaction, she didn't know what was.

When she didn't respond, he continued. "Well, if your plan fails, Josie and Matt will still be married. No harm done."

Shaking her head, she ran slightly trembling fingers through her hair, then brought the left down to stare at the diamond weighing so very heavily on her hand and her heart.

His explanation was fine as far as it went, but she suspected there was more to this than what he was leading her to believe. What kind of man married a total stranger ten minutes after they'd met?

"I can't believe you did that," she said. "You're sure the marriage was real? I mean, you could have just slapped a ring on my finger to play along, and I wouldn't have known the difference."

Without warning, Ryder shoved his stool back and stood, shifting nervously. "You're making it worth my while."

Monica narrowed her eyes, wondering why he seemed so uncomfortable. The man had married her—actually married her rather than just pretending, which is what she'd have done had she been in her right mind—but suddenly he felt ill at ease? Too bad that case of nerves hadn't come up *before* he said "I do."

"Worth your while?" she asked warily. "How exactly am I going to do that?" If it had anything to do with sex, she was going to claim insanity brought on by the consumption of alcohol and hop the next flight back home. If he tried to hold her to a devil's bargain, she'd have every lawyer in Chicago on retainer before her plane touched solid ground.

He speared her with a sharp glance. "You know what you promised—a fifty-thousand-dollar investment in my ranch."

She clutched a handful of shirt over the region of her heart. "*Fifty thousand dollars*? Where am I supposed to get fifty thousand dollars?"

And then it dawned on her. Her jaw dropped into a long *O*. "Oh, *that* fifty thousand dollars," she said quietly. "But I don't have it anymore. Matt ran off with every penny I had to my name."

Ryder kicked his stool out of the way, causing it to teeter precariously on two legs before settling again, and moved closer to the counter. He loomed over her, making Monica wish she could sneak out of the room and finish the rest of this conversation via Skype—with an ocean and three continents between them.

"What do you mean you don't have the money?" he asked through clenched teeth. He yanked a worn leather wallet from his hip pocket and tossed some folded papers at her. "There's our marriage certificate and the agreement you signed, so don't even think of backing out," he added with a growl. If his fists tightened any more, his knuckles would pop off like the buttons on David Banner's shirt as he turned into the Incredible Hulk.

"I mean I don't have the money. I don't have *any*

money," she said as she unfolded the papers in front of her. Sure enough, there was a brand new, bona fide marriage certificate—signed by her and Ryder, sealed by a modern-day minister-slash-officiant, and delivered by one very ticked-off new husband. There was also a random envelope with the previous day's date scrawled across the top, followed by the words, *I, Monica Blair, do hereby promise to invest $50,000 in the Rolling Rock Ranch in return for Ryder Nash agreeing to marry me for an unspecified amount of time.* There was some additional information about accruing interest on top of a fifty-fifty split once something called EAT started making money. The majority of it may not be in her handwriting, but that was definitely her printed name at the top and her signature at the bottom.

She threw her arms up in supplication. "I'm sorry if I told you I had this much, and even sorrier if I said you could have it, but except for last month's paycheck, I honestly don't have two nickels to rub together. Matt convinced me to give him my life savings, and then he up and ran off with that...with your sister."

Ryder's molars ground back and forth in fury. She could almost hear them being worn down to nubs. With shoulders tense and feet spread, he looked prepared to fight. And all Monica could think was that if he took a swing at her, she should duck and run for cover.

"Why would you give that man your life savings and then let him run off with another woman?" he charged.

She almost rolled her eyes, then thought better of it. Ryder probably wouldn't appreciate such a gesture in his present mood.

"I didn't *know* he was going to run off," she answered, with just as much accusation in her tone as he'd used with her. "I *thought* we were going to be married. I *thought* we were going to start a new fashion magazine together. I *thought* I was going to be the head photographer of that magazine."

She thrust out her chin and stuck clenched fists on her hips in a mirror image of Ryder's own defensive stance. The papers crinkled in her grip. "I *did not* think my fiancé was going to run off with another woman and leave me high and dry. So excuse me very much for making plans for the future."

Ryder stared at her a moment with crazed rage in his eyes. Then he snorted at her. A leave-it-to-a-woman-to-screw-up-this-badly, I-should-have-known, you-idiot snort.

Monica inhaled so deeply, she thought her lungs would burst. "Don't you snort at me," she demanded, all but shaking a finger in his face. "I'm not the one who married an intoxicated woman after my own sister's wedding. Just how drunk were *you* to believe I was going to give you fifty thousand dollars just to marry me? I could have had any man in Chicago for fifty bucks and a six-pack of beer!"

He took several deep breaths, relaxing enough to cross his arms over his chest instead of letting them hang like two-by-fours at his sides. "Are you finished?" he asked quietly.

His sudden turn from anger to almost unbothered left her momentarily speechless. Then she let her own arms drop and shrugged. "I guess."

He slipped the papers from the tight fist at her side and tucked them back into his pocket. Then he turned away and headed for the fridge to root around in one of the compartments.

"So what do we do now?" she asked tentatively, taking a small step forward.

"About what?" he asked over his shoulder.

About global warming and the fate of sea turtles in Portugal, what do you think? But she didn't say that. "About us," she stressed instead, slipping her hands into her front pockets.

"I don't know about you, but I have a legally binding

piece of paper that says you'll be putting fifty thousand dollars into my ranch. One way or another, I plan to collect." He straightened, a slice of bologna in his mouth. "But for now, I have work to do."

Her nose wrinkled at the sight of that disgusting piece of processed meat by-product hanging from between his teeth. She didn't particularly like meat, and bologna was the worst. Snouts and beaks and assorted rat parts, she was sure.

He crossed the kitchen again, heading for the front door, totally ignoring her.

"Wait," she called after him, pulling her hands from her front pockets as though that would stop him. "We haven't figured out what to do about this mess yet. And what am I supposed to do while you're working?"

Pausing on the threshold, he finished chewing the bite of lunchmeat. "Whatever floats your boat, darlin'," he said, fixing her with a cocky, too-sexy grin. "Cook, clean, go bungee jumping with that little belly button ring of yours." His eyes fixed on the small silver hoop above her navel for a moment before sliding up to meet her gaze.

"Or maybe you can sit down and figure out some way to come up with that fifty thousand dollars you owe me. 'Cuz you aren't leaving until I get my money."

Chapter Six

If you're in doubt about whether to kiss someone, give 'em the benefit of the doubt.

"Excuse me?" Her mouth went as wide as her eyes, and she was sure she'd heard him wrong. She wasn't leaving until he got his money? That sounded eerily like a threat to her. Like he planned to hold her hostage until she paid up.

She expected him to turn around and explain what he'd meant, but he kept walking with that damn infuriating, careless stride of his, acting as though he hadn't heard her half-shriek.

"Wait a minute," she called after him. He ignored her. She caught the front screen door before it could swing closed behind him and stepped onto the front porch. He still didn't stop.

Since she wasn't wearing shoes—and Ryder didn't seem inclined to slow down so she could run back to the bedroom for the satin pumps she'd worn with her wedding gown—she clamped down on the tiny bit of dread she felt at the thought of going barefoot just to follow him and sank her feet directly onto the warm, dry ground.

The sun hit her full force the minute she stepped off the porch. She threw a hand up to block the rays and tried not to squint. Squinting caused crow's feet. Sun caused other assorted wrinkles, not to mention dry skin, sunburn, age spots, and cancer. Dirt seeped between her toes and a sharp stone bit into the sensitive flesh of her instep. She grimaced but said nothing.

The glare of the sun turned Ryder into a dark outline of human form a yard or two ahead of her as she tried to keep up.

Covering her eyes with one hand, holding her jeans up with the other, she tiptoed a few steps, loathe to grind even more dirt and grit into her soft, once-white feet. She wobbled and winced with each step, and probably looked like a dizzy penguin.

Pavement. That's what she needed. Nice, flat pavement that wouldn't bruise the bottoms of her feet and put her in line for an emergency pedicure.

"Will you wait just a damn minute!" she ground out, determined to catch his attention before her feet were worn down to stubs.

He stopped suddenly, turning to face her so fast that she nearly bumped into him. The look he gave her made her feel like a three-year-old caught scribbling on the walls with permanent marker.

"You don't have the sense God gave a goose," he snapped, motioning to her shoeless appearance.

She opened her mouth to argue—she *did* have the sense God gave a goose, she just wasn't used to running out of the house without shoes on to chase after rude cowboys—but he cut her off.

"Come out here in your bare feet and you're likely to

need a tetanus shot."

Monica glanced down, searching the ground around her feet for sharp, dangerous objects. She didn't see any.

"We shoe horses out here. There could be a stray nail you wouldn't see until it was stuck in your foot. And those grassy toenails of yours are bound to be a temptation to the cows," he added with derision.

She ignored his comment about her toenails being painted Jolly Green Giant green. If she'd known she was going to wake up in Hooterville, she'd have used Cow Pie brown instead.

"Well, you didn't exactly give me a chance to put shoes on," she said defensively, tugging harder at the loose waist of her pants. "Besides, all I have are my satin pumps, and they'd be filthy just chasing you this far."

He rolled his eyes again. Then he came forward, leaning toward her, and before she had a chance to react, he lifted her into his arms.

Her body stiffened, not only surprised by his actions but by her sudden shift from vertical to horizontal. She wasn't used to not having her feet flat on the ground—even if that ground was dirty, gritty, and crawling with God-knows-what. Then she began to notice the warmth of his body seeping into her skin, the strong arms holding her, and she decided not to protest.

Bumping happily against his chest, she stared at his stubbled chin, full mouth, and the cool azure eyes shaded by the brim of his hat. With a sly grin, she said, "Your mama sure did raise you right, Mr. Nash."

His face remained blank. He didn't even turn his head to look at her. "She raised me to be a gentleman, no matter how flighty a woman might be."

She leaned back as far as his arm would allow, affronted. "I am not flighty." And then she grabbed the edge of his hat and yanked it down over his eyes.

He kept walking, never breaking stride. But he lifted his head and glared at her from beneath the low, oddly angled rim of his cowboy hat.

"Flighty," he said. "And short-tempered."

Before she had time to respond to that, or exact her revenge, he stepped through the doorway of a large, half-dilapidated barn and set her on her feet.

Stray strands of straw—or hay, she wasn't sure which—lined the barn floor and bit into the bottoms of her feet. It also threw up small motes of dust that tickled her nose and eyes.

She took a moment to glance around the building, noting that the back half was completely missing. From the color and texture of the wood, she didn't guess it had been all that much of an architectural accomplishment to being with. But like this, with one corner fallen in a heap of broken boards and the other wall bowing like a weak shelf, it was truly pathetic.

Two men worked in the destroyed corner, holding up new support beams, hammering, cussing, and all around making a racket.

"Hey, Ryder," one of the workers called when he spotted them.

Ryder raised his hand and waved. "Hey, Kevin. Benji."

They didn't seem the least interested in her, simply went back to what they were doing.

"What happened?" she asked, still staring at the destroyed area.

"Tornado. Ripped through here last summer and nearly leveled the whole place." He hitched his head to the side, toward where the men were working. "That's the least of my problems." Then he turned to face her more fully and said, "This is the main barn. We use it for storage and chopping the cattle."

Monica let out a gasp of despair. How could he be so blasé about the slaughter of poor, defenseless animals? "You kill cows in here?" she asked, horrified. She could almost hear their desperate moos for help and was glad a tornado had ripped down the barn, if it meant saving a few innocent bovine lives.

He gave her an odd look, and then his brows lifted and he broke out in laughter. "No," he said. "Chop is the food we give them. When we bring the herd in to feed, it's called 'chopping.'"

She sighed, thinking The Powers That Be could have come up with a better name for cow food than "chop."

Still chuckling, Ryder moved across the barn floor and opened the door to a small, unlit room. From where she was standing, she could see cobwebs hanging in the air and dusting Ryder's hat. She shivered, deciding she would never enter that part of the barn unless she was covered from head to toe with full body armor.

"If you're going to follow me around like a lost puppy, you're going to need something on your feet.

Offended, she put her hands on her hips and opened her mouth to toss back a retort.

"These should fit you," he cut in, turning with a pair of dusty, dirty, knee-high rubber boots in his hands. In his other, he held an equally dusty and dirty cowboy hat. He tossed the boots at her feet, then swiped at the hat with one of his big, gloved hands.

She began to stick her foot into one of the boots when she saw something move. She screamed and threw it back toward Ryder.

"What?" he asked, giving her one of those hysterical-female glares.

"There's something in there," she rushed breathlessly, her heart trying to beat its way up her throat. She *sounded* like a hysterical female, she knew. But until the multi-eyed creature inside that boot was dead as a doornail, she didn't particularly care.

He picked up the boot, turned it upside down, and shook it hard. A large, long-legged spider fell to the straw-strewn floor and skittered away.

"It was just a spider," he told her.

"I can see that," she said, batting at little invisible creatures that she suddenly felt crawling all over her body. "But I'm not putting those things on until you're sure there are no more bugs inside."

He gave a long-suffering sigh, but picked up the other boot and began shaking them both. He slapped them together, banged them against the floorboards, and then reached inside each and swiped the interiors with his gloved hands.

"I think they're safe," he said finally, handing them back to her.

She wasn't so sure, but as long as Ryder had checked them, she felt fairly secure. Still, as she stepped into them, she kept her toes curled under, prepared to jump out at the first sign of arachnid inhabitance.

"Okay?" he asked.

She nodded, shifting warily inside the footwear.

"Good." He slapped the extra hat on her head and pushed it down until it held. "This will help shade your eyes and keep you from getting sunburned."

She smiled then, a little smittenly, she suspected. But how could she not almost want to kiss the man when he'd just given her shoes for her battered feet and a hat for her delicate, Southern Belle skin?

"Think you can manage to keep up now, Rapunzel?"

Risking crow's feet after all, and other assorted wrinkles that might form in her later years, she scowled at him. "I have no intention of keeping up. You're going to stand still while we discuss just what you meant about keeping me hostage."

He laughed, one deep exhalation of breath that could have been a snort if he'd inhaled instead. "I never said you were a hostage."

Her lips thinned. "Then what exactly did you mean when you said I wasn't leaving until you got your money?"

When she stuck her fists on her hips in agitation, her jeans fell dangerously low. She ignored them, but Ryder's focus zeroed in on their downward slide like a trained fighter pilot.

He remained silent for a moment, then cursed. "Lord have mercy, woman, you could give a dead man a heart attack in those things." He took one last look before turning to root around in the closet room again.

He turned back to her, a long length of thin rope in his hand. His eyes went back to the pants riding low on her hips, but he didn't seem quite so distracted this time. "What I meant to say earlier was that you're not getting a divorce until I get my money."

She blinked, not sure how to react to that. She wanted to ask if an annulment was a possibility. If he said yes, then she would know they hadn't done the hanky-panky last night. After all, you could only get an annulment for a handful of reasons, one of which she was pretty sure had something to do with not having sex. If he said no...

She didn't even want to contemplate "no."

Pulling off his gloves and sticking them under his arm, he threaded the twine through one of the belt loops at the front of her pants. With each loop, he moved closer to her body, brushing the bare skin of her midriff. Her stomach muscles tightened instinctively as the air caught in her lungs. His hot breath dusted her cheek, and she let her eyes flutter closed. It felt good, having him lean so close, feathering touch after touch of his fingertips along her sensitized flesh. When he came to the back loops, he didn't bother turning her around, instead slipping both arms around her waist and feeling his way through the motions.

A stuttering jolt of electricity ran down her body, calling every E, F, and G-spot to full attention. Knowing he had to finish soon or she'd melt at his feet, she lifted her head to see how much longer he planned to be. Only to find him staring at her with the same intensity he seemed to be dedicating to the makeshift belt.

His hands moved from the center of her back to her side, ending at the front button of the jeans. Dark eyes still boring into hers, he tugged the rope tight and created some sort of knot or bow that she didn't dare look down at. She might not have been able to see what he was doing, but she felt every agonizing movement as though they were both stark naked and Ryder was playing connect-the-dots with her beauty marks.

Finished tying the rope, his hands stilled and Monica forced herself to breathe before she passed out. Which she was very much in danger of doing.

Slightly dizzy from lack of oxygen and the sexual tension racing around them like honeybees, she reached up and grabbed hold of his upper arms for balance.

Ryder didn't move. Didn't reach out to steady her or shake off her grasp. He simply stood statue-still and stared into her eyes.

And then the back of one finger touched her stomach just above the waist of her jeans. His smooth, hard nail caressed her skin lightly, and she felt it all the way down to her toes. It moved upward slowly, so slowly, she bit her lip to keep from sighing in pleasure. Her chest hitched, and she clutched his arms even tighter as he toyed with the small hoop at her navel, flicking it back and forth, before skimming higher. Up to the knotted closure of her shirt, over button after button after button, until he reached the bareness between her breasts.

He stopped there, almost unsure of whether to go on.

And, oh, lord, she wanted him to. She wanted him to keep sliding that warm, strong finger over her skin, maybe even lean forward and press his equally warm, strong lips to hers.

But that probably wasn't such a good idea.

She blinked. Definitely not a good idea, considering their relationship up to now. Yes, they were *technically* married, but that didn't give them any call to go doing the Mattress Mambo or Macarena or any other euphemism for getting naked and horizontal. They hardly even knew each other. And she wasn't drunk anymore, so she would have no excuse for sleeping with a near-stranger. No matter how much she wanted to.

Breaking eye contact, Monica cleared her throat and took a step back. She looked down at her new belt and fiddled with the simple knot he'd made at the front.

"Now I really do look like Ellie May," she muttered.

"What?"

She lifted her head to find Ryder still studying her closely, though not with as much intensity or raw desire. His mind was obviously elsewhere. And she suspected she knew where.

Shaking her head, she said, "I was just thinking that I look an awful lot like Ellie May Clampett from *The Beverly Hillbillies.*"

"She was a blonde," he pointed out, and his voice sounded gravelly, unused.

She chuckled, tucking a stray curl of her own short, dark hair behind her ear. "Not a natural one, I don't suppose."

"No, I don't suppose."

Monica felt as out of sync as Ryder sounded, like she'd been picked up, spun around, and dropped in a foreign land. And it had nothing to do with where she'd woken up this morning. That, she was actually beginning to deal with. This had much more to do with the fact that she found herself suddenly quite attracted to her husband. Who would have thought?

She racked her brain for something to get them past this awkward moment. What had they been discussing before he slipped the rope around her waist? Something important, about money and being held prisoner.

The image of herself in a harem outfit, tied to his headboard with the same kind of rough twine he'd just used to hike up her pants, flashed through her mind and sent a deep throb to her lower extremities.

I have to get out of here! she thought, shaking off the erotic haze spinning its web around her mind and body. If she didn't, she might just try to put that love-slave fantasy to the test.

Oh, yes, she remembered now. She'd asked if Ryder meant to hold her hostage, and he said she wasn't a hostage; he just didn't intend to give her a divorce until he got his money. Money that she simply didn't have.

She cleared her throat. "I'd better be going," she said, taking a step backward, almost reluctant to move away. "Thanks for the hat and boots. And the belt." Her voice caught on the last word, sensations assaulting her memory.

"Where are you going?"

She began to shrug, then stopped herself, not wanting him to think her indecisive. "Home," she told him. She still had to figure out what to do about Matt stealing her money and marrying another woman, but it could wait until she got home and was back on firmer footing...literally. "I'll just call a cab and see if it can take me to the airport."

"There are no cabs that come out this far."

That caught her off guard for a moment. "Then I'll walk to the nearest Greyhound station and catch a bus."

He grabbed her arm before she could take another step.

"Not so fast," he said, all signs of intimacy gone from his tone and expression. The moment had passed and it wasn't coming back.

Monica frowned. "I thought you said I was free to go."

He shook his head. "Uh-uh. I'm not going to keep you prisoner, darlin', but you aren't leaving, either."

Ignoring the grip he still had on her, she put her hands on her hips and threw him an arched glance. "By definition, not letting someone leave *is* keeping them prisoner. *Darlin'*."

His upper lip quirked at that, and she wanted to smack him for being so amused.

"If you leave, there's a good chance I'll never see you again, which means I'll never get my money. So you're staying."

"I told you," she ground out. "I don't *have* any money."

Letting go of her arm, he turned her in the opposite direction and rested a hand at the small of her back as he guided her forward out of the barn. "Then you'll just have to work off your debt."

Chapter Seven

When a man asks a woman to share his lot, she has a right to know how big it is.

She balked, digging the heels of her too-big rubber boots into the dirt. By "work," he meant sex, she was sure. Good lord, how many times would it take to work off fifty thousand dollars? Even at a hundred dollars a pop, she could be here until the cows came home.

She looked around her. *Bad analogy, Mon. The cows are already home.*

Not that she had any intention of being his sex toy for the next ten or twenty years. She didn't intend to be his sex toy for five minutes. She might have considered the idea a few seconds ago when his warm breath and even warmer fingers were doing wicked things to her mind and body, but not now. Not now that he was keeping her here against her will. If he needed sex so badly, he could go find himself some other dairymaid to diddle with.

She twisted free and started back toward the house. "I

don't think so."

Before she got three feet, he caught her again. "I do." Keeping hold of her arm, he led her past the front of the ugly brown barn toward a much nicer yellow one.

"You're crazy."

"No, desperate. And desperate men take desperate measures."

"Let go of me." She fought, wondering why one hayloft wasn't as good as another for what he had in mind. "I'm not going to sleep with you just because you think I owe you some stupid money."

He stopped like he'd run smack into a brick wall. Turning wide eyes to her, the corner of his mouth began to tilt upward. He let his gaze run down her body and then up again, pausing for a moment at her navel ring. And then he chuckled. "Sorry, Ellie May, I just ain't interested. Frankly, *you'd* have to pay *me*."

She clicked her teeth together to keep from gasping in outrage.

He wasn't interested, hmm? Then what were all those soft touches and blatant looks he'd treated her to in the barn? And the intense scrutiny back in the kitchen? How curious could a man be about a belly button ring and a hidden tattoo if he wasn't even affected by the body that went with them?

She opened her mouth to tell him just how interested he *should* be when a man on a horse rode into the yard. He wore dusty cowboy boots and a dusty hat, just like Ryder, and another one of those long-sleeve plaid shirts with silver-rimmed, fake pearl buttons on each of the pockets. Was there some sort of fashion code for cowboys that they all had to dress alike?

"Hey, Ryder," the man called, jumping down from his mount and throwing the reins over the paddock fence.

"Ned," Ryder returned the greeting, inclining his head.

Ned sauntered toward them, moving quickly despite his slightly bowed legs. He took off his hat, revealing a head of carrot red hair and freckles that covered every inch of his skin. A cocky grin broke out across his young face as he looked Monica up and down.

"Who you got there, Ryder? She sure is a pretty little thing. 'Cept for those boots."

Monica glanced down at the oversize yellow boots and decided they *were* rather hideous. She looked like an extra in the Fireman's Day Parade.

"This is Monica," Ryder said, a hard undercurrent in his tone. "Monica, this is Ned."

She raised her head to see a muscle jump in Ryder's jaw. Her brows knit. Why was he suddenly so tense when all the boy had done was ask her name?

"Ned helps out around here," Ryder offered brusquely.

Ned chuckled, keeping his gaze on Monica. "More than just helping out, these past few days," he corrected. "Haven't seen Ryder doing much of anything this week, what with his sister's wedding and all."

Ryder didn't seem to appreciate that comment, judging from the tautness of his arm around her back and his fingers digging into her side. She ignored his surly mood and extended a hand. "It's a pleasure to meet you, Ned."

He whistled. "Not nearly so much a pleasure as it is for me, ma'am." He bowed over her hand, pressing a soft kiss to the top.

She smiled, surprised to find such gallantry in a kid his age. He looked to be no older than eighteen or nineteen.

"So what brings you to these parts?" he asked her, apparently noticing that she wasn't exactly dressed in this area's style du jour. "Come to buy a mount off the boss?"

Ryder answered for her. "I was just showing her around, explaining some of her chores since she'll be staying with us for a while."

"You're gonna be working here? Really?" Ned looked like he'd just found a shiny new bike under the Christmas tree. "Great! If you need anything, just give a holler. I'm always around somewhere; I'd be happy to show you the ropes."

She started to thank him and explain that she really wouldn't be around all that much longer, but Ryder cleared his throat, squinting at Ned. "She isn't a hired hand," he snapped. "She's my wife."

Ned's mouth fell open, and his eyes all but popped out of his head. When she glanced back at Ryder, he wore a nearly duplicate expression. He seemed as shocked as they that he'd blurted out such a thing.

"Are you kidding me?" Ned's glance darted from Ryder to Monica and back again like he was watching a Ping-Pong game.

"No," Ryder said. And then he tipped his hat back a bit and said in exasperation, "Look, nobody knows yet, so I'd appreciate it if you didn't say anything. Especially to my folks."

Ned still looked astonished. "No. I mean, sure. I won't tell nobody." Then he slapped his knee. "Damn. I can't believe you got hitched. Never thought I'd see the day."

"Yeah, well…" Ryder couldn't seem to think of anything to say. "Don't you have work to do?" he asked pointedly.

The boy shrugged. "I just came in for another coil of wire. It can wait."

"No," Ryder said, brooking no argument. "It can't."

Ned looked at his boss then, finally sensing that Ryder didn't want him around. "Okay. I'll see you both later, then. Welcome to Rolling Rock Ranch, Miz Nash." He replaced his hat and headed for the barn they'd just exited.

"He seemed nice," Monica said. "I can't believe you told him we were married, though. It's going to be awfully hard to get a quick divorce if everyone knows and tries to talk us out of it."

"We'll worry about that later," he said, taking her elbow to propel her forward again.

Instead of entering the yellow barn through the big Dutch doors she'd spotted as they left the house, he took her around to the side where a large, sliding door had been left open. Once inside, he released her abruptly and left her to follow of her own free will. Which she had no intention of doing. She stood her ground and refused to budge, even when he moved several car lengths ahead of her.

"What are we doing in here?" she called out. Her voice echoed in the high rafters and she almost winced. Ryder didn't seem to notice. He just kept walking, leaving her farther and farther behind.

When he turned into a doorway and disappeared from view, she began to panic. She could have gone back to the house now that he wasn't physically restraining her, but her feet wouldn't seem to turn in that direction. She was too curious about where he'd gone and what he was up to.

A low rumbling rolled through the barn, snaking up the back of her neck. She froze for a minute, afraid that if she moved, whatever had uttered that hideous growl would jump out and eat her. Surely he didn't have lions or tigers boarded up in here. Did he?

Curiosity might have killed the cat, but strange noises and invisible monsters were much more likely to kill *her*. She ran after Ryder, her floppy boots scuffling in the dirt and straw of the floor.

She pretended not to notice the musty smell, the dust hitting her nostrils as she breathed, or the soft nickers from unknown corners. When a huge brown head poked over one of the stall doors as she passed, she screamed and jumped back against the opposite wall. Gasping for air, she stayed as still as possible and prayed for Ryder to reappear before she had a heart attack or ran into some other prancing, snorting beast.

Something came from behind and nuzzled her hair right at the nape of her neck. She let loose another blood curdling scream and sank to the floor, covering her head as though she expected something to bite it off.

"What is all the damn commotion?" Ryder stepped back into the main runway of the barn, a scowl drawing his brows together.

Monica pointed upward and took a quick peek herself. A white horse stood above her, head hanging out over the door of the stall. His nostrils flared, the whites of his eyes showing from all the noise she was making.

"That thing tried to eat me," she told him, embarrassed that her voice quavered over what now appeared to be a simple, fairly harmless horse.

Ryder came forward and took her arm, lifting her to her feet. "That's Chynna, and she wouldn't swat at a horsefly if it bit her on the ass. Especially so close to foaling."

Monica brushed a stray strand of hair out of her face and close to Ryder's side, afraid of what else might pop over the edges of those walls with no warning. "Folding what?" she asked.

He gave her a strange look.

She squared her shoulders and brushed dirt from the back of her jeans. "You said she was close to folding. Folding what?"

Ryder stared at her a moment longer, then burst into deep, full-belly laughter. He slapped his thigh and bent at the waist, gasping for breath.

Pursing her lips, she stood back and waited for him to finish finding her so funny. It took a minute, but he finally straightened and ran the back of his hand across his eyes.

"You really are a city gal, aren't you?" he said, amusement still evident in his tone.

She didn't bother answering. Of course she was a city girl. And he was a backwoods, inbred, redneck hillbilly. She'd like to see how he handled himself in Chicago. Those busy streets and skyscrapers would have him crying for his mommy by sundown.

"She's about ready to foal, not fold. A foal is a baby horse. She's pregnant."

"Oh." Monica tried not to look at Ryder and hoped he wasn't looking at her. She just didn't get this farming deal and didn't appreciate being made to feel stupid because of it. If Ryder were in one of her studios, he'd probably be just as clueless about all the lights, cameras, and backgrounds.

Although she did sort of wish she had some kind of cowboy encyclopedia to refer to. For definitions of things like "chop" and "foaling" and "how to kill a cowboy and bury his body where no one will ever find it."

She slanted a piqued glance at Ryder, who was gently rubbing Chynna's nose and murmuring soft words in her ear. *Yeah, be nice to the horse and treat me like chattel. My hero.* Her eyes moved upward in exasperation, but stopped in mid-roll as he looked back at her.

"This is the stable," he said, still stroking the now-calm mare. "We have about a dozen horses here at any one time. Some are mine, some are boarders, some are here for stud."

Her brows arched at that. She didn't know much about horses, but she knew what "for stud" meant. Before Ryder could spot the slight blush heating her cheeks, she turned away and pointed toward the doorway where Ryder had disappeared and then reappeared after her near-death by horse breath. "What's in there?"

"That's the tack room." He opened the door and led her inside.

This room held no similarities to the one in the other barn where Ryder had found her hat and boots. Large where the other was small, this tack room was also neat, free of spider webs (and spiders, she hoped), and filled with saddles so clean, they shone. The smell of leather and saddle soap permeated the air. The dark colors of assorted saddles gleamed in the light from the one bulb in the center of the ceiling. All different styles of bridles and bits hung from hooks on the walls.

"Have you ever ridden?" he asked.

"No," she answered, shaking her head for emphasis. She knew the difference between English and Western saddles, could tell a bit from a hoof pick, but all of that knowledge came secondhand from books and television, or the one western-wear photo shoot she'd done. She'd never been near a horse—except for Chynna back there—and didn't care to alter that situation this late in her life. Having one of those creatures chewing on her hair had been traumatic enough. Climbing on top of one was about as high on her wish list as napping on train tracks.

It wasn't that she disagreed with the lesson behind the saying that when you fall off a horse, you should get right back on. No, her issues came from the thought of falling off in the first place.

"As long as you're here, you should learn," Ryder said.

She didn't bother reminding him that she didn't plan to stick around much longer or share any more of what he was sure to think were overly feminine, city-girl phobias. She simply ran a hand over the horn of a nearby saddle and ignored the suggestion altogether.

When Ryder turned, she followed him out of the tack room, glancing into each of the stalls as they passed. Except for those with very pregnant mares in them, most were empty, and Ryder explained that the horses were let out to pasture during the day. From there, they could be brought in individually or in groups to ride, train, shoe, groom...

The horses were rounded up and stabled each night, but the cows were often left out, called to the barn only when they needed to be chopped or slaughtered. Unfortunately, Monica now knew the difference between the two terms.

Ryder ended his tour where they'd entered the barn and handed her the pair of big leather gloves he'd gotten from the tack room.

"What are these for?" she asked.

"To keep you from getting blisters on those dainty little hands of yours."

She shot him a questioning glare, but he only leaned behind her, grabbed something from beside the wall, and handed it to her. She looked down to find a pitchfork hanging from her fingers.

"What am I supposed to do with this?" she asked. She'd seen pitchforks before, but never actually held one. She didn't have the faintest idea what it was used for.

"Muck," he said.

Her eyes rounded. Had he just cursed at her? "Excuse me?"

He moved something that looked like a bucket on wheels next to the first stall on her right.

"Wheelbarrow," he said, setting the thing down with a thump.

"Pitchfork." He pointed to her hand.

"Horse shit." He motioned toward the floor inside the open doorway in front of her.

"Now muck."

Chapter Eight

When you're pickin' flowers, everybody gets along. When it comes time to muck the stalls is when you find out how true your love really is.

Ryder left Monica to her first dirty stall, walking away as though he didn't care one whit whether she cleaned it or not, or how she was handling what was likely the only bout of manual labor she'd encountered in her entire pampered life. He took his time crossing over to Chynna, giving her a scratch under the chin before reaching into a nearby bin for a handful of feed. While the horse nibbled, he unlocked the door to her stall and let her take her time moving to the middle of the barn, where he hooked the cross ties to her halter.

If anyone saw him, they'd think he was simply moving through the regular motions of his daily chores, but in reality, he was watching his new bride like a hawk. From the corner of his eye, he could see everything she was doing…as well as the way she was doing it.

She might be an uptight city gal dressed in *his* clothes

that hung on her like burlap sacks, but damned if she didn't make them look like million-dollar threads. Or at least like they'd been made for her. The way she tied the tails of his shirt to leave her stomach bare and emphasize her boobs. And though the pants were baggy as hell, they did amazing things to her ass when she bent over...which she did repeatedly as she forked up horse droppings and dumped them into the wheelbarrow.

He could stand here watching her do that all day. Never mind that it gave him a hard-on he had to hide behind Chynna's considerable girth, or that brushing down the mares wasn't really his responsibility. Grooming was normally left to the ranch hands, and there were dozens of other tasks he, as the boss, should be doing. None of which were going to get done standing in the barn.

But even though Monica seemed to have the hang of things, Ryder couldn't find it in him to walk away. He just stood there, running the curry comb round and round in circles over Chynna's soft fur and observing his new wife through the open stall door.

His wife. Now there was a scary thought. He still didn't know what the hell had possessed him to go along with her idiotic proposition. Ryder wasn't usually one to go off half-cocked or follow in the footsteps of anybody who did. But something about her had gotten under his skin from the very start. There were so many things about her that should send him running in the other direction, but she just kept roping him in.

He wished he could blame it on his dick or the fact that he hadn't gotten laid in a while, but though that may be one of his most painful troubles right this second, physical attraction was only part of the problem...and he couldn't quite put his finger on the rest of it. There was just something about her.

How terrible would it be to let her go? Did he really need

to "hold her hostage," as she called it, just because she'd signed a marriage certificate and dubious business deal she had no way of following through on?

Face it, she'd pulled a bait-and-switch. If she was telling the truth about giving Matt her life savings—which he may or may not have run off with; Ryder hadn't decided if he believed that part of her story or not yet—then there was no way he was getting the fifty thousand she'd promised him. And keeping her on the Rolling Rock wouldn't change that. The smart move would be to call it quits on their hasty marriage, tear up the hastily scrawled contract they'd worked out over the hood of his pickup truck, and leave her in his rearview mirror.

Definitely the smart play.

So why wasn't he doing just that?

Hell if he knew. Except that some niggle in his brain told him that if he kept her around, he'd figure out a way to get her to pay up. Or at least find out more about her to give himself a little more leverage.

If they went their separate ways, he got nothing. Worse than that, he'd still be in hock up to his eyeballs, and out a couple hundred more thanks to the newly minted Mrs. Nash's brilliant notion to elope in Las Vegas. She'd paid for the marriage license online, but everything else had come out of his pocket.

Maybe there was no future for the two of them—and by "future" he definitely wasn't thinking along the lines of matching rocking chairs on the front porch while they watched their grandchildren grow. No, the only future that interested him was the one where they stayed hitched until she found a way to scrape up fifty Gs and handed it over. But until he was damn sure there was no chance of money changing hands—hers to his, not the other way around—he just wasn't prepared to cut his losses.

The stall door banged against the wall as Monica came out butt-first, boot heels scuffling on the straw-covered floor, doing her best to steer the ungainly wheelbarrow with its load of horse shit and the pitchfork tossed on top. A decent man would offer to help. A gentleman would offer to take over for her. Ryder stayed where he was, half-hidden behind Chynna's silvery height and width, while Monica lumbered her way to the next empty stall and got back to work.

So maybe he was just okay.

He'd give her one thing—she was no wilting lily. She might fuss, and her mind might flit from one thought to another like a butterfly on the breeze, but she was holding up a dang sight better than he would've guessed. For a city girl, she had gumption.

Maybe that was why he wanted to hold her to their agreement, keep her around a bit longer. He wanted to find out just how much mettle was tucked away in that tempting little package...and if she had any other fun surprises like the belly button ring or the *no, not on my butt* tattoo she'd mentioned hidden in sexy places he hadn't seen yet.

• • •

For the tenth time in five minutes, a cloud of sawdust blew up Monica's nose. She coughed and sneezed and gasped for air. Not that she could breathe in the sweltering heat of this damn barn, even if she'd wanted to. Which she didn't, since every time she inhaled, the most hideous odor known to man scorched her lungs.

God, she hated horses. And barns. And flies. And Ryder.

She slanted a glance over her shoulder to where he was lazily grooming Chynna. The horse stood still, letting him stroke her soft fur, her eyes drifting closed at the pleasant sensation. They both looked entirely too content to Monica.

And the blasted man was whistling. She didn't know what song it was or what he had to be so damn happy about. But he was *whistling* while she was *dying*.

Sweat dripped down her forehead into her eyes. She'd long ago discarded her hat, and the sleeves of her shirt were now completely soaked from wiping them across her face. She'd have taken off the hot, soggy boots, too, if she weren't petrified of what she'd be standing in without them.

Cursing under her breath, she lifted another forkful of manure and dumped it on the growing pile in the wheelbarrow beside her, holding her breath this time to keep sawdust from flying up her nose. She'd done three stalls so far, but it felt more like fifty. Each time she thought she was finished and could go find herself a nice, cool place to pass out, Ryder would move the wheelbarrow to another stall and tell her to keep working.

The one good thing about her predicament was that her debt ought to be paid off by dinner. She figured each stall had to be worth about ten thousand dollars, so she only had two to go.

"This is cruel and unusual punishment, Nash," she called out. "I should turn you in for running a sweatshop ring."

"You think that's bad, wait till you start on the cow barn," he said easily. "You'll need a shovel instead of a fork."

She frowned, thinking about that for a minute. And then her eyes widened as she realized why she would probably need a shovel. Yuck.

"No way," she vowed, dropping the pitchfork and stomping out of the stall. Hands on hips, she glared at Ryder and the horse who seemed to think he was a licensed masseur.

"That's it. I'm done. Consider my debt paid," she said, grabbing her hat and stalking down the walkway. The only reason she'd stuck with it this long was because she was pretty sure he didn't think she would...or could. And, dammit—

she might be a city girl; she might like her mani-pedis and fancy, five-dollar coffee drinks, but she'd wanted to prove she wasn't an entirely useless bit of fluff. She could keep up with the "big boys"—even if those boys were rough and tumble cowboys who'd never seen the inside of a manicure kit or wouldn't know a triple-shot venti half-sweet non-fat caramel macchiato if someone poured one over their heads.

"Hey," Ryder called after her. "Where do you think you're going?"

"Home. Guam. Timbuktu. Anywhere away from you," she threw over her shoulder.

He caught up to her and grabbed the back of her pants to halt her progress.

"Get your hands off of me," she growled, struggling to break his hold. "I'm not mucking anymore stalls. I'm not mucking the cow barn. I'm not doing any other disgusting chores just because you think I owe you something." She slapped at his hands, twisting and turning to reach him. "If anything, you owe me. You owe me new clothes to replace the ones you just made me ruin, you owe me a pedicure for the feet that have probably contracted jungle rot in these damn boots, and you owe me a lung transplant to replace the ones that are now filled with sawdust and horse manure."

He grasped the front of her pants and swung her around, holding her from both angles now. "Settle down," he said, giving them a tug.

"Settle down? *Settle down?*" she all but shrieked. "You're insane. I married a madman, and you want me to settle down." The sides of his mouth turned up, and if she hadn't been so furious, she'd have probably thought he looked boyish or charming.

"If you hate it that much, darlin', you don't have to muck anymore stalls."

She froze. "I don't?" she asked cautiously.

"Nope." His smile widened.

"Then I can go home?"

"If you consider my house home, yes. And while you're in there, you can clean up a bit. I figure your housekeeping abilities ought to be worth something toward your debt."

Her teeth clamped together, blood pounding in her brain. "*Ooooh*," she ground out. And then she stomped on his foot. As hard as she could. Even through his worn leather boots, she was pretty sure he felt it.

He cursed and let her go.

Taking advantage of his pain, she ran away from him and out of the barn.

But she didn't get very far. Her sweaty feet kept slipping inside the rubber boots, causing them to scrape painfully against her heels. She was exhausted from working so hard, and every muscle in her five-foot-four frame screamed in agony—her back, her legs, her arms, even her neck.

When she reached the corral, she stopped, sagging against the top slat of the fence connected to the stable. Breathing ragged, she rested her head on the splintery wood and waited for Ryder to catch up. After all, he only had a stubbed toe, she had a stubbed body.

A second later, he ambled into the sunlight and leaned against the fence next to her. He stared out toward the horizon, not trying to touch or argue with her. She lifted her head to look at him, wondering what he was up to.

"I love this place, you know," he said softly.

"How can you love it?" she asked, awed and more than a little confused by his admission. Her nose wrinkled at the very thought of going back in that barn. "It's hot. The animals are big and stinky, and there are flies *everywhere*," she gritted out, swiping at one of the pests as it buzzed around her face.

He chuckled. "Yeah. Isn't it great?"

She rolled her eyes, sure he really was insane if he could

feel an ounce of fondness for a place like this. Now her apartment in Chicago—there was a home to get dreamy over. Air-conditioned comfort; a beautiful sofa to relax on; soft, thick carpeting to curl her toes into; even a gas fireplace she could sit in front of during the winter, sipping hot cocoa and watching the snow fall outside the sliding doors that led to the balcony. Walking around outside during a Chicago winter was a different story, but for the most part, Ryder didn't know what he was missing.

"I've had my eye on this piece of land since I was about twelve years old," he continued. "It didn't take me more than a heartbeat to lay claim to it when my parents offered to help me start my own homestead. It's so peaceful here."

She bit down on a scoff. Personally, she hadn't had a moment's peace since waking up in his bed, but she decided not to remind him of that fact.

"You can look out across the fields and see for miles."

She turned her head in the direction he indicated. He was right. A wide swath of green dappled with brown stretched out in front of her. Small hills and valleys, with dots that she thought must be horses and cows. It was picture perfect, like a television commercial or magazine layout inviting you to enjoy the beauty of a real farm or dude ranch.

But it was still hot and stinky.

She started to say so when she noticed the expression on Ryder's face. Pride, joy, contentment. He really did love it here.

Monica was stunned. How could anyone find joy or satisfaction in getting dirty and sweaty, working with huge farm animals that could crush you with only one hoof, and coming home with brush burn on his face? The boots and hat were none too comfortable, either, she was learning. The blazing sun beat down on her and perspiration gathered at her hairline, waiting for the moment when she removed the hat so it could come pouring down her face.

True to her classic sitcom-loving nature, the theme to *Green Acres* began thrumming through her brain. She used to think the show was hilarious, with its fish-out-of-water characters and storylines. But much like Eva Gabor, she'd been dragged into the country by her farm-loving husband, with no idea when she'd be able to get back to her normal life in the city…and suddenly it wasn't nearly as amusing.

"Over there is where I want to build the equine therapy barn and corral," he continued, pointing. "It's going to cost an arm and a leg to get set up, but there's a boy in town who needs it. A lot of folks from all around who need it. That's what the money you promised is going for, since the bank turned me down for a loan. Can't say I blame them," he added with a shake of his head. "It'd be my third, and I'm not exactly winning any races at paying back the first two."

Equine therapy. That was downright…noble. And now she knew what that whole EAT thing on their impromptu business contract meant.

Her heart squeezed, and for just a moment she wished she could reach into her pocket and write him a check to cover whatever strange notions had tumbled from her mouth last night. But she couldn't, and there was no time like the present to get her broke ass out of Dodge.

As much as she was enjoying this quiet moment with her new husband—and surprisingly, she kind of was—she didn't think she could handle sticking around much longer. She'd cleaned a few stalls, discovered that farm living was *not* the life for her, and now it was time to head back to civilization. Regardless of his edict that she couldn't leave until she'd handed over the wad of cash she'd promised. While under the influence of alcohol *and* heartbreak, no less. There should be a law against taking a person's word amidst circumstances like that.

"That sounds great. Good luck with everything. I happen to enjoy city life, though, so thanks for the tour and showing me what I've been missing all these years living in the asphalt jungle," she said, slowly moving away from the fence. Maybe if she played it casual, he'd continue his easy-going reminiscence and barely even notice her absence.

A few steps away, she turned and headed for the house. *So far, so good*, she thought, picking up the pace.

The sound of his heavy boot steps caught up to her a split-second before he did. "Hold on there, Rapunzel."

His honey-rich voice rolled over her spine even as her shoulders hunched around her ears at having her departure halted yet again. And as hard as she fought it, she did love the soft way he called her Rapunzel.

"What now?" she asked, frustrated, looking up in to his intense, azure eyes.

"I told you once, you aren't leaving until I get my money. Just because I said you could stop mucking doesn't mean I changed my mind."

"And I told *you*," she stressed, tired of this same argument. "I don't *have* any money. I cleaned three filthy horse stalls for you, isn't that enough?"

He laughed. "Not hardly."

Hitching one hip, she said, "Then how much was all that work worth? Maybe I can send you a check for the rest." She could probably scrape together a thousand dollars or so just to get him off her back.

"About ten bucks," he answered.

"Ten bucks? *Ten bucks?*" she ranted. "But I worked for hours. I cleaned *three* stalls. I *stink*."

He leaned close and sniffed the arm of her shirt. His eyes went wide at the odor wafting from beneath the material. "You do at that. But I've smelled worse. And two hours of work at five dollars an hour is still only ten bucks."

"Five dollars an hour? I was right, you are running a sweatshop. What I did is worth, like, thirty thousand, at least."

He threw his head back and whistled through his teeth. "You sure do think a lot of yourself, sweetheart. But it's not like you scrubbed down the stalls with your toothbrush. You just scooped out the piles of—"

"Never mind." She held up a hand, not wanting to hear the rest. She also didn't want to argue with him anymore. Even at only minimum wage, the work she'd done was worth more than ten dollars, and they both knew it.

"It's about time you came to terms with the fact that I don't have fifty thousand dollars, and keeping me here against my will, making me do filthy, disgusting chores, isn't going to change that. But the least I can do is give you a little something—for your trouble. How does a hundred dollars sound?"

His mouth turned down, brows drawing together in a deep frown. "Like chicken feed. You've already caused me more than a hundred dollars' worth of trouble, and this ranch wouldn't run for one day on that much."

"Well, take it or leave it," she said decisively. "It's the best offer you're going to get, and I really do have to get back to Chicago."

She tried to move away again, but again he stopped her.

"What is *with* you?" she asked with a frustrated huff, stomping one bare, sweaty foot in her floppy rubber boot. She was beginning to understand what his horses must feel like, being led around by leashes and kept in stalls no larger than a kitchen sink.

"Look, lady," he said sharply, his eyes narrowed as he demanded her attention. "I understand that you were drunk and didn't know what you were getting into when you badgered me into marrying you."

"Badgered?" she repeated in a high voice. *She'd* badgered *him*? Well, he was certainly returning the favor now.

He ignored her outrage. "But I asked you a dozen times if you were sure and every time you said yes. And you may be able to survive from paycheck to paycheck as a big-shot photographer, even after Matt ran off with your savings, but some of us aren't so lucky. We have mortgages to pay, stock to feed, barns to rebuild, fields to tend to, and fences to mend." Releasing her elbow, he swept off his hat and brushed the back of his arm across his forehead. "I wouldn't have gone through with your stupid plan if you hadn't promised me enough money to get that new barn up and buy the equipment we need so I can get the bank off my back and this place in working order again. Believe me."

Monica stared at him, speechless. The lines around his eyes looked deeper in direct sunlight, attesting to just how hard it was to run a ranch. Especially with bills to pay. And not just minor expenses like rent and utilities, but mammoth ones like paychecks for his hands and oats for twenty cows and horses, maybe more.

In a drunken stupor, she had promised him enough to get him out of debt. And in the bright light of day, she'd taken it all back.

She looked at the rounded toes of her ugly yellow boots and tried to think of some way to apologize, maybe even help him get the money he needed.

Then it came to her. Not a brilliant idea, she supposed, but considering what this man had already been through and done for her, she didn't think he would be overly surprised when she sprang it on him. He'd gone along with most of her original plan, after all, now she just had to get him to continue along the same path. Which shouldn't be too hard, if she really could give him the money she'd promised.

"Okay, so you really, really need the money." She could

sure use it, but she didn't really, *really* need it. The fifty thousand she'd given Matt had been left over from her trust fund, only a small amount of which she'd used for college before quitting to become a fashion photographer. With residuals and payments for recent jobs trickling in, she wouldn't have any trouble keeping her head above water...at least for the next couple months. Meanwhile, it sounded like Ryder may be going under for the third and final time. If she helped Ryder now, he could eventually pay her back, as their deal specified. With interest. Provided no huge emergencies came up between now and then, she thought she could swing it.

Besides, if they *didn't* do what she had in mind, Matt would still have her money, she still wouldn't, and none of them—except for Matt, of course—would be any better off than they were at this very moment. That seemed patently unfair.

Plus, if it kept her from having to muck any more stalls, it would be well, well worth it.

She took a deep breath and pushed her own hat back on her head. "Fine, I'll stay. On two conditions: I don't have to clean up after any more disgusting farm animals, and you get Ned or somebody to take care of things here while we're on our honeymoon."

Chapter Nine

There are two things a man's gotta do to keep his wife happy: First, let her think she's gettin' her way. Second, let her have it.

Ryder didn't strangle her. He did give her a glare that could freeze ice cubes in Hades, but he didn't strangle her.

Striding over to the corral, he hiked one foot and one arm on the graying wooden slats. When he spoke, his words were slow, with a calculated calm that made Monica want to jump over the fence with the cows, just to be on the safe side. "What honeymoon?"

"Most married couples do have honeymoons, you know," she said, being purposely obtuse.

His gaze settled on her face and by its strength, she wondered if he had X-ray vision. It certainly felt as though he was staring right through her.

"Yeah, I know most people have honeymoons. But we're not most people," he said. "From your reaction when I mentioned it this morning, I didn't think the idea of sharing a bed settled too well with you."

She swallowed and focused on the brim of his hat rather than his cobalt blue eyes. "I'm only opposed to the idea because I'm still in love with Matt," she lied. A part of her still wanted to get even with her ex for what he'd done to her and put her through, and she cringed when she thought of all that was supposed to have been between them. But she didn't think she was truly in love with him anymore. How could she love someone who would betray her so thoroughly, so brutally?

No. If truth be told, she was becoming less attached to Matt and more attached to Ryder. Well, maybe not attached but attracted. He was a damn fine-looking man. And since she'd met him, he'd rescued her from making a fool of herself at someone else's wedding party, married her just to aid her drunken plot for revenge, and carried her across the yard because she had no shoes.

Aside from making her sift around in dirty sawdust and insisting she pay him money she didn't have, he could easily be the hero of every fairy tale she'd ever read as a child— and a few fantasies she'd come up with as an adult. Little Red Riding Him, The Emperor and His New and Quickly Discarded Clothes, The Princess and the Penis...

She cleared her throat and rested her arm on the rail of the fence, cheeks heating at the path her thoughts were taking. "I realize that my original plan to get back at Matt was a little off the wall," she said.

Ryder lifted an eyebrow.

"All right. A lot off the wall," she conceded. "But even though I was slightly tipsy—"

"You were drunk off your ass."

She cleared her throat, wishing he would let her get through this one assertion without interruption. "Fine. Even though I was *quite* intoxicated, you still married me. Frankly, I don't understand that. You could have dumped me at the nearest bus station and never looked back. You could have stuck a ring on my finger and only pretended we were married. I wouldn't have known the difference. But you really did it."

He didn't answer at first, keeping his focus on the horizon. "Just trying to be a good hair climber," he said quietly.

Her brows knit together. *Now what is he talking about?* She shrugged, deciding it probably didn't matter.

But if she'd had any doubts about the legitimacy of their marriage, his comment—however cryptic—erased all uncertainty from her mind. He wasn't spinning tales or creating an elaborate hoax. They really were married. Leave it to her to find the one man on the face of the earth who wasn't afraid of commitment.

"Well, then, we don't have a choice," she said with determination. "We have to go through with the plan."

He shot her a questioning, apprehensive glance. "What plan?"

"The plan to hit Matt where it hurts, of course. His bank account. The only way you're going to get that money from me is if I get it back from him," she told him frankly.

Ryder's lips went flat. "How do you plan to do that?" he asked, and she could see the skepticism in his eyes.

She took a deep breath and admitted, "I'm not sure exactly. But I'll think of something. If Matt won't return my money voluntarily, maybe we can find some sort of proof that I gave it to him in the first place in case I need to take legal action to get it back. I'll call *Inside Edition* and make it a national scandal, if I have to." Her molars had begun to grind together, and she had to take a deep breath before deliberately relaxing her jaw. "Anyway, he carries his attaché case and laptop with him everywhere, so if there's a record of the money changing hands and showing that it was supposed to be a *loan*, then that's where it will be."

He snorted and gazed back across the pasture, all but

dismissing her.

His disregard made her bristle. "I don't need your help, you know. I can track down Matt and get my savings back all by my lonesome. You can stay here and brush your horses, and I'll FedEx the money to you once I have it."

One brow shot up on Ryder's bronze face. "I don't think so. Don't take this the wrong way, darlin', but you've caused enough trouble already. I'd have to be loco to let you try something like this on your own. You'd probably end up in Tijuana with a belly full of tequila and a new husband on each arm."

She glared at him, shooting daggers for that last comment. "Do you have a better idea?" she asked crossly. "Because if you do, I'd love to hear it."

"I told you, you can muck some stalls and groom some horses, and we'll call it even."

She was already shaking her head. "Uh-uh. No way. That is not an option. If you want your money, you have to help me find Matt and get *my* money back."

He continued to study her. "And you think we can do that?" he asked doubtfully. "Just the two of us, trying to convince Matt to repay the money he took from you."

Taking a deep breath, she avoided his gaze and quietly said, "We have to. We don't even know each other; we can't stay married. You have a life here, one that means a great deal to you, and which I know nothing about. And I have a life back in Chicago, one you would hate. I think the best thing to do is go our separate ways. Since you won't allow that until you have your precious money, this is our only option."

She turned to him then, spine straight, hands on hips. "Now, are you in, or are you out?"

Please say yes.

He took a deep breath, looked out across his fields of grass and livestock, and nodded. "All right, I'm in. I just hope you know what you're doing, darlin'. 'Cuz if you don't, we're in one steaming heap of trouble."

"I'm very good under pressure," she said by way of an answer. She didn't think it made either of them feel any better. "First things first. We have to track down Matt. Do you know where he and your sister are honeymooning?"

He thought a moment. "They're staying in Hawaii for a few days before moving on to visit France or Rome or something like that."

Her jaw snapped closed. She and Matt had talked about going to Hawaii for their honeymoon. It seemed he meant to drive that stake through her heart as far as he could.

That knowledge steeled her resolve. If even an inkling of doubt had remained in her mind, it dissolved like sugar in water. Oh, she'd get her money back, all right. And along the way, she might just make her vermin of an ex pay, big-time. For marrying another woman, jetting off to an island paradise, and getting her into this mess with Ryder.

She glanced his way and forced back her thoughts of revenge. "We don't have much time, then, and Hawaii encompasses a lot of vacation spots. Where, exactly, did they go?"

He concentrated again, his eyes narrowing to a squint. "Waikiki would be my guess."

Of course, Waikiki. That's where she'd wanted to go. "Where are they staying?"

He thought for a moment, then sighed with defeat. "I don't know," he said with a shrug. "I'd have to ask my mother."

Monica grinned, undeterred. "I can call her. What's her number?"

He gave her another look. Not "hysterical-female" or "petulant child"—the two she recognized. This one was new and seemed to say, *Are you out of your ever-lovin' mind?*

"Are you crazy?" he shot at her, letting her know her

guess had been on point. "My mother doesn't even know you exist yet, and I have no intention of introducing the two of you over the phone."

He pulled on his gloves, making sure that each tan leather finger fit snuggly against his own flesh ones. "I'll call her later and find out where Josie and Matt are staying. Okay?"

Fixing her with a pointed gaze, he seemed to be waiting for her to respond. She shrugged a shoulder and said, "Sure."

"Good." With a nod, he headed for the stables without a backward glance.

"Can I go in now?" she called after him.

"Be my guest," he tossed over his shoulder. "And while you're in there, see if you can't clean the place up a bit. Miz Nash."

Monica gave him the evil eye for all of ten seconds before deciding it must not work on someone when his back was turned. Rude hand gestures probably wouldn't have much effect, either, but she was sinfully tempted to give it a shot.

And then she remembered that she'd been granted a reprieve, released from bondage. She was free! No more breathing sawdust or standing in the hot sun.

Monica didn't bother hiding her smile. Not only was she dismissed, but she now had a plan. Another one, or an addendum to the original, whatever. The point was, she'd be getting her money back from Matt the Rat. And rubbing his nose in it if she got half a chance.

As quickly as the floppy rubber boots would carry her, she ran back to the house and dumped the footwear at the front door, thankful to be free of the sweaty, uncomfortable things. If she ever had to go out to the barn again—which she sincerely hoped never happened—she'd put socks on before the boots.

She ran into Ryder's bedroom to pack her things—and then remembered that she didn't *have* any things. A slightly used wedding dress and a still-damp bra and panty set didn't exactly warrant the use of luggage.

She stood in the middle of the room for a minute, feeling futile. And then she shrugged to herself, deciding that she would simply have to do some airport shopping or stop somewhere along the way to pick up a few things. Clothes, for sure, but also necessities like deodorant and a toothbrush of her own.

But without needing to pack, she didn't really have anything to do. No small tasks to occupy her time. She went back to the kitchen and dug through the cupboards, finding a pack of saltines to nibble on and almost, *almost* considered straightening up Ryder's kitchen.

It wouldn't take much, just gathering up all the assorted glass and plastic containers to be recycled, running a wet cloth over the countertop. But her feminist side balked, asserting that if Ryder had made the mess, then Ryder could darn well clean it up!

So she wandered toward the living room with her little waxed paper bag of crackers. As she passed the phone, she wished she could call Ryder's mother to press her for details about Matt and Josie's honeymoon. Patience wasn't her strong suit, and having to bide her time with just about anything gave her hives. But it really wasn't her place to approach *his* mother, and she not only needed to respect those boundaries, she needed to trust him.

Trust him, a near stranger. Also not something she excelled at. But this near stranger happened to be her new husband, and though the ink was barely dry on that dubious merger, she had to admit that Ryder had been nothing but honorable so far.

She couldn't claim to remember every moment of their association—except for waking up in bed with him, both half-naked, and not being entirely clear on whether or not they'd shared the intimacies of a wedding night—but she was pretty sure he'd only ever been 100 percent honest with her. Granted, Matt was a prime example that she might not be the best judge of character, but where he'd been smoothly charming and slick in gaining her confidence, Ryder seemed to be more of a forthright-to-a-fault kind of guy. If she Googled "painfully honest," she wouldn't be the least surprised to see it pop up with a full-color photo of Ryder right there to illustrate the term.

Maybe that was why she leaned toward having faith in him. She'd been worked up and emotionally wrecked over Matt's betrayal and what to do about it for what felt like decades rather than only a few days; it would be nice to take a deep breath and let someone else take care of things for a change. Not forever—she was too tightly wound in general to take her hands off the wheel for that long. But it wouldn't hurt to push her troubles to the side and relax for a couple hours.

To that end, she returned to the fridge and grabbed a can of Coke, then headed for the living room to plop herself down in front of the television. Picking up the remote, she started flipping through channels, hoping to find something interesting…and anything but *Green Acres*. Normally, it would be one of her go-tos, and she'd be delighted to discover that Ryder had a channel that carried the oldie-but-goodie. Now that she'd managed to fall into the alternate universe that was "farm living," it didn't hold nearly the same appeal.

• • •

Ryder heard the house phone ringing from across the yard, but didn't alter his stride. Voicemail kicked in after five rings, so even if he hurried, he wouldn't catch whoever was calling.

His cell phone was hooked to his belt, but everybody

knew coverage was sketchy the farther you got from town. He could make and receive calls right around the house and usually in the barns, but if he rode into the pastures or past the row of trees along the far side of his property, it was hit or miss. The landline was far more reliable, which is why he kept it and used it to collect messages while he was working.

Sure enough, the trills stopped before his foot hit the step of the porch. He'd check to make sure it wasn't an emergency, but grabbing a beer and washing up was higher on his list than checking voicemail right now.

And then there was the matter of checking up on the missus. He shook his head, still not used to the idea. He also wasn't used to anyone being around when he came in for lunch, but knowing Monica would be waiting gave him a tiny punch of anticipation low in his belly. His life would be easier if it didn't, but there it was.

His next thought was that maybe she'd taken him up on his suggestion about cleaning the kitchen. As much aggravation as she'd caused him already, it sure would be nice if she'd made herself useful while he was working outside. Then again, it was probably too much to hope that Monica was *that* kind of woman. And after roping her into cleaning stalls this morning, he doubted she was of a mood to make his life easier in any way, shape, or form.

So maybe she was doing something harmless like taking a nap or watching TV. Whatever the case, he just hoped she'd managed to keep herself out of trouble. More than once since they'd parted ways out in the yard, he'd caught himself wondering if leaving his new bride to her own devices had been the wisest course of action. After all, Monica did have a habit of getting into hot water. Like showing up in a wedding gown at someone else's reception, marrying the first man she stumbled into, and coming up with the half-assed idea of tracking down her ex-fiancé to get back the money he'd absconded with. Not to mention giving the man her savings in the first place.

With all of those less-than-sensible images of Monica running through his brain like water on a mill wheel, he'd decided it might be smart to keep her with him the rest of the day. Even if he didn't put her to work mucking stalls, he intended to drag her back with him after lunch. She could certainly curry one of the horses or polish some saddles—something non-strenuous that wouldn't cause her to chip a nail or split an end.

The first thing he noticed when he stepped into the house, screen door banging closed behind him, was that he'd been right on the housekeeping front—she hadn't bothered. Everything was exactly as he'd left it...and not in a good way.

The second thing that caught his attention was voices. One of them came from the living room and was indistinct enough that he placed it as the television.

Whew. He'd lucked out...Monica had camped out in front of the TV and actually managed to keep herself out of trouble.

Releasing a breath, he removed his Stetson, but before he could hang it on one of the hooks on the wall beside the door, he heard laughter—a light, breezy chuckle that was unmistakably Monica's coming from farther back in the kitchen.

"No, ma'am, I'm not the new cleaning lady."

Who was she talking to? Ryder spotted the empty phone charger and his gut clenched, everything in him going cold.

"I'm not sure when he'll be back, but I'd be happy to give him a message."

Dammit. Why hadn't she let the call go to voicemail? She really shouldn't be answering his phone; it was only going to create more problems than it would solve.

"I'm not Stephanie, but he definitely knows I'm here. My

name is Monica."

Shit. Whoever it was knew about his relationship with Stephanie and now knew he had a woman named Monica hanging out at his house. Neither of those boded well.

"Oh, hello, Mrs. Nash."

Chapter Ten

Try not to make a ring around the finger feel akin to a rope around the neck.

"No!" Ryder thundered, Stetson falling from his grasp as he lurched toward the sound of Monica's voice. She'd been standing with her back to him, but spun around at his shout, eyes wide, phone still pressed to her ear. And he was almost there, almost had his fingers wrapped around the handset to take over the conversation before things got ugly.

"Don't you dare tell her we're married!" he barked, snatching the phone from her.

"*What?*"

He realized his mistake almost immediately, and his mother's shrieks from the other end of the line confirmed it.

Dammit-dammit-dammit. Shit-shit-shit.

Slapping a hand over his eyes, he dropped his head and cursed his own stupidity. He'd been so worried about how Monica was going to screw things up that he hadn't noticed the trap of his own making lying right in front of him. Son of a bitch.

With a heavy sigh of regret, he lifted the phone and did what he could to stomp out the blaze he'd set with his own big, fat mouth.

"Mom. *Mom*," he nearly yelled to be heard over her high-pitched, rapid-fire questions. "Mom, listen. Mom—"

"Jordan! Get the truck," she ordered, her voice carrying clearly despite the fact that she wasn't talking—or listening—to him.

"Mom, that's not necessary," he tried one more time. "I can explain."

The line seemed to go dead then, and he waited a moment to see if he could hear anything. "Mom? Mom, are you there?"

Smart enough to know a lost cause when it hung up on him, Ryder slowly crossed the kitchen and set the phone back in its base. Biting back a groan, he forced himself to breathe deep and count to ten before turning to fix Monica with a steel dagger glare.

"What the hell did you think you were doing?" he ground out.

She opened her mouth, a hand going to her heart. Shirley Temple couldn't have looked more innocent. "All I did was answer the phone. You're the one who blurted out that we were married loud enough for her to hear."

Yeah, he got that. She didn't need to rub it in.

"But why did you answer the phone to begin with?"

"Um…because it was ringing?" She made the statement a question, her expression clearly implying that the sun had baked off a few of his IQ points before he'd come in. "I was going to let it go, but when it kept ringing, I thought you might not have voicemail, and I didn't want you to miss a message. It might have been an emergency."

Well, it is now.

It was hard to stay mad at Monica, or even continue to blame her, when her explanation made perfect sense. He hadn't warned her not to answer the phone or let her know calls would go to voicemail. And if he'd just kept his mouth shut, taken the phone away from her, or created some kind of commotion in the background to disrupt the exchange, Hurricane Ruth Ann wouldn't now be bearing down on them at record speeds.

"Okay." Scrubbing a hand over his face, he sighed in resignation. "My parents are definitely on their way over, so before they get here, there are some things you should know."

He couldn't decide if Monica's expression was fear or acceptance or a mix of both. Since they didn't have much time, he didn't ask, just barreled ahead in an attempt to prepare her for what was to come. He had a very close-knit family, and his parents were more than a little overprotective. On the verge of suffocating, he often thought.

When they'd found out Josie was getting married, his parents had gone nuts. They'd alternately cried and celebrated every other night right up until the ceremony. Discovering that he had not only eloped, but with a total stranger, would send his mother into high gear. He'd never hear the end of it. Even if Mom and Pop both fell instantly in love with his new bride, they would still hold it against him—that he hadn't brought Monica home to meet them...hadn't let them fuss over her and plan the entire wedding...that there hadn't *been* a wedding. And the fact that he'd broken the news of his nuptials over the phone in a less-than-polished manner...oh, his mother was going to take a switch to him for that one.

In all honesty, he'd been toying with the idea of not telling them about Monica at all. Not only to avoid the "how dare you" elopement lectures, but because he wasn't sure how long she'd be around and didn't want his parents getting any wild ideas about him finally settling down or—God forbid—

starting a family.

Yes, he'd married her, but she also planned to divorce him as soon as they got her money back from Matt. That could take a week, a month, six months…he didn't know. But once they did, she would go back to her bright lights, big city life, and he would still be here, living his calmer, much more normal one. She'd said as much out at the corral, and she was right. No way did he want to share the flashier aspects of her world with parents who would undoubtedly question him about his relationship or press him to work things out. Not when his marriage to Monica was never meant to last forever.

Which was exactly what he liked about it—no pressure, no commitment, a light at the end of the tunnel. A ball, but no chain.

But now his parents knew he was married and were about to swoop down on them like crows on road kill. Except he wasn't dead—he only wished he were.

He pressed two fingers to his temple where a rhythmic pounding had begun to echo through his brain. *Lord, I need a horse-size dose of Excedrin.*

As quickly as he could, he gave Monica a rundown of his parents' personalities and what she was likely to face when they arrived. The more worried she started to look, the more he considered grabbing her up and high-tailing it before the Wrath of Ruth Ann materialized on the doorstep. But they'd never make it. His folks only lived over the next rise, and even if they did manage to escape for a while, his mother would hunt them down and demand the truth.

"I don't feel very well," she said, swaying a bit on her feet. "Do you think I could go lie down?"

"Not a chance," he answered—never mind that he'd been thinking something awfully similar only seconds before. "We're in this together."

"What are we going to tell them?" she asked anxiously.

"About being married, I mean. I can't imagine your parents will be too happy to know the truth—that we left your sister's wedding for our own. Or that we've known each other a total of thirty-six hours, most of which were spent passed out cold."

She rubbed her temples with the tips of her fingers, and Ryder figured she was wishing for a nice, big bottle of aspirin herself at the moment.

"Speak for yourself," he replied. "I was sober and only slept for eight of those thirty-six hours. Besides, I'd be more worried about them finding out you're the one I had to carry out of Josie's reception."

Her eyes widened like a horse about to spook. "Do you think they'll recognize me?"

He considered that for a moment, then grinned. "Nah. Your face was in my butt most of the time."

The wide eyes narrowed to irritated slits.

"What's the matter?" he asked, grin widening a fraction. "Don't you remember sinking your teeth into my cinnamon buns?"

"Oh God." She groaned and sank forward, letting her body fold in half until it threatened to flip her all the way over.

"Oh God," Ryder echoed with dread, eyes glued to her hair.

• • •

Monica lifted her head to find him staring, his mouth hanging open, his eyes blank with astonishment.

"What?" she asked, unsure what could have caused such a reaction when his parents hadn't even arrived yet.

"Your hair is pink," he said slowly, succinctly, and with more than a little derision.

Her hand flew to the back of her head, just now remembering the magenta streak dyed there. She had pretty much forgotten that tiny detail in all the confusion of the past few days.

"It's no big deal," she assured Ryder. "You can only see it when my hair is up."

His eyes widened. "Well, your hair is up now," he said. "And my parents *will* think it's a big deal."

"Okay, okay." She tugged at the rubber band to rid herself of the ponytail, but the thin, sticky cord caught, knotting in the thin strands of her hair. "Ow," she gasped.

"What's wrong?"

"It's stuck. I can't get this stupid rubber band out."

Ryder came forward, examining the mess before adding his fingers to the jumble. "Why did you use the damn thing if it was going to get stuck?"

"I didn't *know* it was going to get stuck," she snapped. Though she'd had a good idea, she admitted silently. Rubber bands were notoriously bad hair care accessories.

"*Ow!*" she screamed. "Stop pulling so hard. You're going to pluck me bald."

"We have to get your hair down," he said. "My parents can't see that my new wife has bright pink hair." He paused a moment, then added, "They can't see that belly button ring, either. Take it out, cover it up, I don't care. Just do something. They can't see it."

A car door slammed in front of the house, and they both froze.

"Damn, they're here." Ryder hurried across the kitchen to glance out the window.

Monica couldn't help herself; she followed and tried to peer around his wide shoulders for an advance glimpse at what she'd be up against. Before she managed it, though, he spun back around, then spun *her* around, and started tugging at her hair again.

"Hurry up!" he demanded.

Her ponytail now hung haphazardly at the back of her head, and he gave the rubber band another hard yank. "Ow! That hurts, dammit," she said between gritted teeth. "Don't you have a knife or scissors or something?"

He grumbled under his breath, but let go of her hair and dug into the pocket of his pants. While he did that, she began to untie the knot at the front of her shirt.

"What are we going to tell them?" she asked frantically. They hadn't had a chance to cover that, and now she wished they'd started there and he'd filled her in on his parents second.

"I don't know." Slipping the blade into her hair, he sliced the tiny brown band. "Just...try not to say anything incriminating, and follow my lead."

She rolled her eyes, suspecting that he didn't have any better idea of how to handle his parents in this situation than she did.

Footsteps sounded on the porch and they both straightened, stiff as boards. She smoothed the tails of her shirt, knowing they were wrinkled beyond redemption, only to have Ryder whirl her around again to face the door. She'd barely regained her balance and was quickly running a hand through her hair to grab the rubber band and shake some bounce back into her battered, so-called carefree 'do when the front door swung open.

Monica didn't even want to consider what a hideous picture they made—her hair a mess, her clothes making her look like a throwback to *The Beverly Hillbillies* on a bad day; Ryder standing behind her looking guilty and uncomfortable, she was sure. It probably didn't help that he was still holding the pocketknife, blade open, either.

His mother entered first, barreling into the house like a steam-driven locomotive. She wore an outfit similar to Monica's, except that her jeans fit and her shirt was tucked neatly at her belted waist. She was also wearing shoes, which was a big plus, as far as Monica was concerned. Her short, silver-streaked hair looked windblown, her cheeks rosy.

A moment later, a tall, gray-haired man followed. The moment she saw him, Monica knew he had to be Ryder's father. She imagined Ryder would look exactly like him in twenty or thirty years.

Ryder's mother stopped several feet away, taking in the scene before her. Then her hands moved to her hips and she fixed Ryder with a parental glower that made even Monica quake in her boots...well, if she'd been wearing any, she would certainly be quaking in them.

"Just what in blazes is going on here, Ryder Winthrop Nash?" she demanded.

Monica's eyes widened and she bit back a chuckle. Turning to Ryder, she whispered over her shoulder, "Winthrop?"

"Don't ask," he answered sotto voce. Then to his mother, "Hi, Mom."

"Don't 'Hi, Mom' me." She came forward a few steps, but kept her stance rigid. Her eyes narrowed as she studied Monica. "Who is this woman? Is she the one who answered your phone? The one who wasn't supposed to mention that you're *married?*"

Ryder started to explain, but Monica cut him off by moving forward, hand extended. "Hello, Mrs. Nash. I'm Monica. And, yes, I am the one who answered the phone."

His mother seemed to relax a bit, her shoulders lowering as she thought it over and decided it would be safe to shake Monica's hand. "You look familiar," she nearly accused. "Do I know you from somewhere?"

"No," Monica and Ryder answered at the same time, perhaps a bit too quickly and a bit too loud.

"No," Ryder said more calmly, "I don't see how you could. Monica is from out of town. She's never even been to Nevada before this," he added, as though making sure to cover all the bases.

His mother squinted, studying Monica a moment longer. "You still look terribly familiar." Then she released a breath and carefully asked, "Is it true the two of you are married?"

Again, Monica spoke before Ryder had the chance. "I'm afraid so."

"Oh." Tears came to the woman's eyes, and her shoulders slumped even lower than before. "I can't believe it. My oldest child, married. And he didn't even have the courtesy to tell his very own mother. When did all of this happen?" she rushed, clearly trying to grasp the situation.

"You'd better have a good explanation for this," his father added sternly. "Your mother nearly had a heart attack when she hung up the phone."

"Mom, Dad," Ryder said softly. "Why don't we have a seat, and Monica and I will explain everything."

Monica turned to face him, noticing that he used his body to block the kitchen entranceway, gesturing toward the living room instead. He probably didn't want his parents to see the mess on the counter.

As his parents passed ahead of her, he lifted his brows heavenward. Then he took her hand, and they moved together into the living room.

Ryder took a seat in a wide, comfortable chair, urging Monica onto the arm next to him. She assumed he wanted to project an air of true love and newlywed bliss. His parents sat on the sofa adjacent to them and exchanged a somewhat curious, mostly worried glance.

"You've already met Monica," Ryder began. He put a hand on her knee. "Monica, this is my mother, Ruth Ann, and my father, Jordan."

"It's a pleasure to meet you," she said, giving them a lopsided grin. They didn't quite concur, she knew.

"I know this is a shock," Ryder said. "And I wish you didn't have to find out this way, but the truth is, Monica and I were married yesterday."

"*Yesterday?*" his mother all but shrieked. "But yesterday was Josie's wedding."

Ryder nodded. "Why do you think we didn't tell you? We didn't want to spoil her big day."

"But...but how could you get married the same day as your sister? Why didn't you tell someone so we could make plans and—"

"That's exactly why we didn't tell anyone. We didn't want you to fuss. We didn't want parties and fancy clothes and a bunch of guests milling around. We just wanted to get married." He turned to Monica. "I guess we got kind of caught up in the wedding fever. Didn't we, sugar?"

She blinked at the smoldering gaze he cast her way, then choked out, "It was a fever all right, *sugar.*"

Ruth Ann's lips flattened.

His father leaned forward, his brows knit in a frown. "You could have at least told us about her, Ryder. We didn't even know you had a sweetheart."

Monica smiled. She'd never been referred to as someone's sweetheart before. The term was quaint, polite. She liked it.

"We haven't known each other all that long," Ryder said, skirting the truth. "Matt introduced us a while back, and we've kept in touch ever since. Phone calls and such. And then when we got to talking at Josie's reception...well, it just felt right. So we drove to Las Vegas and tied the knot."

The corners of his mother's mouth turned down. "But you left the reception with that awful girl in the wedding dress who tried to ruin the entire thing."

Monica's grip on Ryder's hand tightened.

"Who?" Ryder asked, with such feigned ignorance that Monica almost believed he didn't know what Ruth Ann was talking about.

"That woman. She was drunk, and she climbed up on the dais and went on about how she was supposed to marry Matt instead of Josie."

"Oh, her." Ryder gave an unconcerned snort. "I took her outside for a while, then called a cab and sent her on her way. Monica and I left half an hour or so after that. I hope that woman's tirade didn't upset Josie too much."

Monica squeezed Ryder's hand again, this time as a warning to watch what he said about "that woman."

"No, no," his mother assured them. "She was upset for a few minutes, but Matt assured her that the woman was out of her mind. She must have been to barge into a wedding reception like that."

Every muscle in her body growing tense, Monica had to grind her teeth to keep from launching a blistering retort. So Matt had told everyone she was out of her mind, hmm? Just wait until she got a hold of him. She'd draw and quarter the lying bastard.

Ryder's thumb began a gentle, calming stroke against the palm of her hand, silently warning her to keep her cool. It worked. She flexed her shoulders and reminded herself to play along, no matter what was said.

With a slight sniffle, Ruth Ann dabbed at tears. "I just wish you'd told us, dear. Your father and I would have loved to plan a beautiful wedding for the two of you. We wanted to see you standing at the front of the church while you waited for your lovely bride to walk down the aisle."

"You know better than that, Mom. You'd never have gotten me married off that way. One of the reasons I suggested going to Vegas is because it was a no fuss, no muss elopement." He lifted his head and smiled at Monica. "Monica didn't want a big wedding, either, did you, darlin'?"

Frankly, she had. She'd wanted a huge wedding with

Matt, complete with bachelorette party, matching bridesmaid gowns, and a band that knew the "Chicken Dance." But she smiled serenely and answered, "No."

Apparently coming to terms with her only son's sudden marriage, Ruth Ann took a deep breath and slapped her knees. "Well, you have to at least let us throw you a reception. Nothing fancy—a barbecue maybe, with all of our friends."

Monica was already shaking her head, not wanting to dig an even bigger marital hole that might become difficult to crawl out of later.

"Actually, Mom," Ryder said smoothly. "We were planning to leave right away for our honeymoon. I was going to let you know as soon as I got everything stowed away for the ranch, but then when I came in for lunch, you were already on the phone with Monica and I went ahead and ruined the surprise with my outburst," he explained. "Since Matt and Monica are such good friends, and he's the one who introduced us, we actually thought we'd try a few days in Hawaii, too, maybe even hook up with them while we're there. We just need some details about their trip."

His mother beamed. "What a wonderful idea! I'm sorry to see you leave so soon after finding out about all of this, of course, but every newlywed couple deserves time alone." She glanced at her husband. "Your father and I will make all the arrangements. Think of it as our gift to you, since we didn't have the opportunity to plan a big wedding."

"That's not necessary, Mrs. Nash," Monica rushed out.

"We insist. Don't we, Jordan?"

"Absolutely," the unusually quiet man agreed. "I'll see if I can't get you seats on a flight that leaves first thing in the morning."

Monica glanced at Ryder, wondering at the thoughts going through his head right now. She'd be willing to guess they weren't nice ones. But since he wasn't contradicting his parents' plans, she decided he must want her to go along with them, too. With a nod, she said, "That's very sweet of you both—thank you. Morning would be great...you can leave that soon, can't you, darling?" she asked, turning her best smitten gaze on Ryder.

He met her eyes, revealing nothing but agreement and adoration of his new bride. But she didn't miss the muscle in his jaw that jumped before he spoke. "I'll have to clear up a few more things with the hands first, make sure someone can oversee the herd while I'm gone, but, yeah, I think we can leave in the morning."

"Don't worry about the workload, son," his father said. "Until we get the barn rebuilt at our place, there's not much work for the boys to do. I'll send them over here to make sure everything's taken care of."

"Thanks, Pop. I'd appreciate that."

His mother gasped suddenly and covered her mouth. "Oh, I still can't believe my baby boy is married. And to such a pretty girl." She hopped up and wrapped her arms around Monica.

Monica sat like a statue for moment, both stunned and touched by the gesture. She was the only child of two rather standoffish parents; as much as she loved them, they weren't big on showing emotion. In high school, her best friend had insisted that every outrageous act Monica insisted on performing—from her Goth phase to the time she'd gone skinny-dipping on a dare—were simply a need to rebel against her parents' uptight way of life.

Her friend was probably right...and Monica hadn't changed much over the years. She still enjoyed doing her own thing, and obviously continued to act rashly from time to time, or she wouldn't have woken up in bed with a cowboy she'd never met before and be planning a honeymoon she didn't really deserve.

Displays of affection continued to throw her off-balance more often than not, but when Ruth Ann squeezed tight, Monica experienced only a brief flash of discomfort before raising her arms and hugging Ryder's mother in return. By the time they pulled apart, they were both blinking back tears. Monica turned her head to hide her reaction, hoping Ryder wouldn't notice. He would never understand how such an open, loving gesture could affect her so much. Especially when she knew that this marriage business was all for show.

But very few people in her life had ever been as affectionate with her as his mother. It didn't seem to matter to Ruth Ann that Monica was a virtual stranger who had married her son under very odd circumstances. Because Ryder had chosen her, Ruth Ann automatically—well, almost automatically—accepted her. It warmed a place deep in Monica's heart and made her feel a thousand times worse for the charade she and Ryder were acting out.

Ruth Ann wiped at her eyes and sat back down beside her husband—after Jordan, too, had given Monica a gruff, breath-stealing, welcome-to-the-family embrace.

"So," Ruth Ann said slowly, a smile accentuating the lines at the corners of her mouth. "When do you think I'll get my first grandchild?"

Chapter Eleven

There are two theories to arguin' with a woman. Neither one works.

"Hold this." Monica brushed the once-beautiful, now annoying lei around her neck out of the way and swung the "Dirty Little Slot" carry-on satchel she'd purchased before the first leg of their trip in Ryder's direction while she juggled the handful of shopping bags and tried to get the flat plastic key card to unlock the hotel room door.

He'd talked her out of buying the rhinestone-studded T-shirt with the same tongue-in-cheek phrase, but she hadn't been able to resist the tote. For one thing, the tiny dot of an airport they'd flown out of only had one gift shop filled mostly with kitschy souvenirs. It's what came from being situated within a hundred-mile radius of Vegas, she supposed. For another, she'd needed something to stuff all of her other purchases into as they went along. And finally, if nothing else, she wanted at least one fun, Monica-esque reminder of this adventure.

Ryder gave a grunt of displeasure as the bag hit him in the solar plexus. "I hope you're not going to be this bossy the whole time we're here, sugar, or I may have to dump you down the nearest active volcano."

She slanted an annoyed glance in his direction and barely kept from sticking her tongue out at him. "Try it, and they'll be scraping little pieces of your miserable hide off the hooves of your cows until Christmas," she shot back. The green light flashed and she turned the handle, bumping the door open with her hip and letting the momentum propel her into the air-conditioned room.

Her new hubby had been a phenomenal pain in her butt since before they'd left the ranch. First, he complained about how long she took to get ready, despite having no luggage to pack, no makeup to apply, and no wardrobe to choose from. Then he griped about having to make the trip at all when he was needed at home, and he continued to bitch about whatever caught his attention—the crowded plane...the long flight...the lousy food...the long wait for a cab...the difficult check-in at the hotel's registration desk... The list went on and on until Monica wanted to drop him in a volcano of her own.

And the only thing that shut him up for even a smidgen of time was the reminder that they were doing all of this for the grand sum of fifty thousand dollars, which would be going directly into his pocket. If he was really set against the trip, she'd told him through gritted teeth, they could just go their separate ways and forget all about this devil's deal they'd made.

To which Ryder gave one of his signature snorts and told her, "Not on your life, darlin'." Probably because he suspected—and rightly so—that she would go ahead with The Plan, with or without him. And if he wasn't right there to annoy, irritate, vex, and all around piss her off, she might get *the* money back, but he wouldn't get *his* money.

So she was stuck with him. For better or worse. *Ugh.*

Okay, she thought with a twinge of guilt. *So I owe him. I may have gotten him into this mess, but I'm also trying to get him out.* That had to be worth something, didn't it?

She breathed a sad sigh of resignation and dragged herself to the king-size bed in the center of the room, letting her body fall face down on the mattress. A moment later, she heard the door click shut and rolled to her side to see Ryder standing over her, his carry-on and hers hanging from his shoulder.

"Here," he said, dropping the bag he found so offensive on the bed beside her with a heavy plop. "You may have talked me into this asinine trip, but I'm not your personal assistant—or your bellhop." With that, he set his own bag in a corner beside the entertainment system and removed his hat, swiping a hand through his sandy blond hair.

This time she did stick her tongue out at him. "You know, for fifty thousand dollars, you'd think you could be a little nicer to me." She lifted her upper body with her elbows and propped them behind her. "Not to mention the fact that I'm your wife."

He hitched a thumb into his belt buckle and fixed her with a look that told her his definition of "wife" was on the same plane as Mad Cow Disease, at least where she was concerned.

"You show me the fifty thou and I'll show you just how nice I can be." His voice lowered with the last part of his statement, and one brow lifted with a suggestive wiggle. "Until then, you can thank your lucky stars you're not up to your ass in horse shit. Where I wanted you."

Monica bit her lip, more from the struggle to come up with an appropriate comeback than to keep from saying something she'd regret. At this point, she couldn't imagine regretting much of anything. The louse.

Ryder picked up his single black duffel bag from the floor and slung it over his shoulder. "I'm taking a shower. Do you care?"

Only if he drowned in the process. "Not at all," she replied sweetly. "I'll just sit out here anxiously awaiting your return."

"You do that," he tossed out as he headed for the oversize bathroom.

She fell back on the bed with a ragged sigh. Oh, this was going to be a real thrill. She wondered if she could bind and gag him and leave him in the closet until she took care of this problem with Matt. But, no. Ryder was a cowboy. And didn't cowboys know all about knots and such? He'd probably just untie himself, break down the closet door, and come after her like...like a cowboy after an ornery cow.

Rolling her eyes at her less-than-creative simile, she got up and began unpacking the motley assortment of clothes she'd managed to buy along the way. Short layovers and a limited number of rather unimpressive shops had left her scrambling, but hopefully she'd purchased enough to wear the first couple of days. After that, she supposed she could do a little more shopping. Waikiki would definitely offer a wider assortment of stores, but she also couldn't go crazy. Thanks to Matt, she was currently living on an uncomfortably snug budget and had already spent more than she should have with inflated airport prices.

She'd found some skirts and tank-like blouses at one shop and bought one of each. The skirts were bright florals, the tops matching solids. She might end up looking like a catalog model, wearing practically the same thing every day, but it was better than continuing to dress out of Ryder's closet.

Underwear-wise, she'd found *one* bra in her size and had chosen a six-pack of Hanes bikini-cut panties over the individual thong styles, because she'd never been fond of feeling like she had a string of dental floss rubbing between her butt cheeks. The rest of her finds included a surprisingly cute swimsuit, sarong, and sandals set, and a goofy one-size-fits-most nightshirt stamped with both the front and rear view of a super-sexy woman in a short grass skirt and coconut bra.

Monica had just finished stuffing her few new belongings into one of the dresser drawers when the bathroom door opened and Ryder emerged in a fresh shirt and jeans. He was barefoot, with his boots clasped in one hand. She tried not to stare at his long toes or the way his damp hair clung to the nape of his neck. How was it possible that he could be covered from neck to ankle and still send her pulse skittering? He was smoking hot, but that was *not* why they were here.

Swallowing hard, she leaned back against the dresser, jumping slightly when her hip bumped the open drawer and it slid closed with a sharp slam. "All finished?" she asked, even more annoyed with herself when her voice came out in a squeaky rush.

"Yep." Setting his boots on the floor, he grabbed his duffle and moved to the bed.

"I'll go take a quick shower myself, then. Can you call your sister's suite and ask them to meet us for dinner?"

He raised an eyebrow. "You really want to get into this so soon? Can't we just wait until tomorrow?"

She shrugged a shoulder. "I don't know. I'm sure your parents have told them by now that we were on our way, so it might seem odd if we don't contact them as soon as we get in, don't you think?

"Nah." His eyes sparkled with roguish mischief. "If this were a real honeymoon, darlin', I'd be nailing my new bride to that cute little headboard, not hooking up with another couple for a boring-ass meal."

Her eyes widened at his callousness, but she managed to smother an indignant gasp. Especially since she'd had similar thoughts about him only moments before. "Well, the sooner we get started, the sooner you can go back home to your cows," she added, knowing the reminder of his precious ranch would be the deciding factor.

"Fine. But for the record, I still think the idea you cooked up on the plane is one of the stupidest I've heard since Ned suggested we use razor wire to keep the cattle in the pasture." He shook his head as though that idea still boggled the mind.

"Yes, I know," she huffed. "If I had a dollar for every time you've mentioned what a ridiculous idea this is, we wouldn't have to go through with it at all because I could just hand you the fifty thousand dollars you want."

The frustrating part was that she didn't disagree with him. She might not categorize the plan she'd hatched as *stupid*, but it wasn't terrific, either, and if there were any other way... But she wasn't even sure this would work, let alone anything else.

"We just have to hope your sister doesn't recognize me from the reception, and I need to get Matt alone so I can press him for information about my money."

Ryder reached for his boots and started tugging them on. "Then maybe I'll take up ostrich farming and you can tie a string to that belly button ring of yours and go flying around the islands."

Ignoring that sour statement, she added, "And remember that we're madly in love. You adore me. Worship me. Kiss the ground I walk on."

He snorted and gave her a look that said he'd be more likely to spit on the ground she walked on. "Don't expect too much of that lovey-dovey crap. Josie wouldn't believe it, anyway."

She clamped down on the urge to throttle him. "Do your best. I'll change for dinner."

• • •

When she returned twenty minutes later, Ryder was stretched out in the center of the bed, a pillow stuffed behind his back, remote control in his hand. He'd stopped on ESPN, but wasn't really paying attention to the noisy dirt bikes racing around in a pit of mud.

"Did you talk to Josie?" Monica asked. Just like a real wife—nag, nag, nag.

"Yeah," he said without bothering to look at her. "We're meeting them in the outdoor dining area at six."

"Great. I hope we can pull this off," she added nervously.

Ryder didn't much care if they did or not. He was more inclined to just come right out and ask Matt if he'd taken Monica's money. And if he had, where the hell it was. Nor was Ryder opposed to the idea of grabbing the man by the scruff of the neck if he gave him any guff.

He lazily lifted his gaze, as if Monica were only slightly more interesting than what was on TV...and then his jaw dropped. He closed it quickly, hoping she hadn't noticed, and hit the power button on the remote, casting the room into sudden, almost painful silence. She was definitely more interesting than dirt bikes.

Her hair was slicked back in a short ponytail at the nape of her neck and somehow darkened into a "wet look," she'd used a heavy hand with the makeup around her eyes, and her skin had somehow been turned at least two shades darker from hairline to tippy-toes—all in an effort to alter her appearance enough to keep Josie from recognizing her. The insta-tan was somewhat jarring at first, but he had to admit that the efforts to disguise herself were likely to work. He didn't know how anyone who'd seen Monica with curly brown hair, porcelain skin, and in a full-length wedding gown could possibly suspect she and the woman standing before him now were one and the same.

She'd also changed from the tight black leggings and fire

engine red Sin City "I feel a SIN coming on!" T-shirt she'd picked up at that first airport gift shop to travel in, to a gold bikini and some sort of short—*very* short—wrap-around skirt. Knotted on one hip, the black-and-red flowered material left little to the imagination. He could practically see right through the damn thing, to the tiny slip of gold beneath. A small triangle that covered the most important part of her anatomy. The rest of the suit he couldn't even see. He hoped there were straps somewhere on her hips to hold the blasted triangle up, but he couldn't be sure.

Then when she leaned over to retrieve something from one of her bags, he discovered that way too much of her rear end was visible through the skirt thingie, especially since the suit bottom only covered about half of each of her butt cheeks. He was a fan of string bikinis, of course, but living where he did, he didn't get many chances to see them up close. And while he was fine with them in general, he wasn't sure he liked the idea of his wife walking around in one. Not when she was out to get her ex-fiancé.

She turned back to him and his eyes zeroed in on the bikini top. More blasted triangles! This time it was two smaller ones pointed upward rather than downward, connected by spaghetti-thin straps that wrapped around her neck and back. And those triangles left nothing to the imagination. He could see every inch of cleavage—if you could even call it that when there was nothing to hide the smooth valley or shadow the view—and the tiny, pearl-like ridges of her nipples under the cloth. Ryder knew Monica photographed models for a living, but in this get-up, she could easily pose for the cover of *Sports Illustrated* herself.

It didn't help that her belly button ring was displayed perfectly on the slight curve of her abdomen, just above the tight, knotted skirt. He never thought he'd be particularly interested in a woman with body piercings, but—*damn!*—

he'd had more than one erotic fantasy about that silver hoop since Monica had stormed into his life. And the thought of other men entertaining those same thoughts didn't sit well with him.

"You're not wearing *that* to dinner," he blurted out. Her brows lifted and he hurried to add, "Are you?"

"Of course." She smiled sweetly, slipping her feet into tiny sandals with black crisscross straps. Then she picked up a pair of sunglasses and hooked one of the stems over the thin string between her breasts.

"This is Hawaii, Ryder. Everyone dresses this way, even for dinner. Besides, I want to throw Matt off-balance and keep your sister from connecting dots."

He felt a scowl settle into the deep lines of his forehead. Monica hadn't painted a very pretty picture of Matt to begin with, and the idea of the guy ogling her in her current outfit didn't exactly endear the man to Ryder. Never mind that Matt and Monica had supposedly been engaged and surely saw each other naked. Never mind that Ryder didn't have any real interest in Monica. Brother-in-law or no brother-in-law, it left a sour taste in his mouth.

Lifting her gaze back to Ryder, Monica gave him a quick once-over. "You're the one who's going to look out of place, you know."

"I don't give a rat's ass what people think," he said, knowing how she felt about his clothes, since she'd mentioned more than once that one simply did not wear a cowboy hat and boots in Honolulu.

Right now, he was more concerned with how Monica was dressed. He didn't like the idea of her traipsing around the hotel in that get-up, but he didn't know what he could do to stop her. Even if they were a real married couple and his opinion meant something to her, it wasn't exactly his place to tell her or any other woman how to dress.

She checked her watch. "It's almost six now. Shall we go?" she asked.

"I guess," he said reluctantly, grabbing his Stetson and shoving it down on his head. He didn't like this. Not one tiny bit. But he held the door open for her and followed behind her down the hotel corridor, watching as her firm little fanny swayed left to right with every other step.

She stopped suddenly, turning to face him, and he knew he'd been caught. It took some doing, but he refused to blush. If she insisted on walking around like that, she ought to be used to men checking her out.

"Why are you smiling?" she asked suspiciously, one eye narrowing while her hands lifted to her hips.

Was he? He gave a mental shrug. Well, there sure as heck was enough to smile about. His grin widened at the very thought.

Lifting his gaze from her bikini top—isosceles triangles, if he remembered anything from high school—he drawled out, "Sorry, darlin'. I was just rediscovering my fondness for geometry."

Monica's brows arched at that, but she didn't bother to ask what he meant. Good thing. Chances were she wouldn't like the answer.

Her lips thinned into a straight line as she turned and stomped off ahead of him. Which only took him back to his original hobby...staring at her tottering behind.

Chapter Twelve

When the herd turns on ya and you're forced to run for it, try to look like you're leading the charge!

"Ryder!"

The minute Josie spotted him—and how could she not spot full cowboy regalia in the midst of Bermuda shorts and flowered shirts?—she raced between umbrella-covered tables scattered across the restaurant patio and threw herself into his arms. While Ryder stepped forward to meet his sister, Monica stopped at the wide entrance to the outdoor dining area, slightly uncomfortable with the exuberant family reunion, but also wanting to take stock of the other couple in the moments before she made her "grand entrance" as Ryder's new bride.

Although she didn't remember much about the sister from their first, embarrassing encounter, the woman was a smaller version of Ryder, with ash blond hair and high cheekbones. She was wearing a plain black one-piece bathing suit with a long, flowered sarong tied at her small waist. Very similar to

Monica's outfit, but a bit more demure. And, actually, Josie would probably be better off with a shorter skirt. Having worked in the fashion industry for so long, Monica knew that showing some leg would make the petite Josie look taller, more reed-like. But she was very pretty, and it was obvious she thought the world of her brother.

Ryder took off his hat and held it while he hugged Josie tightly around the waist. If she weren't his sister, Monica thought she might be a tad jealous.

"I can't believe it!" Josie exclaimed breathlessly. "When Mama and Daddy called to tell us you'd gotten married and were on your way here...why, I almost fainted dead away. Didn't I, darling?"

"Darling"—a.k.a. Matt the Rat—came to her side, a wide smile on his even-more-tan-than-usual face. Of course, given the spray-on tan she'd given herself, she could hardly criticize. "You sure did. I didn't know what she was screaming about, but she was certainly excited."

He held out his hand. "Good to see you again, Ryder."

"You, too." Ryder took his hand for a quick shake.

Still hanging back, Monica bristled at Ryder's friendly response to Matt's greeting. She'd told Ryder about Matt. Why was he being so nice to the lousy cheat?

"So where is she?" Josie asked. "I can't wait to meet her. Where did you meet her? None of us even knew you were seeing anyone since Stephanie." She slapped his chest in a teasing gesture. "Shame on you, Ryder."

"What's the matter—didn't Mom tell you all about her?"

Josie shook her head. "We didn't get to talk long. Matt and I were already late for our couple's massage at the hotel spa, and she only called to let us know you were on your way. All she said was that you'd run off to Vegas to elope and would arrive in Honolulu sometime today. So where is she?"

That was her cue. Taking a deep breath, Monica pulled

herself up as straight and poised as possible, then stepped forward, glad they'd overlooked her in their excitement. Or maybe they'd expected Ryder to show up with someone more his speed—a country girl in cutoffs and a straw hat rather than a gold lamé bikini. She did so love the element of surprise, especially when it came to knocking Matt for a loop, and this was one look he'd never seen from her.

"Right here," she called out, stepping forward to plaster herself to Ryder's side. Then, as an explanation for why she hadn't been by his side all along, she said, "I just stopped in the lobby for a book of matches. I want as many souvenirs from our honeymoon as I can carry." Turning a beatific smile on Ryder, she coughed up her best madly-in-love voice and asked, "Aren't you going to introduce us, sweetie?"

His arm tensed at her cooing tone. Not that she blamed him; faking blind adoration made her a little nauseous, too.

"This is Monica," he said without elaboration. Monica pinched him under the arm, and he quickly added, "My wife."

The words came out so strangled, she thought it sounded like he'd rather be swimming with piranha than introducing her to his family.

"Monica," he continued, "this is my sister, Josie, and I'm pretty sure you already know her husband, Matt."

Matt turned three shades of white beneath his fresh tan, then drifted into a sickly gray until Monica thought he might lose the dinner they hadn't even eaten yet. His eyes, however, were as dark as obsidian and twice as cold.

Monica smiled as brightly as possible, envisioning herself as the bulb in a lighthouse. "It's a pleasure to meet you," she told Josie before turning to Matt with the same grin plastered on her face. "Hello again."

Nothing more. No ranting about his betrayal, no accusations about the money he'd stolen from her, no threats to tell Josie what her new husband was really like. Just a simple hello. Let him stew. Let him wonder and worry over when, or if, she'd say anything. Let him live in fear.

"You two know each other?" Josie asked, glancing first to her husband, then to Monica.

"We, uh…uh…"

Monica just blinked innocently, letting Matt squirm like a worm on a hook. Secretly, his nervousness and irritation filled her with an almost unholy glee. *Ha! Take that*, she thought and gave him a mental punch to the gut.

After a full minute, when it seemed all he could do was stutter, she said, "We've worked together. I'm a fashion photographer, and Matt and I have discussed the idea of starting a new magazine together." She shot a pointed look at her ex-fiancé, pleased to note a touch of color slip into his cheeks while the rest of his skin faded to nearly translucent.

Josie apparently didn't notice the change in her husband's pallor. "I had no idea," she said. But she didn't sound the least bit suspicious. She simply took Monica's hand and leaned forward to kiss her cheek. "Well, welcome to the family. I'm so happy for both of you. I hope you and Ryder will be very happy together."

If Monica had been holding a grudge against Ryder's sister for stealing Matt from her, it quickly disappeared. Feelings of anger molded themselves into instant esteem and maybe just a bit of sympathy for this pleasant young woman who had wound up with the likes of such a rat bastard.

And now that she knew Josie wasn't some gold-digging tramp who'd purposely stepped in to ruin her life, Monica could focus her hostility exclusively on Matt, who truly did deserve her animosity. Not to mention a little payback. Okay, a lot of payback.

Josie leaned back suddenly, an odd expression on her face as she studied Monica. "Do I know you from somewhere?" she asked. "You look familiar."

Thoughts of revenge against Matt dissipated as Monica's heart slowed just a bit and she felt Ryder's fingers dig into her wrist. First Ruth Ann, now Josie. And if Josie recognized her through all of her cosmetic adjustments, her whole plan would be ruined.

"I don't think so," Monica answered. And then, because it was the first thing that popped into her mind, she added, "But some people do say I look a lot like Julia Roberts. Not so much with the hair"—she touched the side of her darker-than-usual, slicked-back 'do—"but in the face and figure."

Ryder made a rude sound of disbelief at her side. "Julia Roberts?" he whispered just above her ear. "So who does that make me—Richard Gere?"

"More like Lyle Lovett," she shot back under her breath.

"Maybe I saw your picture on Ryder's phone or something," Josie suggested, completely missing their low-key battle of wit. Then she waved a hand, as though shooing the thought away. "Shall we find a table and sit down?"

Monica released a pent-up breath. Ryder was getting on her last good nerve, but the most important thing was that his sister didn't seem the least suspicious. Whew.

"That sounds great," Monica replied. "I'm starving." Even though she'd eaten her lunch and half of Ryder's on the plane, it still seemed like weeks since she'd had a decent meal.

Josie insisted she and Matt pick up the tab and urged everyone to have the lobster special. But while the other three at their table took her up on the offer, Monica stuck with an order of fettuccine Alfredo sans seafood, a Cobb salad, and tropical fruit sprinkled with coconut.

They made small talk until their drinks were served—a domestic beer for Ryder, double Scotch on the rocks for Matt, Mai Tai for Josie, and a very non-alcoholic iced tea for Monica. She hadn't been lying when she told Ryder alcohol did a number on her, and considering the mess she'd gotten into the last time she drank, she was putting both feet firmly on the teetotaling wagon for a while.

"So, Monica... Tell me a little about yourself. How did you and Ryder meet?"

Monica stirred a bit of artificial sweetener and fresh-squeezed lemon into her tea as she tried to formulate a flawless response. She much preferred the dull small talk to being cross-examined. Of course, she'd known people would be curious, and that she and Ryder would have to come up with some type of tale to recount, but as much as they'd tried to brainstorm exactly what they would tell people, almost every suggestion had only led to an argument, so they hadn't cemented any brilliant ideas.

But before she could utter a word, Ryder took over with an anecdote of his own. "You know, that's a funny story."

Yeah, Monica couldn't wait to hear it. She held her breath.

"Monica called one day, looking for Matt. He was visiting you, and when she couldn't reach him, I guess Mom gave her my number."

The waiter came then with their meals, and Ryder paused while everyone was served. "Anyway, she started to give me a message for Matt, but it got complicated and she told me to forget it. But after all that, we had to laugh over the time we'd wasted to begin with." Ryder spread the cloth napkin over his lap, gave it a couple absent strokes, then reached for his beer. "We got to talking, and the next thing I knew, I'd missed feeding time."

Josie's eyes went wide. "*You* missed feeding time?"

From the tone of her voice, Monica assumed this was big deal. The equivalent of blowing off a meeting with the mayor or forgetting to pick your child up from soccer practice.

"Yep." Ryder gave a little chuckle. "Good thing Ned was there to take up the slack or we'd have had a stampede on our hands."

Josie leaned her cheek against the back of one hand, fork dangling from her fingers. "It must have been love. Ryder never misses a feeding," she told Monica, a mischievous twinkle in her eyes. "He even warned me before my wedding that he'd have to leave the reception early enough to get home and take care of the horses and cattle. And sure enough, he disappeared right after he took care of that hideous woman."

Josie's teeth clicked angrily on her fork after she finished speaking, and Monica's eye twitched. Just a quick, almost imperceptible spasm in the corner of her right eye. She smiled and pretended to brush a speck of dust from her lashes as she smoothed away the tick.

What was it with everybody dumping on her about that blasted reception? Okay, so she'd been a little tipsy. So she'd crashed her ex-fiancé's wedding reception and accused the groom of being one rung below pond scum on the ladder of life. It's not like she'd killed someone.

And, frankly, her opinion of the groom hadn't changed. If more people would open their eyes and take a good, hard look, she suspected they'd realize what a weasel Matthew Castor was, too.

"Actually," Ryder said, leaning toward her, letting his sleeve-covered arm brush her bare one, "I didn't get home in time for feeding that night, either." He flashed a grin unlike any Monica had ever seen on him. His eyes sparkled and his teeth gleamed. All thirty-two of them. His smile was so beguiling, she actually began counting.

"I'd invited Monica to the wedding, and after I put that other woman in a cab..." He stroked the inside of her arm, sending shivers straight to her spine. If he was trying to distract her from getting worked up about being called *that woman*, he was doing a damn fine job. "Monica and I decided to leave and attend a little ceremony of our own. Isn't that right, dumplin'?"

Dumplin'? She forced her lips to curve. Two could play at this game. "That's right, sugar lips." And before she could think about it, she leaned forward and planted a big, fat kiss on his mouth.

Ryder's eyes widened in surprise, and Monica gave a silent whoop of satisfaction. For one-tenth of a second...right up until Ryder wrapped his arms around her back, pulled her flush with his warm body, and opened his lips.

Chapter Thirteen

*When a woman makes up her mind, you can always be sure
she's gonna do exactly what she says—or not.*

Tongue. That's all Monica could think as they sat there at the
dinner table, sucking face like a couple of teenagers under the
bleachers. Josie and Matt were staring, she was sure. Probably
so were the other diners. But all Monica could think was
that Ryder had the warmest, softest, trickiest tongue she'd
ever had the pleasure of having in her mouth. He did wicked
things to her lips and the inside of her mouth, and his hands
were doing soft little stroke-y things to the skin beneath the
strap of her bikini top and the nape of her neck. Lightning
struck and zigzagged its way straight to her toes, hitting every
erogenous zone in its path. She went limp, letting Ryder do to
her what he would—audience be damned.

Then, just as she turned herself over to him, to the
sensations he was creating, he let go. If it hadn't been for the
protective curve of the patio chair, she'd have slumped back
and fallen flat on the ground.

"Sorry," Ryder said, giving his sister and brother-in-law an apologetic nod as he reached for his beer. He took a long swallow before going back to eating as though he hadn't just seared Monica's insides and left her steaming.

She stared at him, snapping her jaw shut to keep from looking too stunned. After all, she was supposed to be used to Ryder's lusty attentions.

"He does that all the time," she said with a lopsided grin.

When she looked in Matt's direction, she saw his lips tense into a thin, disapproving line. She wanted to snap at him, ask what he was staring at or what right he had to look put-out when he'd run off with another woman in the first place. But she merely lifted a pinky to slowly wipe the corners of her mouth, as though Ryder had smudged her lipstick or left too much of a trace of passion behind.

In contrast to Matt's reaction, Josie gave her an impish smile and wink that said she understood all too well.

Monica tried to work up a kernel of jealousy or anger, thinking she ought to feel something over the fact that Ryder's sister was so obviously sexually satisfied by Monica's ex-lover. Funny, but it didn't seem to bother her. All she could feel was the heat of Ryder's kiss and the lingering need for completion.

She took a sip of tea to wet her suddenly dry throat and then dug in to her salad, trying to pretend everything was normal. Just another day of wedded bliss.

"So are you going to live at the ranch with Ryder?" Josie asked.

That wasn't something she and Ryder had covered, so Monica took her time chewing while she thought up a decent answer. Laying her free hand over the top of Ryder's, she rested her head on his shoulder and said, "Absolutely. I'm used to traveling, so I can take short assignments anywhere in the country and still be back home in under a week."

She tipped her face to look at Ryder and batted her lashes adoringly. "I couldn't bear to be away from my honey-bunny longer than that, I don't think."

Ryder pressed a kiss to her forehead and ran his fingers down her bare spine...and farther. She jerked and bit down on a squeak as his hand curved over her left buttock and squeezed. "Nor I you, darlin'."

Her eyes narrowed. He was definitely up to something. Playing happily married was one thing. Copping a feel at the dinner table was something else entirely. Not that the copping didn't feel mighty good.

But she could hardly drive her fork into his leg or throw her tea in his lap, now could she? So she'd just have to give him a taste of his own medicine.

She ignored the placement of his hand and went back to her meal. Ryder did, too, except that he used his left hand to eat, leaving the other comfortably stationed on her derriere. And every once in a while, when she least expected it, he'd pat or squeeze or tweak and almost drive her out of her skin.

It took her a few minutes, but she finally came up with an idea. *Can you say, "Tit-for-tat?"* she thought wickedly.

"Mmmm, that rice looks delicious," she commented innocently, zooming in on the pilaf on Ryder's plate. She dug out a big scoop and pulled it toward her mouth. And just as she passed over his thigh, she tilted the fork and let a few grains fall.

"Oops." She giggled. As she picked up the grains between her thumb and forefinger and popped them in her mouth one at a time, she made sure to dislodge his napkin with her pinky. She knew Ryder was watching her every move and only hoped he wouldn't notice. By the time she finished, she had the napkin pulled all the way to his knee and gave it one final flip to send it floating to the ground.

"For heaven's sake. I'm such a klutz tonight." She laughed

again and gave her eyes a roll before bending to retrieve the cloth. And as she did, she made sure her hand passed dangerously close to Ryder's crotch, sweeping over the taut denim of his jeans and just brushing the edge of the bulge at the apex of his thighs.

She had to *reeeeeeaaach* for the napkin, so of course she ended up resting her head in his lap for a good fifteen seconds. And she didn't come up for air until she heard his sharp intake of breath and felt every muscle in his body stiffen.

Still under the table, she allowed herself a wide smile of triumph, but as she straightened, she schooled her features and forced herself to look recalcitrant. Lord knew this wasn't the most outrageous thing she'd ever done in her twenty-nine years, but it ranked right up there.

She shook the napkin to remove any lingering bits of dirt or sand from the patio and then replaced it on Ryder's lap, being sure to place it evenly and smooth out all the wrinkles. "There. I'm so sorry, darling. I hope I didn't hurt you by leaning on you like that."

Their eyes locked and Monica could all but read his mind through their dark blue depths. He was thinking hot thoughts—very hot thoughts—and her gaze slid to his lap. Sure enough, her wheedling had affected him. Her breath hitched and she realized she wasn't completely unaffected herself. If she didn't do something to douse their mutual ardor, things could get out of hand—if they hadn't already.

She swallowed hard and made herself turn back to Josie and Matt. "But enough about us—how are things with you two? How's the business, Matt? Are you still planning to start that new magazine we discussed?" She considered tossing a few visual daggers his way, but realized the effort would be wasted when her words alone caused him to choke on a bite of lobster.

Josie pounded his back until he regained his equilibrium

and wiped a dribble of drawn butter from his chin. He looked like he wanted to go back in time and take the conversation in another direction, but Monica didn't let him.

"I know you were looking for investors. Did you find the money anywhere?"

By now, Matt's mouth was hanging open, his lips as white as his face. "I, um...um..."

He was back to stuttering.

"I'd still be interested in being head photographer if you go through with the project. I love my current job, don't get me wrong, but I think it would be wonderful to work with my brother-in-law."

"Well...um..."

"I'm sure you'd be much more understanding about my wanting to stay close to home, too." She stroked Ryder's arm and shoulder before adding the coup de grâce. "Being a newlywed yourself and all."

Josie appeared genuinely charmed while Matt looked like he was coughing up a furball. He sputtered and choked. Then he reached for his scotch only to choke on that, too.

"Darling, what's wrong with you tonight?" Josie patted his back.

He swallowed hard several times, clearing his throat and gazing anywhere but at Monica. "Nothing, I'm fine. I just swallowed a little funny is all."

"Don't you just hate it when things go wrong like that?" Monica remarked innocently.

And finally Matt met her gaze. "Yes," he said roughly. "I do."

Something told Monica he wasn't referring to her rhetorical question. He still looked slightly stunned by her presence, but through that she detected a modicum of genuine fear and more than a hint of annoyance.

Matt was very self-assured and didn't like being

questioned, as his angry glare attested. Sitting across from him now, Monica suspected she wasn't the first "investor" to be bilked by him, and that having people poke around, asking for details, threatened his fragile house of cards. She'd often heard him use the term "OPM," but hadn't made the connection before. Now she knew it was an acronym for one of his favorite things: Other People's Money. The bastard.

From his reaction, she doubted many of the folks who'd been taken for a ride had bothered to confront him, either. Or maybe they just hadn't been able to *find* him.

Lucky for her, she'd ended up tying the knot with someone who knew exactly where he'd be. But what about the others? Because she felt sure there were others. For the first time, she wondered if anything could be done for them. To help them recover what they'd lost or at least attain some type of retaliation against Matt.

One thing at a time, and she had to tread carefully, but maybe after she'd gotten her money back, she'd try to find out who else he'd hurt and see if there was a way to aid them, as well.

Of course, what she most wanted was to ask him point-blank where the hell her money was, but knew he wouldn't give her a straight answer. Besides, she didn't want to drag Josie into this if at all possible.

They were just finishing dessert, and before Monica had a chance to put him even more on the spot, Matt stretched dramatically and placed his arm around Josie's shoulders. "Boy, it's been a long day. I'm exhausted. What do you say we go back to the room early, sweetheart?"

"Oh, but I thought we could all take a walk on the beach," Josie said with a frown.

"What room are you in, by the way?" Monica put in blithely, seeing an opportunity to gather more information about Matt.

"We're on the tenth floor, Suite 1052."

Monica's eyes widened. "You're kidding! We're right next door, then, in Suite 1054."

"That's wonderful!" Josie exclaimed, clapping her hands together. "Mama said she was going to try to find you a room near ours, but I had no idea she'd manage to get you so close." She laughed. "That means we share a lanai, too. I wondered who we'd meet out there, or if it would pose a privacy problem."

Monica smiled. Not so much because she was excited about sharing a lanai with her new sister- and brother-in-law, but because having a room right beside theirs might make her plan of searching through Matt's things easier to pull off.

"I have an idea," Monica suggested. "Why don't we call it a night but meet back here first thing in the morning for breakfast?"

Josie tugged on the strap of her one-piece suit. "That sounds like a great idea. What do you think, Matt?"

Matt swallowed hard and Monica suspected he'd be pulling nervously at his tie by now if he were wearing one. Instead, he only worried one of the buttons of his Hawaiian shirt. "Fine with me."

"And you simply *must* leave the balcony doors open in the morning," Monica added quickly, before they could run off. "When you come back from breakfast, your room will have the most heavenly ocean scent you've ever smelled. You'll want to bottle it and take it home with you." The corners of her mouth lifted in what she hoped was a trustworthy expression.

"Great idea, thanks," Matt said quickly and stood. He took Josie's arm, all but lifting her out of the chair. "We'll see you in the morning, then."

Monica grinned and waved and gave herself a mental standing ovation for her spark of last-minute genius. If they followed her advice, it would make getting into their room to snoop around so much easier.

"What was that about?"

Still smiling, she turned to Ryder—who wasn't smiling at all. He didn't look angry, but he didn't look particularly pleased, either. "What was what about?"

"That crap about the room smelling like the beach." He picked up his Stetson from the extra chair and leveled it on top of his head.

"It wasn't crap, it's true. Doesn't it smell beautiful out here?" She took a deep breath to prove the point. "I just thought they might enjoy it if their room smelled like something other than stale air conditioning."

"Yeah, right. And if I believe that one, I'll bet you have a prime piece of swampland you'd sell me, too."

"You're so cynical." She rolled her eyes at him. "I'm implementing our plan, here, Ryder. Do try to work with me."

He shifted on the patio chair to face her. "It's not our plan, it's your plan. And I was working with you until you went off-script. Care to clue me in on this fresh twist to your operation, Agent Zero?"

"I'd be happy to." Ignoring his sarcasm, she bounced forward on her own seat, her breasts coming dangerously close to touching the side of his arm as it draped over the side of his chair. "You see, if they leave the lanai door open in the morning, I'll be able to sneak into their room and go through Matt's briefcase while you keep them occupied down here."

He snorted and looked at her like she'd just grown a second head. "This is your brilliant plan?" he asked. "Why not call hotel security tonight and turn yourself in for breaking and entering? Save them the trouble of coming for you tomorrow."

Biting her tongue to keep from sticking it out at him, she plopped back in the chair and crossed her arms over her chest. "I am not going to get caught. And even if I did, Matt and Josie aren't going to press charges. Not against their new sister-in-law. I just have to get in there, find some proof of the money I lent him, and get out."

He seemed to think that over for a minute. "Well, you're not doing it by yourself," he said finally. "You'd probably fall off the balcony or get your little muumuu caught on a doorknob and end up naked." He gestured toward her outfit in disgust.

"For your information," she returned in a tone so haughty, it put his to shame, "this is not a muumuu, it's a sarong. You'd know the difference if you ever left your precious farm. And I have no intention of pulling a Lucy-and-Ethel. I can handle this without you."

She expected him to say "yeah, right" again—in which case she planned to slug him, husband or no husband. Let him report her for spousal abuse; she'd press a few charges of her own for his hostage-keeping, stall-mucking, indentured servant stunt.

Instead, he snorted. A sound she was getting really tired of. She almost wanted to hand him a lozenge to help fight off the cold he seemed to be catching.

She kicked back her chair and stood, for once towering over him, hands on hips. "I don't need your help or your approval, Ryder *Winthrop* Nash. And take off that stupid hat!" She tore the offending article off his head, slapped it on her own, and stormed away.

Chapter Fourteen

About half your troubles come from wantin' your way; the other half come from gettin' it.

"Monica!" Ryder watched his wife storm off the patio and down to the beach, tossing sand up behind her with every step. Granted, she had a great behind—especially in that tight little peek-a-boo skirt number—and watching it sway back and forth would be high on his Dying Wish list. But she also had his hat and that just plain ticked him off.

He drained the last of his Michelob, pushed his chair back, and headed after her.

Boots, he quickly learned, weren't ideal footwear for the beach. The heels sank into the damp sand with every step, slowing his progress. He could still see Monica ahead of him, having much less trouble in her flappy little sandals. Cursing her every time he yanked his foot up and nearly disconnected his ankle bone from his shin bone, he continued following her, letting his anger build to a nice, slow boil. When he caught up with her, he'd tan her creamy white hide. That'd teach her.

Moving into a bit of a jog, Monica abandoned the beach and started onto a sidewalk that led to a side entrance of the hotel.

He swore. He really would tan her hide if she led him right back to the hotel after making him chase her all this way. If he'd known she was headed back to their room, he could have just cut her off at the pass.

Ryder increased his pace to keep up, glad when he could put good, old-fashioned pavement under him again instead of blasted quicksand.

Inside the hotel, he caught sight of Monica in front of a set of elevators. He called her name and tried to catch up. If she heard, she was definitely ignoring him. She stepped into the first available car and left him standing there.

His hand slapped the metal doors in frustration and then he punched the Up button like it would launch enough missiles to defend against all enemies, foreign and domestic. He rode the elevator up to the tenth floor and stomped down the hall to their suite. He knocked, but got no answer, so he got out his key card and opened the door himself, grumbling the whole time.

"Monica," he said as soon as the door closed behind him. She was nowhere to be seen. Neither was his hat. "Monica," he said again, a little louder.

"I can't hear you, Ryder," she called from behind the closed bathroom door. "I'm in the shower." And then the water kicked on and he heard her humming.

He looked around the room, hoping she'd thrown his hat on the bed or dresser before going into the bathroom. He even looked in the closet and on the lanai. No hat.

And she'd just taken a shower before dinner. How dirty could she be? Unless she wanted to wash off all that fake tan gunk before crawling into bed.

"Monica," he ground out, rapping a fist against the door.

"Is my hat in there with you?"

"I told you, I can't hear you, darling. I'm in the shower."

"Monica," he bit out, grinding his teeth together to keep from bawling her out. "Open this damn door!"

No answer.

"Do you have any idea what steam will do to that hat?"

Still no answer.

Dammit. He wouldn't mind so much if it were his work hat. His work hat had been through worse things than a little bathroom steam—like thunderstorms, tornadoes, and being dropped in the muck. But this was his good hat. His Sunday-go-to-meetin' hat, and being in the bathroom while she stood under a spray of hot water was liable to warp the material. He'd have a hell of a time working it back into shape, if it could be worked back into shape at all.

With a curse, Ryder considered pounding on the door until she opened it. Or kicking it off its hinges so he could talk to her face-to-face and get his damn hat before she ruined it. Of course, if he kicked the door down, he would end up confronting her while she was wet and naked.

He closed his eyes, trying to blot out the mental picture that thought conjured. No, kicking the door down was definitely not a smart idea. Waiting for her to finish, dry off, and dress was a better one. And while he waited, he wouldn't think of her naked. He wouldn't.

He'd seen her in her little gold triangle bikini and handkerchief-size sarong; naked wasn't more than a stone's throw from that. So he didn't need to picture anything else. No high, pert breasts with dusky raspberry nipples. No smooth, curving hips that led to long, lithe thighs. No ugly frog tattoo that was...no, not on her butt.

It was the tattoo that did it. The belly button ring, he was almost getting used to. He still wanted to drop to his knees and lick tiny circles around her navel every time the light created a sparkling glint off the tiny hoop, but he'd seen it before—hell, he could see it *always*, considering how many times it peeped from beneath the hem of her tops.

But the tattoo...the tattoo intrigued him. He knew she had one because she'd mentioned it, but he'd never set eyes on it. He was curious to see just how ugly a frog could be, and where, it was, exactly, since she'd made a point of saying it was...*no, not on her butt.*

Ryder put the heels of both hands to his eye sockets and pressed until little red, green, blue, and white stars sprang to life behind the lids. Pain and blindness was better than picturing Monica wearing nothing but her belly button ring, her frog tattoo...and his Stetson.

Lord have mercy.

He had to get out of here. Had to get off this roller coaster that had been speeding out of control and threatening to send him flying ever since this woman had stumbled her way into his life. Running his hands up from his eyes, through his hair, he made his way to the lanai and sank gratefully into one of the white metal lawn chairs facing the now-black ocean.

A moment later, the sliding door to the next suite opened and Matt stepped out onto the balcony. He turned to close the door and spotted Ryder. For a second, Ryder thought Matt looked as though he wanted to bolt back inside. But he slid the door all the way closed and moved to lean a hip casually against the railing.

"Hi, there," he greeted.

"Hey." Ryder inclined his head, not feeling much up to a conversation, especially with a man who may or may not have stolen Monica's money, and who may or may not be taking his sister for a ride.

"I thought you and Monica would be inside. Or out on the beach." He gave Ryder a leering grin, suggesting he knew exactly what they'd be doing if they were inside or on the beach. Ryder tightened his fingers around the arms of the chair and told himself it wouldn't be polite to bloody his brother-in-law's nose outside their honeymoon suites.

"Monica's in the shower," he said simply, hoping Matt would take the hint and let it drop. And then Ryder speared him with a stare that he expected was appropriately intimidating.

"So, Matt," he began.

"Yeah." Matt pulled a second chair a few feet from Ryder's and sat.

Out of reach. Smart man. "Monica tells me she lent you some money a while back."

It was dark out, but in the light cast through the curtained glass door, Ryder saw Matt blanch. His face drained of color and left him looking like a Halloween ghost costume.

"She said that?" he asked, his voice rising a bit with the last word.

"Yeah. For that fashion magazine the two of you planned to start. Of course, she hasn't seen any signs of that happening and is beginning to wonder what's going on. I think she may want her money back."

If Matt's face had blanched before, it went deathly pale this time around. For a minute, Ryder thought the other man might pass out from lack of oxygen. Add that to how he'd acted at dinner, and Ryder knew without a shadow of a doubt that Monica had been telling the truth all along. However it had come about, Matt did indeed have her money.

Although he was glad to know Monica hadn't lied to him, Ryder wasn't sure what to think of Matt now. He'd thought Matt was a pretty decent guy, a good husband for Josie. But if he'd taken Monica's money under false pretenses, then he clearly wasn't as upstanding as Ryder had first thought. That didn't sit real well with him. And he had to wonder—if Matt wasn't all he seemed to be—what did his sister have that the man might want?

When Matt didn't say anything, he repeated his last comment. "Think you could get her money back to her anytime soon? Just to clear the air," he added in a friendly, brother-in-law fashion.

"I...I don't have any money," Matt stuttered nervously.

Ryder sat forward in his chair, causing Matt to sit back in his. Ryder hoped the look on his face was enough to warn Matt not to try lying.

"I mean, I have it, but I don't have it...handy." He shifted again, getting to his feet by all but leaping over the arm of his lawn chair rather than getting too close to Ryder to stand up. "Like Monica told you, it was for a new magazine. I already invested it. There's no way I can pull the funding now."

With his back against the balcony railing, Matt edged closer and closer to the door of his suite, trying to act casual, Ryder was sure. Except he looked anything but. He looked scared. And guilty as hell.

"I hope you understand. The money's being put to good use, and Monica is behind me one hundred percent on this venture. I'm sure she told you that. It's going to make us both very rich."

Ryder didn't say anything, just kept a steady bead on the other man. Which seemed to make Matt most nervous of all.

"Sorry if there was any misunderstanding," he offered, then darted inside with a quick, "G'night."

Ryder shook his head, trying to decide how worried he should be over Matt's deception. Any claim that the money had been invested and Monica was on board with it was bullshit, he knew. If there was a chance for her to make back her money—and then some—in a legitimate business venture, she wouldn't be so upset or willing to go to such lengths to try to get it back.

But was that enough to raise doubts about Matt's true

feelings for Josie? Was the trouble with Monica's money an isolated incident, or was it all tied together, with his sister being the man's next target? He honestly didn't know what to think.

Behind him, he heard the bathroom door open inside the suite. Monica's humming soon followed. She didn't sound the least bit guilty over making him chase her all the way up here, or ruining his best Stetson.

Pushing himself up from the lawn chair, Ryder stepped into the room, sliding the door closed behind him. Monica stood at the foot of the bed, drying her hair with a fluffy white towel. Another towel—one that looked much smaller to Ryder's eyes—was wrapped around her body, tucked closed above one breast.

Even as he told himself to look away, his gaze lingered. On the slope of her shoulders, the smooth skin of her neck and chest that disappeared within the confines of that towel. Down over everything the soft terrycloth covered, to the area he suspected of being home to one ugly green tattoo of an amphibious nature.

His heart lurched. Not even to her legs yet, and already he was contemplating how she would react if he whipped that towel away from her breasts, tossed her down on the bed, and put good use to their honeymoon suite.

Better to avoid the temptation, he thought, and headed for the bathroom. Two could play this game.

"Where are you going?" she asked, her hand pausing in the act of fluffing her dark, wet hair.

To hell with the waste of water. To hell with his hat. He turned to face her, meeting her eyes. "Sorry, darlin', I can't hear you. I'm in the shower."

And then he stepped into the bathroom, closed the door behind him, and twisted the shower knob to full cold.

Chapter Fifteen

When you're workin' a horse or dealin' with a man, take it slow, take it easy, and don't rush 'em.

Still wearing the towel from her shower, Monica sat in the center of the king-size bed, trying to block out the sounds hitting her from both sides. If she rested her head against the headboard, she was way too close to what sounded like sex noises, and picturing her jerk ex with Josie made her want to barf.

But if she concentrated on the other side of the room, all she could hear was the sound of water running. Which made her think of Ryder. Which made her think of Ryder naked. Which made her think of smooth dark skin, sexy bulging muscles, the tightest butt she'd ever seen outside of a *Buns of Steel* video, and the fact that all those attributes belonged to her.

Husband, she amended frantically. *They belong to my husband.* She threw a hand over her eyes and dropped her face to rest on her knees.

She was losing her mind. Her ex-fiancé was on one side of the wall making love to his new bride—which happened to not be her. And on the other side of the *other* wall was her husband, who was far sexier than any man had the right to be. And she wanted him.

Her head snapped up. *WTF? You want him? Are you crazy?*

Maybe she was. All she knew was that Ryder was her husband. For convenience's sake or not, they were indeed married. He'd helped her when no one else would, when everyone thought she was simply drunk and insane. He was sweet and kind, even if those moments were interspersed with longer periods of him being aggravating and stubborn.

And frankly, she was having a good time with him. Downstairs during dinner, when she'd only been pretending to be madly in love with him for Matt's benefit, she'd found herself actually enjoying herself. Teasing him was fun, and he made her laugh—sometimes by doing something as simple as locking his jaw when she got on his nerves or said something he didn't appreciate.

He wasn't like Matt, who oozed charm and good breeding but was really a sleaze. Matt had always complimented her on everything from her hairstyle to her footwear. Ryder looked her over from head to toe, then asked if she was actually going out in public in *that*, not even trying to hide his disapproval. Matt offered to wine and dine her, treated her like a queen, and made promises he never intended to keep. Then ran off with another woman. Ryder fed her stale saltine crackers (which she'd had to hunt for herself), made no promises of any kind, and told her in no uncertain terms that he'd only married her for the fifty thousand dollars she'd impetuously offered. But he also made her feel like more than a decoration to be led around on his arm.

The way he looked at her sometimes made her feel

attractive whether she was trying to be or not. Like the way he'd stared at her in the barn that first day when she knew darn well she'd looked like something the cows dragged in. And he was candid to a fault. Where Matt said whatever he thought someone most wanted to hear, Ryder said what he was actually thinking no matter the reaction it might elicit. She appreciated that, because she never had to wonder if he was being honest or not. Until she'd discovered what kind of man Matt *really* was, Monica hadn't realized just how refreshing it was to know she was being told the truth at every turn. Even if it stung. Even if it *wasn't* what she wanted to hear.

And he'd come to her aid when no one else would.

Oh, he had his own reasons for going along with her not-always-the-most-sensible plans. She'd promised him a hefty payout for marrying her, only to find out the money was all but nonexistent. Now, unless he stuck with her, he never would get the money.

He might not agree with her plan, but he'd gone along with it, anyway. He might not approve of her fashion sense, but he didn't tell or even ask her to change, as Matt so often had. And he may not love her like a true wife, but he sure as hell wanted her. One look in his eyes when he'd walked in from the lanai, and his desire had been evident.

She just hoped her own had been a little less obvious.

The water in the bathroom shut off and Monica's spine snapped ramrod straight. The noises in the next suite, she noticed, had also grown quiet. Thank God.

A few minutes later, Ryder emerged fresh and clean from his shower. With a towel wrapped around his hips. Her mouth watered. Monica snapped her teeth together to keep from looking like a sex-starved maniac. *But, damn, he looked good*, she thought with a mental whimper.

Light, springy blond hair dotted his chest and trailed

down to the edge of the towel and beyond. Droplets of water from his wet hair dripped onto his shoulders and back and coasted over his sun-darkened skin. She licked her lips, thinking how easy it would be to catch those little drops on her tongue and lap them up like a cat with cream.

Her gaze lowered, but the steady thumping of his hat against his thigh captured her attention and pulled it away from what was hiding beneath the towel at the end of that tapering blond path.

The thumping sounded angry, and she raised her head to look at his face. His brows were drawn as he frowned at her.

"Nice job," he commented, lifting the hat for her perusal.

She studied it, but didn't see anything wrong. The rim looked a little more wrinkled than before, but the brown hat he'd worn in the barn had looked far worse.

"It looks okay to me," she said.

If possible, his brows drew even closer together, making him look like one of the Billy Goats Gruff. Unfortunately, she'd always had a soft spot for those billy goats, and even the mean little troll under the bridge.

"It's ruined," he snapped and slammed it down on top of the entertainment center.

Getting out of bed, she walked to where the hat rested, picked it up, and worked the edges a bit, smoothing the fabric. "It's not that bad. Look, it's fine." She held it up, but he only rolled his eyes at her and stomped away.

"Okay, then I'll wear it." Placing it on over her still-damp hair, she did a pirouette, posing like a runway model. "How do I look?"

He turned from the closet, took in her appearance, flushed from the neck up, and turned back.

Monica turned away, too, not wanting him to see her satisfied smile. He'd blushed, actually blushed, when he'd seen her in nothing but a towel and his black hat. She took a deep breath to keep from jumping up and down.

She hadn't planned to keep the towel on until he finished his shower, but she hadn't rushed to change, either. And now she was sort of glad because she finally knew for certain that he wanted her. She'd eat his hat if he didn't.

Now, she just had to figure out what to do about it.

"I talked to Matt tonight," Ryder said a few minutes later, after they'd both taken turns in the bathroom again, changing into sleepwear.

Ryder wore a simple pair of navy blue cotton boxer shorts that did nothing to hide his extremely attractive, bounce-a-quarter-off-me heinie. Meanwhile, Monica was stuck in the rather ridiculous nightshirt with the headless hula dancer image on both the front and back. It was more suggestive than she'd realized when she added it to her pile at the airport gift shop and had her wondering which Ryder found sexier—*her* half-naked form or the cartoonish, yet perfect, hourglass figure. Not that it mattered. After all, the hula dancer was just a cold, one-dimensional scrap of material, while she was flesh and blood and very real curves. If she decided to do anything about the heady charge surging between them, she imagined he'd appreciate that.

He sat on the very edge of one side of the bed, scribbling on a hotel notepad. She stood on the opposite side, staring at his broad back, fighting the urge to reach out and give it a stroke.

"About what?" She filled her palm with the unscented moisturizer the hotel provided and began rubbing it on her arms and legs to counteract the drying effects of her shower.

"Your money."

Her brows rose. Ryder had asked Matt about her money?

The same Ryder who didn't particularly believe her story to begin with? "What did he say?" she asked cautiously.

He glanced over his shoulder at her. When he saw her smoothing lotion onto her knees and calves, he turned back to his writing.

"You were right." His words sounded gravelly, and he paused to clear his throat. "He has your money."

Monica wanted to do something childish like stick her tongue out or say "I told you so." After all, she *had* told him so, even if he hadn't been quick to believe her. But she retained her maturity and calmly said, "Good. Then he can write me a check and we can go home all the sooner."

"I don't think it's going to be that easy. He claims the money is tied up in the magazine venture." He tossed the pen he'd been using down next to the tablet and stood. "But he was jittery as a Mexican jumping bean when he said it. I don't trust him any more than I would an angry rattler. Which doesn't exactly tickle me pink that Josie married him," he grumbled, almost under his breath.

"So you believe me now." Monica lifted her right foot to the mattress and started spreading lotion around her ankle and over the top of her foot, surprised at how little accusation those words contained. She didn't care who was right and who was wrong, she was simply happy to hear him acknowledge that she wasn't making this up. That Matt really had run off with her money.

"Yeah." Ryder didn't seem the least uncomfortable with his admission, only with the fact that she was moisturizing. Although he kept his body turned toward her, his eyes darted anywhere else. Over her head, at the television—which wasn't even turned on—at their empty travel bags that still stood beside one of the dressers.

With his eyes focused on the alarm clock and the red dots between the numbers, blinking away the seconds, he said,

"Except that he claims you're in this thing with him all the way. One hundred percent behind him, I think he said. That you want him to have the capital for the magazine so you can both start raking in the dough."

Monica's eyes narrowed and she put both feet flat on the floor, hands on her hips. "That son of a bitch. That jackass. That *slime*. I gave him the money to start a new magazine *before* he ran off and married another woman, and he damn well knows it. If he thinks I'm going to let him take my fifty thousand dollars to do with as he pleases, now of all times... well, he's got another thought coming, I can tell you that."

She stomped around the bed, past Ryder, to the second nightstand where she'd left her cell phone to charge. Grabbing it up, she started punching in numbers like she really wanted to punch Matt.

"I don't care if he is investing it in a new magazine, I no longer want him to have it. The jerk."

"Who are you calling?"

"Brooke," she answered. And then her friend's voice came on the line and she said, "Brooke. Hey, it's Monica. Listen, I need you to do me a favor." She wasn't exactly sure of the change in time zones, but if it was after midnight in Honolulu, it had to be almost quitting time in Chicago. "Do you have Simon Farraday's phone number handy?"

She waited a minute and then scrawled the numbers on the same pad Ryder had been using. "Thanks. What time is it there? Okay, I think I can still catch him. And I'll fill you in on everything later, I promise."

She ended the call, then started dialing the number Brooke had just given her.

"Now who are you calling?"

Ryder stood behind her, at a complete loss, she was sure. But she was too angry and in too much of a hurry to go into detail with him. "Matt's accountant, who's also done some work for me—if I can catch him before he leaves the office for the day."

The phone rang about ten times before a man finally answered. He must have let his receptionist go home already, because he sounded none too happy about being bothered at this hour. "Simon Farraday," he snapped.

"Hi, Simon, this is Monica Blair."

"Monica. What a surprise."

She was sure. Especially if he'd seen the same *Tribune* she had—the one with Matt's wedding announcement in it.

"Yeah, I know. I need your help with something, Simon. A couple months ago, I loaned Matt fifty thousand dollars to put toward launching a new fashion magazine. Now that he's... now that we're no longer engaged, I'm really not comfortable with the idea of going into business with him or having such a large chunk of *my* money on *his* side of the table. And I know that any investments Matt makes go through you, so I was hoping you could help me get my money back."

"Monica," Simon said her name slowly and his tone caused her stomach to clench. "I'm sorry to hear about you and Matt, but Monica...he never gave me any money for a new magazine initiative. He never even brought up wanting to get into something like that. Are you sure he said he'd given the money to me?"

Covering her eyes with one hand, she lowered her head and her voice. "No, he never mentioned you, but I know he makes other investments through your office and just assumed..." She blew out a breath. "Is there anyone else he might be working with?"

"Not that I know of. Do you have documentation of the money you loaned him?"

"No," she said simply. Because she was an idiot. Because she'd trusted the man she'd thought she loved, thought she was going to marry. Because she'd had dreams and plans for the future, and never imagined anything like this could ever happen to her. "I'm sure everything is fine. I just have to talk to Matt about it, that's all. Thanks, Simon."

"No problem. I wish I could have been more help."

"Yeah. Me, too. Good night, Simon. Thanks again."

"You're welcome. And Monica... If you plan to tell anyone else about this, be sure you find some sort of proof that you lent Matt the money to begin with. Things could get sticky otherwise."

Didn't she know it. "I'll do that. Thank you."

When she hung up, she didn't know whether to smash the phone against the wall or throw herself across the bed and cry. "Damn him."

"What did he say?" Ryder asked, having been perfectly silent through both conversations.

She turned away from the nightstand to face Ryder. "Surprise, surprise! Matt never mentioned anything about a new magazine enterprise or borrowing money from me."

"He never intended to start a new magazine," Ryder stated matter-of-factly.

Monica shook her head and blinked back the tears that stung at the corners of her eyes. "I guess not. God, I'm such an idiot."

Ryder came forward and put his hands on her upper arms, his fingers squeezing in a gently supportive gesture. Then he lifted her chin and met her gaze. "No, you're not," he said solemnly. "You had no reason to believe Matt was being anything but honest with you when he asked for the money. And you thought you were getting married—why wouldn't you trust your future husband?"

He gave her arms one more soft stroke and then stepped back, pacing to the end of the bed. "Matt's the idiot here. I just hope he's not planning to screw over Josie the way he did you."

Monica sniffed and crossed her arms over her chest. "Does she have any money he could run off with?"

Ryder frowned. "No. But when I wanted to start my own ranch, my parents gave me the land to build on. Josie's never wanted land, so they always planned to give her the cash equivalent. When she settled down."

"Like now. When she just married Matt."

If possible, the furrows in Ryder's forehead deepened. Monica suddenly felt sorry for him. Not only was he dealing with her and financial difficulties because of last year's tornado, but now he had to worry about his sister being married to a con artist. Sprinkle in a dash of adultery and alien abduction and they could all go on *The Jerry Springer Show* and throw chairs at each other.

"Look, maybe we're projecting here. Maybe Matt truly loves Josie and will never do anything to hurt her. Maybe running off with my money was an isolated incident."

The look in Ryder's eyes told her he didn't believe that for a minute. Once a cheater, always a cheater. Once a con man, always a con man.

"So what do you want to do?" she asked. "Do you want to tell Josie, warn her about him? Confront Matt again and demand he return the money?"

"Do you think he would?"

Monica snorted. "Not likely."

Ryder nodded. "I don't want to upset Josie if we can avoid it. Once we have proof, or if Castor does something else, maybe we can break it to her. But until then, I'd rather we kept this to ourselves." He released a deep breath and ran splayed fingers through his sandy hair. "I don't know what Matt is up to, but he's got your money and I'm not sure there's any way to get it back."

He fixed her with a determined glare and rested his hands on narrow, boxer-clad hips. "Do you still think your plan for tomorrow morning will work? Getting them out of the room and searching through his things?"

Monica smiled. For the first time all evening, her spirits buoyed. "Is a frog's ass watertight?"

Ryder's lips thinned, whether in confusion or distaste, she didn't know.

"Yes," she clarified. "The answer is yes. Matt never goes anywhere without that damn messenger bag, and usually his laptop. There has to be *something* in there showing I gave him that money. As long as Josie leaves the lanai door open, we'll be able to sneak in and out and they'll never know the difference."

With a sigh, Ryder said, "Then, as much as it pains me to say this, I think your plan may be our best course of action."

He moved around her to his side of the bed and pulled back the covers. Monica followed his lead and then continued smoothing on moisturizing lotion. Replacing the cap on the small bottle, she crawled under the covers and turned off the lamp closest to her. Ryder rolled to his side and did the same.

"Good night, Ryder," she said into the darkness.

A heartbeat passed and she thought he might have already drifted off.

And then his deep voice carried across the wide bed. "'Night, Mrs. Nash."

It took Monica a long, long time to fall asleep.

Chapter Sixteen

Don't wait to get to know somebody better before you kiss 'em. Kiss 'em and you'll know 'em better.

Monica awoke at the crack of dawn the next morning. She'd tossed and turned most of the night, too excited and nervous about today's venture to sleep soundly. As soon as a touch of morning light filtered through the drapes, her eyes popped open and she began to sit up—only to realize that her face was plastered to Ryder's warm, bare chest.

She blinked, wondering how she'd ended up so close to him when they'd fallen asleep on opposite sides of the bed last night. Even rolling around like she had, she didn't remember rolling into him. And that was something Monica thought she would most definitely remember.

Then she became aware of his arm curled around her waist, his hand on the side of her breast. Her leg was draped over his thigh, her knee resting very close to his—

"Morning, sweetheart. Care for a quick tumble?"

Her heart jumped into her throat as her eyes swung to his

face. Ryder looked completely content, staring up at her with drowsy amusement.

If she weren't so embarrassed about unconsciously drifting into him last night, she might have been amused, too. Her face flushed and she threw back the covers to climb out of bed.

"No, thank you."

"You sure? You'd be surprised at what a cowboy can learn, spending his days around all that rope and hay."

The images his words created burned themselves into her brain and caused every inch of her skin to tingle with sensual awareness. She dug down deep for a healthy dose of sarcasm and shot back, "Yeah, I'll bet you and your friend, Ned, can get real creative."

His self-assured grin slipped a notch at that and she hurried on. "It's time to get dressed. We have to be ready and listening when they leave the room."

Sifting through her drawer of limited clothing choices, she gathered a few things and hurried into the bathroom. When she emerged, wearing a short floral skirt and sleeveless periwinkle blue top, Ryder was propped against the headboard, his pillow folded behind his back, one leg thrown out over the bedspread.

He looked picture perfect—if you liked those sexy pictures they put on dirty playing cards—and good enough to eat. Her stomach growled in agreement and she quickly turned away, stuffing her discarded nightshirt in the first drawer she reached.

"All yours," she gestured toward the bathroom, then busied herself with making a huge production of folding and rearranging the bulky bit of cotton.

More leisurely than she'd have liked, Ryder got out of bed and moseyed—yes, he definitely moseyed, damn his cowboy hide—into the bathroom. Two minutes later, he came back out, still wearing nothing but his navy blue boxer shorts.

He opened one of the dresser drawers that contained his clothes and pulled out jeans, fresh boxers, and an undershirt, then headed back to the bathroom. Stopping just short of the doorway, he turned to stare at her, letting his gaze wander from the low V-cut of the blouse's bodice, to the inverted V-cut at the hem that left a portion of her midriff bare, to the ropy sandals she'd just slipped onto her feet.

"What?" she asked, becoming anxious under his intense scrutiny. It was bad enough she'd had to stand there and watch him digging around for clean clothes while he was all but nude. Now he seemed to want to touch the outfit she had on. She looked down at herself, trying to see if her breasts were arranged crookedly inside her bra or she'd forgotten to put on underwear.

"Do you ever wear clothes that cover more than twenty-five percent of your body?"

She sucked in her stomach, stuck out her boobs defensively, and tugged just the teeniest bit at the back of her skirt. It was fashionably short, but not salaciously so. Clearly he didn't spend enough time flipping through the types of magazines she shot for, otherwise he'd know this sort of outfit was downright demure in comparison to some of the styles that were out there.

Without a whit of apology and daring him to offer another word of criticism, she answered, "Sometimes. Just not when I'm on a Hawaiian honeymoon."

He did another head-to-toe perusal, one corner of his mouth tipping up in a grin. "Thank God," he whispered, then disappeared into the bathroom.

• • •

When Ryder returned to the main room, he found Monica on

her knees at the very head of the bed, the rim of a water glass pressed against the wall, the base to her ear. The position emphasized the tightness of her skirt and shortness of her top, accentuating every hill and valley that decorated her extraordinary female form.

He swallowed and curled his fingers into the pockets of his jeans. He'd known marriage would be hard, but he'd never imagined it would be *this* hard. And damned if it wasn't, he thought as a bolt of sexual awareness shot through his body to pool in his groin.

Arguments over money, vacation disasters, and holidays with the in-laws, he could handle. Watching Monica slither around on a king-size bed in an outfit that wouldn't cover the butt of his Winchester, he wasn't so sure about.

Clearing his throat to keep from doing something stupid, he moved toward the closet for a shirt. "Anything exciting going on over there?" he asked. Even though he was relatively sure nothing could be more exciting than what was going on in their own suite.

"Shhh, I think they're getting ready to go down to breakfast."

She ignored him completely as she pressed her ear even more firmly to the glass and wall. Shrugging into a long-sleeve shirt and tugging on his boots, Ryder allowed her to listen for another few minutes before grabbing the phone and dialing the hotel restaurant.

As he began talking to the hostess, Monica shushed him again, but he staunchly ignored her. "Yes, my wife and I are supposed to meet another couple in your dining room for breakfast," he explained, "but we're running a little late, and I was wondering if you could tell them that we'll be down as soon as we can." He gave a brief description of Josie and Matt, thanked the woman for her assistance, and hung up.

Monica had turned around on the bed to face him, a

strange expression on her face. But it sure as hell beat staring at her rear end.

"What did you do that for?" she asked.

"I don't want Josie and Matt to get worried or suspicious when we don't show up. This way, they'll think we're just running late and will wait."

Her eyes brightened and she smiled. "Good thinking. You're better at this than I expected."

He glared at her for her apparently low opinion of him, then drawled, "Darlin', I'm better at a lot of things than you'd probably expect."

The makeshift eavesdropping device slipped out of her hand as her brows shot up in surprise, and she barely managed to catch the glass before it hit the headboard. With a grip less steady than before, she switched the listening glass to her other hand and pressed her head to the wall once again.

"I think they're leaving," she whispered. "No, wait... wait...yes. The door just closed."

Ryder and Monica both stood, his feet firmly on the carpeted floor, hers bouncing on the mattress as she wobbled to the edge and used his shoulder for support while she jumped down. Ryder put his hands on her waist to help her, then quickly let go when the warm silk of her skin all but singed his fingertips.

Monica must have felt it, too, because she stopped dead in her tracks to gaze into his eyes. Then she seemed to shake off the sensation and raced out to the lanai.

"Yes!" she cried and threw her arms into the air Rocky-style when she saw that Josie had indeed left their balcony door open. The gesture raised her top a good three inches, giving Ryder a prime view of her belly button ring and a tasty glimpse of her where the curve of her hips disappeared beneath the waist of her skirt. His eyes locked on that small portion of her anatomy, and he stood frozen until Monica grabbed his hand and pulled him into Josie's and Matt's honeymoon suite.

The room looked almost identical to theirs, except for a different set of tropical paintings on the wall and the alarm clock on the opposite side of the bed.

Monica immediately set about searching for Matt's bag. It wasn't out in plain sight, though Ryder didn't know why he'd expected it to be. She opened cupboards and drawers, drew back bedspreads, and scoured the inside of the closet.

"Damn it."

"What's wrong?" She sounded so forlorn that Ryder went to stand next to her in front of the closet. On the floor sat a metal safe, and Ryder knew exactly what Monica was thinking. If the bag—or more likely, laptop—was inside, they'd never get their hands on it.

"Don't hotels usually provide a combination for the safe? Or do you think Matt would come up with his own?" he asked.

"He probably used his own," Monica said. "But if he did, he also probably wrote it down somewhere convenient. Let's double-check the nightstands. Maybe the pockets of some of his clothes."

While Monica shoved her hand in and out of every pocket in the closet, he set about running his palms over the surfaces of both bedside tables, even the back of the headboard. His fingers bumped something big and lumpy near the bottom, and he put one knee on the mattress to get a good look behind. On the floor, close to the wall, was a dark brown fabric satchel like the one Monica had described. He grabbed it by the handle and dragged it out.

"What do you think?" he asked Monica. "Is this what we're looking for?"

She lifted her head briefly to glance in his direction, then went back to picking pockets. "No, the combination has to be on something smaller than—"

Her head whipped back around. "Yes! Yes, that's it!" She slammed the sliding closet doors closed and launched herself onto the unmade bed. "Thank God. Where did you find it?"

While he told her, she propped the case against her legs and threw it open, pulling a lightweight laptop from inside.

"Anything important is probably password protected. Do you know what that might be?" Ryder asked.

"If he hasn't changed it since we broke up."

Ryder rolled his head away, about to tell her Matt most likely *had* changed his password. It was a smart thing to do every couple of months, anyway, and if Matt was as devious as Monica claimed, the guy probably changed his passwords every other day or so. But a second later, the top popped open and Monica flashed him a wide smile, like a prospector who'd just struck gold.

Then again, maybe his new brother-in-law wasn't the sharpest tool in the shed.

Falling to her butt on the bed, she propped the tablet on her knees and began tapping the keyboard, running her fingers over the touchpad as she searched file folders and documents. Ryder sat next to her and studied everything over her shoulder. A lot of words and codes he didn't understand zipped past his vision, and the speed at which Monica worked didn't help. But he began to realize that Matt was playing with a shit-ton of money and had his fingers in quite a few pies. The cash may not be liquid, and he may not have even told anyone how much he had stashed away, but judging by what he could make out, the man had accounts—big ones—all over the world.

"This is it," Monica said suddenly, her voice unnaturally low. "I think this is it."

Ryder leaned right while she leaned left, and they sat with their shoulders touching, reading the document on the screen. It appeared to be an email confirmation from an offshore bank verifying that fifty thousand dollars had been successfully transferred to MAC Holdings, LLC.

"Is there anything else?" he asked.

Monica did a bit more scrolling, then shook her head. "I don't see anything else for fifty thousand even."

"Do you think that will be enough?"

"I don't know, but I'm not taking any chances. I'm downloading everything."

Dipping into her blouse, she produced a flash drive and stuck it into the USB port on the side of the laptop. *More tricks from Monica and Her Magic Cleavage*, he thought wryly.

"If the money is still there, we may be able to get it back," she said. "If not, I'd assume he'd have a statement of the transfer to another account somewhere in here, too."

Just then, they heard a sound outside the hotel room door. The scraping of a key card, feminine laughter. They looked at each other, panic racing through them.

"Take this." Monica shoved the laptop at Ryder's chest. She quickly shoved everything else back in the messenger bag, leaving no trace that they'd been poking around.

"Come on, come on, come on." She stood behind him, one hand on his back, eyes darting nervously toward the door while she begged the download to hurry and finish.

Ryder glanced toward the lanai as the door handle started to turn. They'd never make it out in time. Grabbing Monica's hand, he yanked her down to the floor and all but pushed her under the bed, sliding in beside her, laptop and all, only seconds before someone bounced onto the mattress.

"I can't believe you forgot your wallet," Josie said.

"If you hadn't been rushing me, I probably wouldn't have. Good thing Ryder and Monica are running late so we could come back up for it."

"Good thing I had my key," Josie returned.

And then the mattress lurched again and muted laughter reached their ears.

Ryder flinched and Monica lifted her hands to her ears, muttering, "Oh, no. Not again."

• • •

Springs squeaked. The mattress moved above them, coming very close to hitting them both in the head. Monica turned to bury her face against Ryder's shoulder, then caught a whiff of his cologne on her first deep inhalation of breath. The scent brought to mind images of him back at the ranch, in his dirty jeans and boots, leather gloves, and dusty hat, smiling crookedly even though a cow had apparently kicked him in the jaw. Not to mention the sight of him that morning in nothing more than boxer shorts and smooth, bronze skin.

Those thoughts, combined with the noises above them, turned the blood in her veins lava hot. She covered her ears and tried to roll away, wanting to be as far from Ryder as possible when she went up in flames, but his arm stopped her. With a vise-like grip around her waist, he kept her next to him. With his other hand, he tipped her chin toward the computer screen, which had finished downloading onto the flash drive.

She was torn—did she uncover her ears long enough to eject the thumb drive and shut down the laptop, or did she wait out the X-rated activity taking place above them and hope she could get everything taken care of before Matt noticed his messenger bag was missing? To her surprise, Ryder grabbed her hands and yanked them to his ears, then placed his over hers...the buddy system of blocking out what neither of them wanted to hear.

He jerked his head toward the screen, urging her to take

care of things before they got caught. And though she knew he was right, she was also keenly aware of how close they were.

His gaze was hot, smoldering, and she knew it mirrored her own. She clapped her hands even more tightly over his ears, hoping he would take the hint and do the same for her. Although in a second, he was going to be a sitting duck for whatever noises trickled down to the floor. Squeezing her eyes closed, she shook her head, then made sure that when she opened them again, she was looking at the laptop and only at the laptop.

As quickly and quietly as possible, she ejected the flash drive and stuffed it into her bra where she was sure it wouldn't fall out. Then she closed Matt's email program and anything else she'd opened while snooping, then stuffed it all back in the bag. Reaching around her, Ryder returned the tote to exactly where he'd found it on the floor, hidden behind the bed's headboard.

Now they were both unprotected, every sound in the room seeming to echo off the walls and bounce straight to their hiding place. The second their eyes met, Monica knew it was too late to try to block them out again. The raw, naked longing in his eyes made the rest of the world cease to exist, because she felt exactly the same way. She no longer heard Matt and Josie above them, doing whatever it was lousy ex-fiancés and brand-new brides did at nine o'clock in the morning. She no longer cared that her marriage to Ryder was a convenient one, supposedly in name only. She wanted him, and from the rigid press of his arousal against her hip, she knew he wanted her, too.

He held her gaze a moment more before his eyes drifted to her mouth, and he leaned forward to touch her lips with his own. The soft heat of them drove even the simplest thought from her head. His hands moved from her arm to the back of her head, from her waist to the curve of her breast, and she yearned to get closer to him, to mold her body with his in every possible way.

Her fingers clutched at the front of his shirt, sifted through the soft satin of his hair. She looped her leg with his and tried her best to move on top of him. Unfortunately, the solid base of the box springs right above them stopped her halfway across his body. His lips continued to wreak havoc with her senses, sending electric shocks to harden her nipples and pool low in her belly. She lifted her leg, gently caressing the bulge of his sex with the crook of her knee while his tongue darted into every nook and cranny of her mouth, teasing her and leaving her breathless.

She drew her hand down his chest, feeling the sinewy strength beneath the fabric of his shirt. When she reached the waistband of his jeans, she tugged slightly to loosen his shirt, then began pulling at the button. She got it loose and was just beginning to unzip the fly when his strong grip on her hand stopped her.

They broke apart, both gasping for breath. Monica tried to free her hand, go back to loosing him from the confines of his jeans, but he held her still and arched his head toward the mattress above them. The heavy haze of arousal cleared slowly as she listened, but she realized Ryder was trying to tell her that Matt and Josie were no longer on the bed.

"We'd better get down there or they'll be wondering where *we* are," she heard Josie say.

And then Matt chuckled and said, "They were probably running late for the same reason. I don't think they'll mind too much. Maybe we should just cancel breakfast altogether. We could..." His voice trailed off as they moved into the hall and the door clicked closed behind them.

Monica and Ryder stayed where they were for another second, then he released her hand and eased out from under the bed. She crawled out after him, running a hand over her hair and clothes while he tucked in the loose tail of his shirt and refastened his jeans. They kept their eyes averted, neither of them brave enough to say a word about what had happened beneath the bed.

"We'd better get downstairs," Ryder finally worked up the courage to say.

She nodded and followed him to the lanai. "I should fix my hair and make sure my tan isn't splotchy."

Back in their suite, Monica refused to look at the bed that took up a good portion of the room. If she looked at the bed in here, she would remember the bed in there. And if she started thinking about the bed in there, she would remember all sorts of things better left forgotten.

Apparently, the close confines had played havoc with Ryder's judgment, too, because he seemed less than eager to recall the situation himself. He moved across the room toward the door, never sparing her a backward glance. Never mentioning that what had happened between them beneath that bed was either a huge mistake or the start of something very special. Never showing signs that he was either completely repulsed or compulsively eager to pick up where they'd left off.

And if it hadn't affected him, then it sure as hell hadn't affected her.

Ryder went to the door, crossing his arms over his chest and his legs at the ankles, leaning back to wait for her. Rather than darting into the bathroom to get ready, she stayed where she was, on the other side of the room.

"You go ahead," she told him, centering her gaze on the smoke alarm above his head. "I'm not much in the mood for breakfast."

Even though she wasn't looking at him, she caught his frown in her peripheral vision.

"Don't you think Matt and Josie will think it's odd that I called to say we were running late and then show up without you?"

She met his eyes then and tried not to recall the deep, hot passion she'd seen there only moments earlier. With a shrug, she said, "I don't really care what they think. Tell them I'm sick. Tell them we had a fight and I'm not speaking to you."

Surprisingly, he didn't argue with her or order her to accompany him. Instead he asked, "What are you going to do up here by yourself?"

She thought about that for a moment. Then, biting down on the dread that threatened to launch itself up from her belly, she reached into her cleavage and removed the thumb drive. The move reminded her too much of what they'd shared under the adjoining suite's king-size bed.

Nothing happened between us. Nothing happened, nothing happened, nothing…

"I'll run down to the hotel business center and print out everything from this drive. Then maybe we can call Simon to see if he can use any of it to get my money back."

For the longest time, he didn't respond. Then he turned the knob, opened the door, and stepped into the hall.

"All right," he agreed. "But we might as well share an elevator on the way down."

She'd been trying *not* to get close to him…to get him out of the room so she could do a bit of hyperventilating without an audience, then get a firm hold on her hormones before having to face him again. But she had no ready excuse for why they shouldn't leave the room together, and it really would be stupid to follow two steps behind.

With a nod, she slipped past him, doing her best to stay out of reach as they moved down the hall, stepped into the elevator, and pressed the buttons for their respective floors.

Chapter Seventeen

Women have to be in the mood. Men just have to be in the room.

Ryder stood alone in the elevator after letting Monica out at the ground level. He leaned against the metal bar at the rear of the car, dragging in deep gulps of air and fighting the urge to drag his wife back to their suite to finish what they'd started. The sounds of Matt and Josie above them had been hugely awkward at first; the last thing a brother ever wanted was to catch his sister getting lucky. But it had taken him only a second to block that out entirely, his attention zeroing in on Monica until all he could think of was kissing her and touching her, and much, much more.

Close confines and the power of suggestion were good excuses, but he doubted even Monica would be able to look him in the eye and deny that they'd done what they'd done because they'd *wanted* to do it.

But then, she hadn't been able to look him in the eye at all once they'd crawled out from under the bed. That's when he'd known they couldn't simply pick up where they'd left off, no matter how fast his heart was still beating or how hard he was to be inside her.

When she'd told him she didn't want to go down to breakfast with him, he'd been almost relieved, thinking that what they both needed was a little time apart to put things into perspective. Now, though, he wasn't sure there was any perspective to be found. They hadn't spoken or come within a foot of each other the entire elevator ride down, yet he couldn't seem to get her out of his head. Her scent continued to tease his nostrils. The remembered feel of her silken flesh tickled his fingertips, the taste of her keeping him painfully aroused. It took every ounce of willpower—and a list of about three thousand parts of a horse's anatomy—to keep from hauling her back up to the room, tossing her down on the bed, and showing her what a real man could do to a woman. He doubted her ex had ever made her moan in even half the octaves Ryder had in mind.

Throwing a hand over his eyes and rubbing his temples, he pushed himself away from the wall as the doors slid open and strolled toward the dining area.

When he reached the restaurant, he spotted Matt and Josie right away, ignoring the hostess station to head in their direction. Rather than sitting down, he gripped the back of an empty chair at their table and smiled ruefully.

"Sorry about this, but we're not going to be able to join you for breakfast," he told them, knowing he wouldn't be able to get through a meal while wondering what Monica was up to and whether she was making progress in her efforts to track down the money Matt had stolen.

Josie looked immediately worried and started asking if something was wrong.

He fell on the first excuse that came to mind. "Monica isn't feeling well and I don't want to leave her alone for long.

You'll be all right without us, won't you?" he asked, meeting Josie's eyes and ignoring Matt altogether. He may not be ready to tell his sister her husband was a snake of the lowest order, but the more time he spent with Monica, the less he liked his new brother-in-law.

"Of course," she answered. "I hope Monica's all right. Do you think it's serious?"

He shook his head. "Naw. Probably just something she ate."

A mischievous glint entered Josie's eyes and she smiled brightly. "Maybe it's morning sickness."

It took a full minute for her meaning to sink in, and when it did, Ryder pushed himself away from the chair he'd been leaning on so fast it hit the edge of the table before settling back on all four feet. Not because it was a real possibility— God knew it wasn't, at least not with him—but because the sudden image that popped into his head of Monica pregnant with his child, cradling his child, was real and solid and not nearly as abhorrent as it should have been.

His face grew warm, and he swallowed past the lump that had suddenly formed in his throat. "No, it's not that. Definitely not that."

She gave him another mischievous smile and shrugged one shoulder. "I hope she feels better soon. Tell her we're thinking about her. And if you need anything, we're right next door."

Ryder nodded and made his way back through the restaurant to the lobby of the hotel. He passed the elevators without slowing down and headed outside into the bright sun of a beautiful Hawaiian morning. He didn't want to have breakfast with his sister, but he wasn't going to stare over Monica's shoulder while she fiddled around at the computer, either. Out on the street, he looked one way down the sidewalk, and then the other. With no idea of where to go, he started walking.

A couple hours later, Ryder returned to the hotel, hoping his walk had helped him build up a resistance to his wife, who would no doubt be back in the room by now. It sure as hell hadn't helped him forget the feel of her knee rubbing back and forth across his crotch or the sound of her impassioned moans in his ear as he teased her nipples to tight little peaks. Closing his eyes, Ryder shook his head and admitted he'd need to walk the length of Oahu and all seven of its surrounding islands to work off the energy still bubbling just beneath the surface of his restraint.

Against his better judgment, he slipped his key card into the door lock and walked into the suite. Monica was nowhere to be seen. He moved slowly into the room, not wanting to startle her, but not wanting to be startled by her, either. Considering the clothes she chose to wear in public, there was no telling what kind of cardiac situation he'd be risking by invading her privacy.

The bathroom door was open, lights off, so he knew she wasn't there. That left one more space where she could be hiding. Unless she was still out, she had to be on the balcony.

Pushing the heavy curtains aside, he opened the door and stepped onto the lanai, immediately spotting Monica. She was lounging on one of the long beach chairs, her sandals dangling from the tips of her toes, a pair of dark sunglasses shading her eyes. A bottle of suntan lotion sat on the cement floor beside the chair, and she'd rolled the hem of her blouse up to just below the swell of her breasts, encouraging the sun to kiss as much warm, white skin as it could reach.

Ryder thought the sun was a lucky son of a bitch.

She rolled her head to the side, looking at him from

behind dark lenses. "I wondered when you were coming back," she murmured, but didn't sound overly concerned about his welfare. "How was breakfast?"

"I skipped it and took a walk instead." Glancing over his shoulder, he checked to make sure Matt's and Josie's lanai doors were closed, then asked, "How did it go with the bank stuff?"

Throwing her legs over the edge of the lawn chair, she stood and cocked her head to one side, motioning for him to go back inside. She followed, closing the glass doors behind her and pushing her sunglasses up to rest in the soft cushion of her hair.

"It went okay," she said, but didn't sound terribly enthusiastic. She kept her voice low so no one else would hear—unless they had their ear pressed to a drinking glass against the wall. But Ryder doubted anyone other than Monica would resort to such means of eavesdropping.

"The account exists, so I have to believe the money is still there, but I had to pretend to be Matt's secretary and give some of his personal information just to find out that much. For anything else or to have the money transferred to another account, I'll need a lot more. Like his social security number, answers to security questions, etcetera." She pulled a face. "Unfortunately, I don't think I can fake my way through all of that. Do you?"

He shook his head. "Probably not. And if he's swindled money before, then he's probably got multiple social security numbers and different answers for different security questions, depending on the account."

Monica blew out a breath, ruffling a few strands of hair that had fallen across her face. "I was afraid you'd say that. And I think you're right."

Silence filled the room as seconds ticked by. Then Monica inhaled deeply, squared her shoulders, and dug down to the base of her gut for every ounce of self-assurance she could muster.

"As long as Matt doesn't suspect anything, we don't have to rush. I mean, I'm sure his radar is up now that we've crashed his honeymoon, but he doesn't know we hacked his laptop and made copies of his files, so if we play it cool, we may be able to lull him back into a false sense of confidence."

"Okay," Ryder agreed slowly. "Then what?"

"I'll call Simon Farraday again. He's a forensic accountant, and from everything I've heard, highly respected. To be honest, I don't know how he got hooked up with Matt to begin with. But he has to have account information, and if there's any way to access them or prove Matt took my money under false pretenses, Simon can figure it out."

"You trust this Simon guy?" Ryder asked, crossing his arms and hitching a hip, making it clear he had his doubts.

"I don't know. I think so," she told him honestly. "I'll feel him out a little when I call, and I won't give him any pertinent information unless I think he'll be a good ally. How does that sound?"

Ryder shrugged. "I don't suppose we've got much choice."

She shook her head, but he could see the doubt in the lines between her eyes and around her mouth as she chewed nervously on the nail of her thumb.

"Hey," he said, reaching out to cup her shoulder and give her a reassuring squeeze. "Whatever happens, we won't be any worse off than we are now, right? Follow your gut the way you have this whole time, and we'll handle one thing at a time."

It occurred to Ryder that in the short time he'd known Monica, his opinion of her had done a full one-eighty. He'd gone from thinking she was crazy—or at the very least, taking him for a ride—to realizing she'd been right about everything: the money, Matt, the data they'd found on his laptop. The way her mind worked, the ideas she came up with, could be outlandish and sound borderline bizarre, but at the root of it all, she knew what she was doing.

Just because she went about things differently than just about anyone he knew didn't mean she was a space cadet. She was smart and gorgeous and giving him a run for his money—literally.

Wondering exactly when Monica's skewed logic had begun making sense to him, he reached into his pocket and pulled out the gift he'd brought back for her from his walk.

"I almost forgot," he said, handing her the small white box. "I got this for you."

She took the box, but didn't open it right away. Instead, she stared at it as though it were some foreign object she didn't quite recognize. "For me? What is it?" she asked.

He almost grinned. "Why don't you open it and see."

She rolled the box over in her hands, touching each side and corner before turning it back again and lifting off the lid. A pair of earrings rested inside. The bright red hibiscus flowers were carved out of wood and would hang almost to her shoulders. As soon as he saw them, he'd thought of Monica and known they would go perfectly with her short, dark hair and killer outfits.

"They're beautiful." She ran a soft finger over one of the petals and then lifted them out of the box to slip the fish hooks through her earlobes. "How do they look?"

Her smile almost brought him to his knees. She looked sexier and more beautiful with that smile on her face than he'd ever seen her—and that included the time she'd strutted around the room in nothing more than a towel and his Stetson.

After staring at her for what must have been a full sixty seconds, it occurred to him that she'd asked a question and was most likely waiting for an answer. Except that he couldn't remember what her question had been.

"The lady at the shop said the hibiscus is Hawaii's state flower. They looked like something you'd wear, and I thought you might like a souvenir to take back with you."

"Other than the 'Dirty Little Slot' tote bag and hula dancer nightshirt, huh?" Her lips curled in a teasing smile as she beamed up at him and then leaned forward to press a light kiss to his lips. "I love them. Thank you."

The kiss might as well have been a hand stroking him all the way down to his groin. Of their own volition, his hands reached out to cup her elbows, bringing her flush with his body, flattening her breasts against his chest until her nipples felt like marbles digging into his flesh. She stood on tiptoe to kiss him fully before he'd even thought of tipping his head down to hers. Their mouths meshed, tangling until he couldn't tell where his tongue ended and hers began.

Dipping at the knees, he curved an arm under her buttocks and lifted her until she had to lean down to continue the kiss. Her arms wrapped around his neck as he started toward the bed, only hoping he was headed in the right direction. He'd make love to her on the floor before he would break contact to see where he was going. When his knee cracked into the side of the bed, he slowly lowered Monica to the waiting mattress, following her down, covering every inch of her tall frame with his own as they continued to kiss.

He bit her lower lip, dragged his tongue across her cheek to the hollow just behind her ear. The earrings he'd given her fell back into her hair, giving him room to tease the sensitive lobe of her ear. She tipped her head and moaned low in her throat while he nibbled a trail of wet kisses down her neck, over her collarbone, to the slope of her breasts. Her fingers twisted in his hair, holding him close and encouraging his enthusiastic exploration of her body.

Slipping his fingers beneath the hem of her shirt, he pushed the fabric up until it caught beneath her breasts. He feathered light touches over her softness, moving downward, stroking the flesh of her belly to the waistband of her skirt.

Ryder's fingers stilled just as Monica's began moving. She ran her hands over his chest and back, and then began yanking the tail of his shirt loose from his jeans. With one harsh tug, the pearl-studded snaps opened from stomach to throat. Pulling his head back to hers, she kissed him, teasing him, driving him as insane as he'd tried to drive her.

She was just beginning to toy with the button of his jeans when Ryder's cell phone rang. For a minute, he ignored it. *They* ignored it, too wrapped up in each other to acknowledge any outside commotion. At the moment, Ryder didn't think he would care if the hotel fire alarm went off.

But the phone continued to buzz, growing more and more shrill with every peal. Reluctantly, and with a groan that told Monica just how sorry he was to be doing this, he lifted himself enough to pull the cell from the breast pocket of his shirt.

"What?" he barked, not caring who was on the other end or how much he might offend them. Although they'd stopped kissing, he still had one arm around Monica, her head resting on his shoulder while she waited for him to finish speaking with whoever had dared to interrupt them.

"Ryder, sweetheart," his mother said, throwing the proverbial bucket of ice-cold water on his raging libido and effectively putting a halt on the fun he and Monica were about to have. "I hate to bother you like this, especially on your honeymoon, but I thought you should know that your father had a little accident."

"*What?*" This time the word was more worried than angry. "What happened?"

"It's nothing serious, dear. You know how your father is. He was helping some of your men repair the back wall of your barn when he lost his footing and fell over a pile of boards. He's going to be just fine, but he did break his leg in two places. The doctor says the cast will have to stay on for six to eight weeks."

Ryder heard something in the background and then his mother's failed attempt to cover the mike. "Hush up, Jordan. It's that ornery streak that got your leg broken in the first place." Returning to the phone, she said, "He says the doctor doesn't know what he's talking about, that he'll be up and about in a couple of days. You know how he is," she offered in a low undertone.

He did know what his father was like; nothing could keep the man out of commission for long. But the fact remained that he'd been hurt—while working on Ryder's ranch, no less. He would need his family around him, and Ryder would need to be home to pick up the slack, not only at his place, but at his father's, too.

"I'll be on the next flight home."

"That's not necessary, darling. I only wanted you to know—I didn't mean to interrupt your trip."

"Mom," Ryder said firmly, leaving her no room to misinterpret his intentions. "I'm coming home."

Monica lifted her head and sat back as he ended the call. "What's wrong?"

He turned to meet her eyes. He'd have given just about anything to go back ten minutes and pick up where they'd left off. She still looked tousled, her skin showing the rosy glow of being well-kissed and almost as well-loved.

Damn.

"Dad broke his leg. I hope you don't mind, but I need to get back." He stood, ignoring the fact that Monica was straightening her clothes and running a hand over her hair while he entertained thoughts of throwing her back down on the bed and having his way with her.

"Of course I don't mind. Is he all right?"

"He'll be laid up for a while," he answered with a nod, "but otherwise, he's fine, I guess. I'd still feel better if I were there, though. In case they need me and to take care of the extra work that's bound to pile up at both ranches." He paused. "You can stay here if you want."

It surprised him how difficult those words were to get out, and he swallowed hard afterward. It was a legitimate offer—no reason for her vacation to be cut short just because his had been. But the sharp stab of regret he felt at the idea of heading back home while she remained in Hawaii was foreign to him. And he wasn't sure he appreciated the sensation.

He didn't even particularly like it here, no matter how often she reminded him that it was paradise. At least he *hadn't* liked it until about ten minutes ago. Then he'd started liking it a whole hell of a lot.

When he looked back at Monica, she shot him a withering glare and rolled off the bed to her feet. "I can't believe you think I'd stay here while your family is in trouble." She crossed her arms under her breasts and tapped one foot in irritation. "What kind of woman do you think I am?"

He thought she was perhaps the most perfect creature God had ever put on this earth. Physically speaking. And the fact that she had just offered to cut her trip short to go home with him—had jumped down his throat for suggesting otherwise—raised her another notch in his estimation. She may be flighty and annoying and too headstrong for her own damn good, but she had a heart. Not to mention a body that wouldn't quit.

His pulse leaped, and he forced himself to take another step backward before he forgot he needed to get home and made a grab for Monica.

But he didn't need to make a grab for her. She touched him of her own volition. Taking a step in his direction, she laid her hand on his arm and gave a little squeeze. "I'll start packing," she said. "You call and see how soon we can leave. This will give us a chance to let Matt think we've given up on worrying about the money, and I can do the rest of trying to track it down from anywhere."

His head moved up and down, but he stood stock-still, his brain refusing to send messages to any other parts of his body.

"Do you think your sister will be going home, too?"

He shrugged. *Good. I've got the head and one shoulder working. Throw in an arm and she may not think I'm a complete moron.*

"Call the airline," she repeated. "You can talk to her after we get our seats. She and Matt may not want to go back, since they really are on their honeymoon."

She gave his arm another pat and went into the bathroom. He heard her gathering things and throwing them into different travel cases while he dropped down on the edge of the bed with a heavy sigh.

When had he started falling for this woman? When had she become almost important to him? When had his body suddenly decided that it could go longer without food or air than it could without touching her?

As he used his phone to check flights and book tickets, he realized he had six long hours in coach with too little leg room and too much being pressed against her like the cream in an Oreo to come up with the answers.

Chapter Eighteen

You don't need fancy words to make yer meanin' clear. Say it plain and save some breath for breathin'.

Ryder and Monica arrived home late Friday night. They stopped at his place first to drop off their luggage, then headed over to his parents' house.

When Josie heard about her father's accident, she'd insisted that she and Matt return home, too. Matt hadn't seemed thrilled with the idea, but he hadn't argued too much. They were due in on a later flight, Saturday morning or early afternoon.

Except for a cast covering his right leg from hip to toe, and the fact that he had to be pushed around in a wheelchair, Ryder's father seemed fine. He insisted he was and chastised his son for cutting his trip short.

When he apologized to Monica for ruining her honeymoon, he looked so dejected that she could only laugh and kiss him on the cheek, telling him she'd think of a way for him to make it up to her later.

"You really charmed Pop," Ryder said a bit later on the ride back to Rolling Rock Ranch.

Monica raised a brow. "What do you mean?"

"When you leaned over to kiss him and told him he could pay you back later for disrupting our trip, I thought he was going to jump out of that wheelchair and run off with you. Mom would have killed him for it, but he was too smitten to see straight."

She laughed. "I like your father. He's a sweet man. I just hate that he feels so badly about ruining our honeymoon when the whole thing was a sham to begin with."

"Yeah, well, his broken leg did interrupt something awfully honeymoon-like." Ryder shot her a grin, one side of his mouth turned up as he wiggled his brows devilishly.

"I suppose his timing could have been better," she admitted with a chuckle. "But then, you didn't seem too eager to pick up where we'd left off, either."

His wicked grin disappeared as he stared at her, ignoring the road ahead.

"Watch where you're going," she cried, and he swerved to miss a particularly deep hole in the rutted dirt road.

Keeping half an eye on the road, he continued to toss disbelieving glances her way. "Do you really think I didn't want to keep doing what we were doing? If that's what you believe, you don't know jack shit about men, sweetheart."

She glanced out the window into the inky darkness, feeling suddenly uncomfortable with the turn of the conversation. "I know about most men," she said carefully. "I'm not so sure about you."

He hit the brakes so hard she almost flew through the windshield. She threw an arm against the dashboard, and the seat belt jerked hard against her breastbone.

"What are you doing?" she shouted. She looked around for a rabbit or deer that might have run out in front of the truck, but saw nothing.

Instead of answering, Ryder unsnapped his seat belt, then hers, and dragged her across the seat into his lap. Without warning, he gripped the back of her head and brought her face down to his. His tongue ravaged her mouth, touching, scalding every inch while his hands roved over her body. His touch was like a brand, marking her flesh with invisible symbols of ownership. No one had ever touched her like this, ever made her feel this hot and bothered and wanted.

As quickly as the kiss began, it stopped. Ryder pulled away and set her back on the vinyl seat, giving her a little push to her side of the cab. He pulled the seat belt across her waist and rebuckled it, then did the same to his own.

"Be sure," he said, then shifted back into gear and drove the rest of the way home.

Several minutes later, Monica's lips were still tingling as they entered Ryder's darkened house. He tossed his keys on the countertop and flipped a switch, casting light through the kitchen and parts of the entryway.

"Wow. Either you hired a new cleaning lady or your mother spent some time here while you were gone, too."

The counters were blessedly clear, and the sink was not only empty but sparkling clean. All of the dirty dishes and recyclables were gone, and she couldn't resist opening a couple of the cupboards to see if things had been put away or thrown away. But there were stacks of plates and cups exactly where they should be, and both the dishwasher and trash were empty.

"My money's on Mom," Ryder said. "She never liked me wasting money on a housekeeper when she claimed she could come over and clean up just as easily."

"Looks like she finally got her way."

"Yeah—for as long as it lasts." Sweeping his "good" black hat—which Monica still maintained was only slightly worse for wear—off his head, he traded it for the work Stetson hanging inside the front door. "I'd better go out and check the stock, just to make sure everything's okay. Will you be all right until I get back?"

She smiled at his unwarranted concern. If Ryder was anything, it was protective—of everything and everyone in his life. Including her, it seemed. The idea warmed her insides faster than a cup of cocoa on a cold winter morning, though she had no intention of analyzing her feelings along those lines anytime soon. No, it would be better to concentrate on the matter at hand.

Glancing at her watch, she said, "It's too late to try to reach Simon, but I think I'll call my friend Brooke. She'll be wondering what's going on, and maybe I can have her ship some of my stuff. You don't mind if I snap a few pictures of your ranch, do you? I'm getting kind of itchy without a camera hanging around my neck."

"Be my guest. But if you ask me to pose in my birthday suit, you'll have to keep those shots to yourself." A corner of his mouth quirked up as he moved toward the door. "I'll be back in a bit."

Like some kind of lovesick fool, Monica watched him leave and even went to the window after the door closed behind him, just to enjoy the view as he walked toward the barn. It didn't last long, but she figured the few seconds of seeing his broad back, lean hips, and long legs before they disappeared into the evening shadows would be enough to tide her over until he returned.

After that, she didn't know *what* would happen. But if that kiss in the truck were anything to go by, she just might have a sexy, steamy night ahead of her.

A shiver of anticipation raised goose bumps on her arms and legs.

She didn't bother rubbing them away as she retrieved her cell phone and the new charger she'd picked up while they were at the airport. Plugging it in, she gave it a couple seconds to turn on, then texted Brooke. Despite what she'd told Ryder, Monica suddenly didn't feel like filling her friend in on everything that had happened since the last time they'd spoken. It had been a long day, with a lot of exhausting travel. Tomorrow would be soon enough for a chat.

So, through a few brief messages, she assured her friend that she was absolutely fine and would catch her up later…but asked Brooke to box up her beloved Nikon D5, along with a few other amenities, and ship it to the ranch. Finding the address was easy, since all the mail Ryder had missed while they'd been gone was piled on a small desk in the dining room.

Brooke asked one more time if she was sure she was okay, and Monica replied with two words: Vacation Rules.

What had started out as a "what happens on vacation stays on vacation" joke had turned into a code they used occasionally to let each other know when they'd met a hottie and might disappear for a few hours. Once Brooke knew that Monica would only be tied to some guy's bed if she wanted to be, her friend sent one last text: 'Night, followed by a series of emojis, including a thumbs-up, eggplant, wide smiley face, and confetti.

"Ha-ha," Monica responded aloud before sending back a sticking-out-her-tongue emoji of her own.

With a chuckle, she left the phone on the counter to finish charging, then grabbed their luggage from just inside the door to move farther into the house. She put Ryder's duffle in his room, then stood there for a solid thirty seconds, trying to decide if she was brave enough to add her bags to the pile.

Turned out she wasn't. She was a wimp. She wanted him—that had been decided all the way back in Honolulu and more firmly established by the kiss he'd treated her to in his truck.

But she just wasn't gutsy enough to simply move in with him. She could put her stuff in his room, make herself comfortable, probably even greet him naked under the covers, and she knew Ryder wouldn't say a negative word about it. On the contrary. By the looks he'd been giving her all day, he would most likely fall on his knees and thank every god and goddess in creation.

The very idea caused anxious little butterflies to take up tap dancing in her stomach. But she just couldn't do it. She didn't want to make love to Ryder because it was convenient. She didn't want to be at his beck and call. If Ryder wanted her, she wanted to know he *really* wanted her. He would have to make the pivotal move.

With a sigh of regret for her lack of courage, she lugged her things across the hall and into the spare bedroom. It didn't look as homey or comfortable as Ryder's room, but there was a small twin bed against one wall and a dresser against the other, and it would suit her just fine. And if Ryder wanted to pick up where they'd left off...well, he'd know where to find her.

She was back in the kitchen, fussing around with nothing much just to keep busy when Ryder came in from the barn. He set his hat on the counter and came around to lean against its edge.

"How'd it go?"

"Fine." She turned to face him, leaning against the sink in a mirror image of the way he was resting against the adjoining counter. "I ended up texting just to let Brooke know I was still alive."

He raised a brow. "So she won't be sending in the troops

to rescue you?"

"Not unless I send an SOS or fail to contact her again tomorrow."

"Good to know."

She chuckled. "Yeah, right. Seriously, though, I'll need to call Simon first thing in the morning to see what he can do about my money being in that offshore account. I'm just afraid he'll say there's nothing he can do—or that he'll need a signature or something to move things forward."

"Well, Matt and Josie will be here tomorrow, so if he does, we'll be able to get it."

With a snort, she set her hands to her hips and challenged him. "And how, exactly, will we manage that?"

Ryder didn't move, just stood there staring at her as he seemed to mull things over. "I don't know, but I'm sure you'll think of something."

"Me? Why me? I thought I was the one who kept getting you in trouble," she pointed out.

"You do keep getting me in trouble," he conceded with a small half-smile. "Funny, but I seem to be getting used to it."

She rolled her eyes, thinking women weren't the only ones who possessed mercurial personalities. Ryder seemed to change his mind at least as often as she did.

"So *we'll* think of something," he told her.

"Like what?" Pitching her voice an octave higher, she batted her eyelashes in her best impression of a sultan's houri. "Matt, darling, I know you left me at the altar and I've been hounding you ever since, but would you mind signing this itty-bitty little paper so I can take my money back from your secret account?"

The other corner of his mouth tilted up, but he only shrugged, unaffected by her dramatic display. "I'm sure we can come up with something less obvious than that. Pop's hurt. If you need a signature, maybe we can get Matt to sign a get-well card for him—from all of us."

"Ohmigosh, *yes*." Monica's eyes widened as she rushed forward, gripping his forearms with excitement. "Oh, Ryder, that's perfect! And I'm an excellent tracer. We'll get him to sign a card for your dad and then I'll copy his name."

"Whoa, now," he said, moving his hands to her waist and drawing her a tiny bit closer. "You may be getting ahead of yourself. We don't know yet what your friend might need."

"I know, but if we do need Matt's signature, that is a *brilliant* way to get it!" She cocked her head to the side and grinned. "You know, for a cowboy, you're kind of good at this cloak and dagger stuff."

"Cowboys are good at a lot more than just herding cattle, you know." His hands drifted from her waist to her backside and pulled her close. "Care to give me a proper thank you for my ingenuity?"

Her eyes locked with his as exhilaration faded and a whole other sensation swept through her. She licked her lips and swallowed before trying to speak. "What would you consider a proper thank you?"

A grin split the hard lines of his face, and his grip on her butt tightened until she was flush with his body, her breasts pressed flat against the hard wall of his chest. "I was thinking maybe we could pick up where were left off in Hawaii. You know, kind of finish our honeymoon."

His head dipped and his lips touched hers, warm and strong and inviting. She tried to calm the erratic beat of her heart, but the organ was already off on a drum solo that would put Van Halen to shame, and Ryder's tongue was doing the wickedest things to her own.

Her eyes drifted closed on a sigh. Lord, she wanted him.

Without breaking the kiss, he turned her so that she was leaning against the counter instead, and then lifted her to sit on its edge. His hands clamped down on her hips, and she felt the solid ridge of his arousal between her thighs. Wrapping her legs around his waist, she drew him closer. As close as two people could get with their clothes on.

He groaned and ground his pelvis into her body. His hands slid up to cup her breasts, and then to rub his thumbs over the area of her nipples beneath the bra while his mouth moved to her cheek and along her jawline.

She took a ragged breath, striving for some sort of sanity when all she really wanted to do was lie back and let Ryder touch her anywhere he could reach. But she made herself think. Made herself run through the repercussions of making love to this man, husband or no husband.

"Wait." She put her hands on his shoulder and levered away from him until his lips were no longer wreaking havoc with her hormones. She looked him in the eye and made sure he was cognizant enough to understand every word she said. "We may not be able to get an annulment if we do this, you know," she said, her tone firm while her insides felt like Jell-O. "That whole 'lack of consummation' thing will be out the window."

Oh, she had no intention of turning him down if he was determined to seduce her. She was ready to race him to the bedroom at the word "Go!" But she wanted him to be as sure as she was before they did something they could never undo.

A spark of something almost predatory leaped into his eyes as he leaned in and licked a particularly sensitive spot at the base of her throat that made her body go tight. "So we'll get a divorce instead."

And then he lifted the edge of her shirt and pulled the whole thing up and over her head in one quick motion, causing the hibiscus flowers dangling from her ears to rattle. The top disappeared somewhere over his shoulder as he pressed back against her, the thin material of his shirt rubbing against the stiff lace of her bra.

She chuckled and wrapped her arms back around his neck. "You've done this before," she said.

His laugh was low, gravelly, and knowing. "A couple of times, yeah."

He let his fingers trace the edge of her bra, then move in slowly decreasing circles toward the centers of her breasts. Soon his hands were on her skin, nudging the fabric out of his way. When he slipped a finger beneath the edging to touch one puckered, tightening nipple, she moaned low in her throat and arched her back. Then, before he could make a move to do it, she reached behind her and flipped the hook of the bra, letting the straps and material fall away from her arms and breasts.

"God, yes," he whispered in a harsh tone, and then wrapped his hands over her bare flesh.

"Since you've done this before," she managed, almost undone by the soft stroking of his hands on her flesh and his lips trailing a hot, moist path down her neck, "I assume you have a condom tucked away somewhere for just such an occasion."

That stopped him cold. In a single breath, he went from teasing and tormenting to standing ramrod straight and staring at her like a baseball fan who'd just gotten thwacked on the head with a home run ball.

Monica sat back in surprise, bringing her hands up to cover her bare breasts. "What?" she asked.

"Shit." The lines on his face deepened as he scowled, and his fingers clamped into her hips. "Shit, shit, shit," he muttered, banging his forehead softly against hers.

Her eyes widened with surprise. "You've got to have some in your bathroom," she said, her tone thick with disbelief.

He was a hot, sexy, single, and very virile guy…no way did he not have condoms on hand, just in case. Even she carried one in her purse and a couple in her camera bag…just in case.

And if she'd only asked Brooke to ship her equipment *before* they got back from Hawaii, she would even now have Ryder inside her and be screaming his name.

His mouth twisted. "I think I have one in the truck."

She was already hopping down from the counter and the comfortable perch she'd made of his body. "I'll check the bathroom, you check your truck," she said, passing out instructions like she'd been reincarnated from a drill sergeant.

"I'll meet you back here." He pulled her up snug against him and gave her a long, deep, wet kiss.

Her knees nearly buckled from the feel of his tongue alone. And then he released her and started outside. "Hurry," she whispered raggedly.

He stopped at the front door and shot her a hundred-watt smile. "I'm the wind, darlin'."

She watched him go, then laughed at his parting words, as well as their current situation. Who would have thought that after agonizing for days over whether they should or shouldn't sleep together, their final decision would be done in by the Search for the Holy Latex?

Grabbing her discarded clothing from the floor, she shrugged into the shirt, sans bra, and ran back to the master bedroom. She hit the drawer of Ryder's nightstand first... because wasn't that the most logical place for a guy to keep his condoms?

Apparently not.

Moving to the bathroom, she looked in the medicine cabinet, under the sink, and then in each drawer of the vanity, tossing aside extra razor blades, Band-Aids, and all kinds of other personal items. Finally her fingers bumped into a small foil packet at the back of the very last drawer that she prayed wasn't a sample of Tylenol. Unless Ryder couldn't find a condom, either, in which case, they'd probably both need an aspirin.

She yanked it out and sent a little prayer of thanks heavenward. The Holy Grail. *Yes!*

Pushing herself to her feet, she raced down the hall.

Only to meet Ryder coming in from outside.

"Found one!" they cried out at the same time, holding up their treasure like a battle flag.

Ryder was on her in a nanosecond, pushing the open blouse off again over her shoulders and steering her backward toward the bedroom while her fingers loosened the buttons of his shirt. His mouth fused with hers, and they kissed harder and deeper with each step. His feet danced as he tried to avoid stepping on her sandal-clad toes, then they hit his bedroom doorway, and he simply picked her up by the waist and carried her the rest of the way into the room.

She fell back on the bed where he dropped her and began pushing her shorts down over her hips while he struggled with his boots. One after the other, they fell to the floor with a clunk. Then he shrugged out of his shirt and moved to the waistband of his jeans.

Already naked and more impatient than she'd have ever imagined, Monica scooted forward on the mattress and pushed his hands aside. "Let me." She undid the button and then moved to the zipper, slowly sliding it down over the pressing bulge of his arousal.

His eyes drifted closed at the sensation, and she watched him more than what she was doing. Once the zipper was completely down, she slipped her hands into the waistband of the jeans and slid them, cotton boxers and all, down over his buttocks and legs. He kicked them away from his feet and looked down at her, his erection standing strong and proud in front of her face, saluting like a private to a four-star general.

She didn't wait for him to ask or make another move toward her, but put her hand at the base of his penis and her lips to its very tip. The breath rushed out of his lungs as her tongue swept around the crest like it was a lollipop. She didn't know if Ryder had expected her to shy away from this or not, but he looked infinitely pleased with her decision.

Some women didn't like oral sex, she knew. Most men loved it, at least the BJ variety. And so did she. She loved the pleasure it gave her partner, the feel of that steel-hard length of man in her mouth. And she loved the fact that most men, after receiving a little TLC themselves, tended to repay the favor.

Ryder's fingers sifted through the short strands of her hair while she worked her mouth down the length of his penis, then back up, taking the whole thing into her mouth. She continued to roll her tongue around the soft skin, at the same time gently sucking. And while one hand remained at the base of his erection, her other explored the curve of his hip, down his thigh, into the area between his leg and scrotum. He sucked in a harsh breath when she palmed the delicate sack and began gently kneading. And then his hands tensed on the back of her head, and he forced her away. His hot gaze burned into hers as he looked down at her.

"You're very good at that, sweetheart," he said with a soft smile.

Monica stood, his hands falling from her hair to her shoulders. "City girls are good at a lot more than just hailing cabs, you know," she retorted, throwing his earlier words back at him and then wrapping her arms around his neck.

As they kissed, he lowered them both to the bed, his hands skimming every inch of her body. She reached out, fumbling around on the comforter for the condoms they'd both dropped. Her fingers closed over one of the packets, and she struggled to open it behind his back, not wanting to concentrate too hard on anything but the feel of Ryder's lips and caress. Once the condom was open, he sat back a bit and began to take it from her, but she stopped him.

"Uh-uh," she said, pulling it out of his reach.

Amusement lit his eyes. "You just want to be in charge of everything tonight, don't you?"

She pushed out from under him and rolled to her knees on the mattress, moving back toward the headboard. Ryder followed slowly.

"Yep. I'm gonna ride you hard and put you up wet." She had no idea where she'd heard that before, but it sounded like cowboy lingo. And from the looks of it, Ryder appreciated the terminology. A grin split across his face and, if possible, his erection grew even larger.

"Is that right?" he asked, stalking her now.

She nodded weakly, her mouth dry, as he moved across the bed like a panther tracking prey, a wicked glint in his eyes. The bedframe banged against the wall as he pressed his body flush against hers, his hands running from her upper arms to her wrists. He held them against the wall while he stared into her eyes, the light hairs on his chest rubbing against the raw, sensitive tips of her breasts.

And then he released her and plopped back on the bed, fluffing the pillows behind his head as he lay there in all his naked glory. With his arms propped behind his head, he twisted his face to shoot her a devilish grin. "Saddle up, sugar. This is gonna be the ride of your life."

"Arrogant oaf," she muttered.

But she said it as she straddled his body, seating herself on his knees so that she could lean forward and apply the condom—with her teeth.

• • •

When Ryder saw what she meant to do, he drew in a sharp breath. Shit! She already had him harder and more turned on than he'd ever been in his life. Did she really think she needed to tease him with parlor tricks for a good lay? If things got any better, he'd be taking the trip alone—and he didn't like that idea any more than he thought Monica would. He started to say something, warn her that she was treading on thin ice, but she only smiled, the off-white rubber dangling lightly from between her teeth.

Leaning forward, she dropped it on the head of his arousal, then licked a path all the way around its rolled bottom as she fastened it more firmly with her fingertips. And each time she smoothed the latex down a fraction of an inch, she first had to kiss and lick and nibble the spot.

Not that Ryder had a mind to complain. He clutched big handfuls of bedspread on either side of his body while his chest heaved for air and groans of pleasure rolled out of him one on top of another. But he'd have to be chopped up into little pieces and cooked over a spit before he'd ask her to stop.

He'd just about had enough—thought he was about to shoot right up off the bed and stick to the ceiling—when she reached the base of his penis, finished covering him with the condom, and gave the spot an extra flick just for effect. When she stopped touching him, Ryder took his first full breath since she'd begun. Then he opened his eyes.

Monica was perched on his legs, smiling like she'd just won the lottery. Which she was about to, if he had anything to say about it.

"Damn, darlin'. You sure know how to make a man sing for his supper."

One side of her mouth lifted in a smile.

He leaned forward to grab her arms, and she scooted farther up his body, until his throbbing length rested against the soft curve of her mound. Her breasts hung before him like a gift from the gods while her hands fell flat on his chest. His eyes narrowed, and he concentrated hard on her face so the feel of her heat against his groin wouldn't be quite so noticeable.

Yeah, just like a guy with two dicks wouldn't be noticeable in the locker room, he thought wryly.

"But you know what this means, don't you?" He pulled her down until their mouths were a mere whisper apart.

She shook her head and leaned into him, her hands moving to fold over his shoulders.

"It means I'm going to have to make you scream."

His mouth opened and all but devoured her soft, sweet lips. She felt like cotton candy and Kentucky bourbon all rolled into one. And he wanted to be inside her. *Now. Enough of this fooling around.*

He slid his palms over her breasts and waist and gripped the swells of her buttocks, pressing her down against his arousal. And then he lifted her, ready to pierce her hot core.

"Time to ride," he whispered.

But before he could move her down to surround him, she sat up, looking at him with wide eyes.

"Oh, wait a minute," she said. And then she bolted across the room and out the bedroom door.

Chapter Nineteen

Sometimes, you just need to take the bridle off, throw the skillet away, and let the cougar scream.

She disappeared through the door, and it took him a minute to move. But when he did, he was across the room in a shot, his arousal waning a bit but still covered in her expertly applied condom. He had to go after her, not only because she'd left in the middle of something very, very important, but because she was traipsing around naked as a newborn calf.

He wrenched the door open, prepared to barrel down the hall, only to find her strolling in his direction from the front of the house. His good black Stetson—the same one she'd stolen, then showered with—was clutched in her right hand, brushing the side of her leg as she walked.

"What are you doing?" he asked suspiciously. He'd never claimed to be an expert on women, and in this case, he was at a complete loss.

She slapped the hat on her head and put a hand to his chest to push him back into the room. "I needed my hat. It's not safe to ride without the proper equipment," she quipped.

He couldn't help it—he laughed. He let her push him backward until his calves hit the edge of the bed, and he was still laughing. Then he let her push him onto the mattress.

"Scoot back," she told him.

"Yes, ma'am." He offered her a little salute. Well, he'd been saluting her all evening, but this time, he actually used his hand.

She grinned as she knee-walked her way to straddling him once again. "I like compliance," she said. "It's very important for a mount to obey its master."

"Yes, ma'am," he said again. She was up near his chest this time, and he was able to reach out and grasp her elbows, bringing her face closer to his own. "I do have to warn you of one thing, though," he said softly.

"What's that?"

She sounded a bit breathless. He liked breathless.

"Turnabout's fair play."

The tendons of her throat moved convulsively as she swallowed. A slight blush stole over her cheeks, and he was glad to see that she wasn't in complete control of either the situation or her emotions.

While she sat there, looking a little dazed, he took the opportunity to run his hands down to her hips, moving them right where he wanted them. Gritting his teeth, he slowly lowered her down onto his raging erection. There was no other word for it—ever since he'd met Monica, every part of his body had been raging. His thoughts, his blood, his cock... She had a way about her that set every cell of his body on full alert.

A sigh escaped her as he pressed her fully onto his arousal and a look of pure delight darted across her features. Her pleasure nearly sent him over the edge. Not inside her a minute, and he was already grinding his teeth and counting to a thousand to keep from exploding.

"Don't move," he whispered raggedly when she shifted her weight on him. If she did, then it would all be over. Wham, bam, thank you ma'am—and he'd be more disappointed than anyone.

He got all the way to fifty before she moved. Her fingers curled into his chest, and she leaned forward a bit to whisper in his ear.

"Ryder."

The sound of his name on her lips sent him right back to zero. *One, two, three...*

"Ryder," she whispered again.

"Don't say that," he grumbled, eyes tightly closed while he counted. *Four, five, six...*

"Don't say what?"

She shifted again and he swore.

One, two, three...

"My name. Don't say my name," he grit out.

She licked the sensitive curve of his ear. His fingers dug into her hips, and his pelvis shot off the bed.

She laughed, low and throaty. "Why can't I say your name?"

He opened his eyes and looked at her, giving up on counting altogether. "Because I'll lose it if you do."

A downright X-rated smile crossed her face. "In that case...*Ryder, Ryder, Ryder.*" And her body clenched around him like a fist.

"Jesus!" His eyes went wide and his body moved of its own volition while she rose and fell on him—just like she was riding a horse. She clenched the walls of her vagina again, and he nearly went through the roof.

"Do you like that?" she asked wickedly. "Do you want me to stop?"

"No." The word was strangled. "God, no."

But he wasn't going to be the only one teetering on the edge. Moving his hands from her hips, he gently cupped her breasts and teased the nipples with his thumbs. She leaned forward and he sat up to capture one straining point in his mouth.

The air caught in her lungs at the touch of his moist tongue on her hot skin, and he gave a silent whoop of satisfaction. Turnabout was definitely fair play.

With a hand on one breast and his mouth on the other, he moved his free hand down over her waist. When he felt it at the side of his thumb, he gave her naval ring a little flick, then continued the route of his hand until he hit the damp, springy curls that surrounded him.

Still teasing her nipples while she moved above him, he slipped one finger into her folds and found the tiny button of pleasure that he knew would send her into total oblivion. Sure enough, the minute he touched her there, she screamed. Her body arched and he released her breast to pull her close, kissing her until there wasn't an ounce of breath in either of their lungs. God, she was so hot and wet, it made him want to weep. And sweep her over the edge right along with him.

He rolled her clitoris beneath his expert fingers, urging her to move faster while they continued to kiss. He didn't want to let go; even to breathe, he didn't want to let go of her.

And then she came. Her mouth opened wide with a high, keening cry, her eyes closed, her back arched. While her body convulsed around him, he came, too, holding her tight against the last few thrusts of his hips.

When the world once again came into focus and every ounce of energy had been squeezed from his more than willing body, he reached up and lifted the hat off her head, setting it beside them on the bed. Then he pulled her down to lie across his chest.

He wanted to say something. Something warm and

tender to comfort her, or funny to break the silence of the moment. But he couldn't think of a damn thing. So he simply kissed the top of her head, tucked her more securely into the curve of his shoulder, and closed his eyes.

• • •

The phone woke her. She didn't know where she was, or even what time it could be. She only knew that she was warm and comfortable and didn't want to be disturbed.

Realizing the blasted phone would keep right on ringing unless she did something about it, she ordered her brain to open her eyes. Modern technology was *not* all it was cracked up to be.

One lid crept open in time to see Ryder reaching toward the annoying object. She was sprawled across his chest, covering him like a blanket. And if she wasn't mistaken...

Her eyes widened. She was definitely not mistaken. They were both totally naked without so much as a top sheet covering them, and Ryder was pressing into her hip, wide-awake from the waist down, at least. Just his stretching for the phone caused a quick bolt of pleasure to race through her body, and she found herself wanting him again, too.

"Hi, Mom," she heard him say. He ran a hand through his tousled hair and sat up a bit more.

While he was occupied with his phone call and before he could try to stop her, she rolled off of him to the other side of the bed. They hadn't even bothered to pull down the covers last night, so there was no sheet to cover up with. Crossing to Ryder's closet, she grabbed the first shirt her hand came in contact with and stuck her arms into the overly long sleeves.

"That's not necessary, Mom. Monica and I don't need—"

The mention of her name caught her attention, and she glanced over her shoulder. Ryder's gaze met hers and he shrugged, as though apologizing for whatever scheme his mother was hatching on the other end of the line. Then his eyes swept over her from head to toe, taking in the fact that his shirt as still hanging open, hiding her arms and breasts, but not much else.

Despite the fact that they were far from strangers at this point, her face suffused with heat and she dashed into the bathroom.

So they'd made love last night. *Gone at it like bunnies on a deadline was more like it,* she thought with a grimace. She was okay with that, truly she was. But that didn't mean she wanted him to remind her of their actions while he was on the phone with his *mother.* Good lord!

She was standing in front of the mirror trying to get short spikes of slept-on hair to lie flat when Ryder rapped on the door and came in without waiting for her to answer.

"Morning, Rapunzel," he said with a sinful grin.

At the sound of his supposed endearment, her arms dropped to her sides. He was still stark naked, and his body left no doubt that the conversation with his mother hadn't dampened his ardor a stitch.

Too bad, cowboy. Until she brushed her teeth and ran a comb through her hair, nobody was getting lucky, not even the Lone Ranger here.

He took a step closer and brushed a hand through her gnarled hair while he bent to give her a good morning kiss. She would have retreated, but with the sink at her hip, there was nowhere to go.

She wasn't uncomfortable with him, exactly, but she looked like hell and hated to have him see her this way. Matt had always told her she looked like Sid Vicious in the mornings. Being compared to a drugged-out punk rocker—and a man, at that—wasn't exactly a stroke to the ego.

Ryder didn't seem to notice her discomfort. Or if he did,

he ignored it.

"I have some good news and some bad news," he said, one side of his mouth still turned up in a grin.

He was the happiest morning person she'd ever seen. Of course, as lucky as he'd gotten last night, he had reason to be in a good mood.

Leaning into her even more, his voice lowered to a conspiratorial hush. "The good news is, we have one condom left and I can get into town this morning for more."

She flushed. And it didn't help that she could feel his erection pressing against the material of the shirt she wore.

"The bad news," he said, moving back a step and returning his voice to normal, "is that Mom and Dad have decided to throw us a wedding barbecue."

Her head snapped up. "A what?"

"A wedding barbecue," he repeated wryly. "To make up for the fact that they weren't able to throw us an engagement party *and* because our honeymoon was cut short." He wriggled his eyebrows suggestively and came in for another kiss. "Well, as far as they know," he said, pressing his lips to her collarbone.

"Did you tell them that's not necessary?" Monica asked, suddenly panicked. She wasn't even sure why.

"I told her. They insist."

"But…but…"

"But nothing. There's no getting out of it." He didn't sound overly pleased, but he didn't sound sorry, either. "Mom has already called half the town and has food on the stove as we speak. They'll be here at six to help us set up for tomorrow."

Set up. God, it all sounded so complicated. Just how many people had Ruth Ann invited? Why couldn't they wait a few weeks before doing something so public and significant? And if *they* were throwing the get-together, why was the event being held here?

"How many people are coming?" she asked, trying to hold on to her trepidation even as Ryder's fingers toyed with the hem of her shirt.

"I couldn't begin to hazard a guess," he said with a chuckle while his lips trailed along her shoulder. "Josie and Matt will come over as soon as their flight gets in, and all the hands will come after work. Other than that, it depends on how many people Mom got ahold of and how many people *those* people got ahold of."

"Oh God." Her head tilted to allow his mouth better access to her neck even as her heart hammered in alarm. "I can't meet all those people. Tell them I can't go."

Ryder raised his head, finally catching the edge of hysteria in her voice. "Can't go? Honey, it's your party. You don't think my folks would throw this big a bash just for me, do you?"

Her stomach plummeted. If he was trying to make her feel better, he was doing a piss-poor job of it.

"I can't, Ryder. I just can't." She shook her head in adamant denial. "It would be a lie."

He ran his fingers over the side of her face and held a hand against her temple. "What lie? It's just a barbecue, darlin', not the Spanish Inquisition."

She continued to shake her head and met his intense, concerned gaze. "No, it's more than that. This is all a lie, Ryder, all of it."

His jaw tensed and his hand fell to her shoulder. "What happened last night wasn't a lie. Was it?"

She closed her eyes, pain searing through her. "No, it wasn't," she admitted hoarsely. Looking up at him, she said, "But that's just between the two of us. By letting your parents throw us a barbecue—a *wedding* barbecue—we're letting them, and all of your friends, believe our relationship is more than it is. How much do you want to hurt them when we finally get divorced?"

His fingers tightened almost imperceptibly on her arms. "I don't want to hurt them at all. But, Monica, our relationship is none of their business. I love my parents, don't get me wrong. But even if we were really and truly married, thinking it was going to be a forever kind of thing, it still wouldn't be any of their business. I don't see why the arrangement we have should affect them any differently."

"Because if we were really married, we wouldn't know whether or not it was going to work out. We *know* this fake marriage is only temporary. And we're leading them to believe it's permanent. Doesn't that bother you?"

He didn't answer, only scowled down at her. "So what do you want to do, tell them?"

She was quiet for a moment. "Maybe we should."

His eyes rolled and he let out a snort of disbelief. "Are you crazy? If you think they're suffocating now, just wait until they find out this whole thing is a sham. They'd be on us like locusts on a wheat field. Nope, no way are we telling them."

"Then why did you ask if that's what I wanted to do?" she asked with a scowl.

"Because I didn't think even you were loco enough to believe something that foolhardy made sense."

Her fists went to her hips while she stared at him, totally affronted. She opened her mouth to tell him off, but he took hold of her shoulders again and gave her a little shake to get her attention—which he had, in spades.

"Sweetheart, trust me on this. We aren't going to tell them, but we aren't going to wreck their lives by going to this party, either. Around here, people look for any excuse to throw a barbecue, to drink, dance, gossip. A hog on a spit is not a lifetime commitment."

Her mouth fell open in disgust. "They're going cook a

pig? A little Babe or Wilbur?"

"Why do you think they call it a barbecue, darlin'?" He winked, then turned and tugged her back into the bedroom. "Now, come on," he cajoled with a wide grin. "Give me an excuse to go into town—help me use that last condom."

Chapter Twenty

If you're gonna go, go like hell. If your mind's not made up,
don't use your spurs.

"Smile."

With one foot propped on the paddock fence, Ned held his beat-up hat over his heart like he was pledging allegiance and gave her a big, sloppy grin. She snapped the picture and lowered her camera, which hung by a strap around her neck.

"How was that?"

"Perfect," she told him. He'd looked young and silly, like the poster boy for a dude ranch instead of a serious cowhand—but he was enjoying himself, and so was she. Man, she'd missed clicking away!

After making good use of that last condom, Ryder had decided he should really go out and check on the horses. Since he usually got up at dawn, letting things go until almost noon was majorly slacking off. Ned had been there, already toiling away, but Monica knew Ryder felt better when he was overseeing the running of the ranch himself.

That had given her a chance to shake off some of the sexual stupor Ryder had lulled her into...with very little opposition from her, of course...and finally put in a call to Simon. He answered on the second ring, thank goodness, and had seemed more than happy to hear her out. To her surprise, he didn't say a word in defense of Matt, instead asking countless questions about her history with him, how he'd convinced her to hand over the money, what he'd claimed he planned to do with it, and the situation she currently found herself in. Then he told her to send him copies of everything she had, keeping the originals somewhere safe and far away from her ex. Simon not only wanted everything she'd copied to the flash drive in Hawaii, but any old texts and emails she could find, as well as her thoughts and notes and ideas regarding her history with the jerk and anything she thought might be pertinent to his possible history of absconding with other people's money.

She couldn't believe how attentive the accountant was, and how earnest he sounded about helping her. It occurred to her that he could be blowing smoke up her skirt the same as Matt had their entire relationship. But something told her she could trust him...hopefully a wiser, more mature sliver of instinct than she'd used to judge Matt. Plus, if Simon was Matt's partner-in-crime, then he would have bent over backward to assure her there was nothing to worry about, that the magazine *was* in the works, and tried to talk her out of looking for ways to get her money back.

Once that was taken care of and she realized she could relax a little on the Operation Trap the Rat front, she'd opened the package Brooke had overnighted to her. It must have been waiting on the porch when Ryder went out, because Monica found it on the kitchen table as soon as she'd headed for the coffee pot.

The Nikon D5 inside was her baby. Oh, she had other,

better, more expensive cameras and equipment for work, but this was her personal camera—the one she'd slept with for a full two weeks after saving for *ages* to finally be able to afford it...the one she carried to take her own photos, even when she was on location, being paid to take pictures for someone else. Thankfully, Brooke was aware of Monica's unhealthy attachment to "Nikki"—yes, she'd named it; so sue her—and had been very conscientious about leaving it inside its case, then wrapping it in bubble wrap, a few layers of the clothing Monica had asked for, and then crumpled paper to fill any gaps between the camera's little nest and the shipping container.

She couldn't help noticing that her friend had also taken creative license with the "extras" Monica had asked her to send, which only made her laugh. Leave it to Brooke to turn "can you send me some underwear?" into an opportunity to poke even more fun at the bizarre situation she'd gotten herself into. But just wait...revenge was a dish best served cold, and the next time something ridiculous happened to Brooke, Monica would be sure to pay her back, big-time.

When she headed outside and started taking shot after shot in a sort of photographic documentary of her Rancho del Ryder experience, it felt almost like Christmas morning. As strange as it sounded, nothing ever looked quite as wonderful to her naked eye as it did through the lens of a camera. Ryder was even letting her use his outdated but still functional computer to download the shots to her private archive program, which she could access online from pretty much anywhere.

"Wanna do some more?" Ned asked, looking eager to keep posing as long as she wanted him to.

But she'd already filled an entire memory card on Ned alone—Ned on horseback, Ned with his hat on, Ned with his hat off, Ned swinging his lasso... What she *really* wanted was to capture Ryder on film. Now there was a fine chunk of photogenic hunkitude.

She'd filled him in on her phone call to Simon earlier, so there was no reason to seek him out, except that she wanted to. And if she was going to fill up another memory card with cowboy pics, she wanted them to be of *The* Cowboy. The one who turned her liquid with a glance and made her want to forget that they were only *playing* at being husband and wife.

"Not right now," she told Ned, sorry to put a damper on his dreams of becoming a studly cover model. "Do you know where Ryder is?"

"In with Chynna, last I seen him." Ned started back toward his horse, and she waved goodbye as she made her way toward the stable.

She found Ryder in a back stall, running his hands over Chynna's sides and belly. Monica knew Ryder was concerned about the mare. She wasn't sure it had anything to do with the horse's health, just that she was close to foaling and Ryder wanted to keep a close eye on her. Of course, she couldn't help but notice the way he filled out a pair of jeans, bent over and facing away from her like that. The muscles writhing beneath his shirt were nothing to scoff at, either; she knew that from personal experience.

Forcing her mind back to less erotic thoughts, she cleared her throat and asked, "How is she?"

Ryder raised his head and straightened. He continued to stroke Chynna's silky coat while taking in Monica's attire in one swift up and down glance. She was wearing one of his long-sleeved plaid shirts, tied in a knot at her belly, and another of those skimpy flowered skirts she picked up on their way to Hawaii. They'd fit right in at the beach, but out here amidst barns and horses, dirt and straw, the cute but awfully short swatch of fabric didn't exactly leave a lot to the imagination.

And he'd heard her out there talking with Ned. The kid had probably been drooling in his boots. Women in these parts tended to cover up a bit more, if only as protection from any number of outdoor hazards, so when one came into town displaying that much skin, men tended to notice.

He frowned. He didn't like the idea of other men getting all worked up over Monica. She was his wife, dammit. Other men shouldn't even be looking at her. Of course, he really couldn't fault them. The way Monica acted and dressed could make Gandhi throw in the towel, and if she were some other man's wife, it would probably take a lightning bolt to the eye sockets to keep him from appreciating her natural beauty.

With a silent huff of frustration, he patted Chynna's flank and moved toward the door of the stall. "Seems fine. She's getting close, though. Any day now."

"Really?" An excited smile broke out over her face. "Can you feel the baby and everything?"

He grinned back at her. Watching a foal being born always gave him that same feeling of wonder and exhilaration. "Yeah, wanna feel?"

He held out an arm for Monica, who looked at him strangely for a second before putting her hand in his. Leading her to the mare, he cupped her hand and ran it over Chynna's belly, using his own to guide her to the right spot. A sharp bump appeared under the flesh and Monica sucked in a breath.

"That's gotta be a knee or hoof," he said. The bulge moved, and he helped Monica follow it with her fingers.

"Ohmigosh," she whispered. "It's really in there." She shook free of his hold and moved to the mare's head, looping a finger through the horse's halter and nuzzling her face against Chynna's. "That's your baby in there," she said, as though the horse understood her words and didn't already know she had a thirty-pound colt or filly moving around in her belly.

A lump formed in Ryder's throat, and he had to stop breathing for a minute before he could swallow past it. Something about Monica clutched at him. Her open appreciation of a pregnant mare, her gentleness with the animal. Something. Whatever it was, it made him want to draw her close and hold her, protect her. Which he could do, if she'd just let him dress her in clothes a bit more appropriate to life on a horse and cattle ranch.

His eyes fell to her feet, and he rolled his eyes. She was wearing those same strappy little sandals she'd worn in Hawaii. And while he had a fair appreciation for strappy anything on Monica at the right time and place, standing next to a twelve-hundred-pound horse with open-toed shoes was just plain stupid. One wrong move and her foot would be broken—or worse.

"I'm heading into town," he offered abruptly. "Want to go along?"

She turned to look at him, surprised by his sudden, slightly off-topic question. "Can I stay here and play with Chynna?" she asked, continuing to stroke the mare's face and neck.

In those shoes, he didn't like the idea. Not one bit.

"What size shoe do you wear?"

Her brows knit. "Seven and a half, why?"

"What size pants?"

"Six to eight. Why?" she asked again, her confusion even more pronounced.

"Something like this will be great for the barbecue, but you keep running around half naked, in bare feet, and you're going to get yourself seriously hurt. I thought I'd pick up a few things for you while I'm in town."

He moved toward the stall door, resting an arm on its edge while he turned back to her. "If you're going to stay in here with her, watch your feet. She steps on you and you're liable to lose a toe."

Monica's eyes widened in alarm, and Ryder nodded in satisfaction. If she was frightened enough of the possibility of severed body parts, she'd be more cautious. After all, she wouldn't look that good with painted toenails if there were only nine of them on display, now would she?

Still, he felt the need to warn her further. "If she does clip you, try not to panic. Pat the back of her leg with one hand and lift her foot with the other, she should step right off. And I'll have Ned stick close to the stables. You need help, just holler."

Monica nodded, a little more solemn than before, and Ryder felt better about leaving her alone. If she had a healthy respect for the power of such a large animal, she'd be less likely to get into trouble.

"Would you mind if I take some pictures of her while you're gone?" She wrapped an arm around Chynna's neck, and the mare lowered her head, snuffling her lips against Monica's shoulder. "I mean, the flash won't scare her, will it?"

To be honest, he wasn't sure. Chynna was as tame a horse as he'd ever run across, but you never knew how an animal would react to something out of the ordinary.

"Come here," he said, gesturing for Monica to move closer to him.

She untangled herself from the mare and moved in his direction. Ryder reached out and turned her away from him, holding her by the shoulders.

"Take a picture." Monica craned her neck to look at him and he nodded. "Go ahead. We're at a safe distance, and I'm right here if Chynna doesn't like it."

From her reluctance, he didn't think she quite believed or trusted him, but she raised her camera nonetheless and focused.

He waited several long seconds for her to snap the picture and when she did, he felt her tense. But Chynna stood there, slowly chewing a mouthful of hay, no more bothered by the camera flash than she was by the flies buzzing around her tail.

"Guess that answers that," Ryder said. "Think you'll be okay while I'm gone?"

She turned to him, her face alight with pleasure. "Oh, yeah."

Then she turned back to Chynna, her camera flashing away, Ryder already forgotten.

• • •

"If you don't hurry up, I'm gonna go out there and tell everyone we can't attend the party 'cuz you're too horny and I have to help you use up this twelve-pack of condoms I just bought." Ryder leaned in the bathroom door and rattled the box of Trojans while his eyebrows did a lascivious little happy dance.

Monica glowered at his reflection in the mirror and continued brushing her hair up into a high ponytail. "You do, and I'm going to tell them that instead of seeing to your horses and cattle like a good cowboy, you turned the herd over to Ned and spent the afternoon boffing your fake wife. Which is why that twelve-pack is now down to only eight."

His brows stopped jiggling with one frozen high above his eye with curiosity. "Care to make it seven? I can run out and tell them you chipped a nail or something and are gonna need a couple more minutes to get ready."

With a snap to the last loop of her elastic ponytail holder, Monica turned and leaned her butt against the sink. "Darlin', with what I have in mind for number five, you're going to need more than just a couple minutes."

He moved into the room, set the packet of condoms

down on the edge of the sink, and rested his forehead against hers while his hands drifted over her hips and beneath the knotted underside of her top. Well, technically *his* top. She was wearing a different floral skirt than earlier in the day, but had opted for one of his western-cut shirts in a nice, mossy green that matched the leaves on her skirt but didn't clash with her toenails. Pinning the sleeves at her elbows and tying the tails to leave a few inches of midriff bare worked surprisingly well—cute and casual, while still being sexy.

She was saving the things he'd bought her today for later, to wear in the barn or for walking around the ranch. In addition to a couple pairs of functional denims and women's tees, Ryder had brought back a pair of shiny black, hand-tooled cowboy boots in town, which she suspected had cost him a pretty penny. They actually didn't fit too badly with the thick socks he'd also purchased for her—though she'd only gotten to try them on for about five minutes in the barn before he'd swept her into the house for a little afternoon delight. And now she was wearing the sling-back sandals that had gotten her through her entire counterfeit honeymoon because they better showcased her brightly polished toenails—the same Jolly Green Giant color she'd been sporting since she first arrived, which just happened to match one of the flowers in this particular skirt.

As his hands slipped over her derriere and his enthusiasm pressed against her stomach, he whispered, "You've gotta stop saying stuff like that. I won't be held responsible for my actions if you don't."

She let her head fall back while he nuzzled her ear. "You're the one who bought every kind of condom you could find. If you expect to finish off the ribbed and move on to the glow-in-the-darks, we have some serious work cut out for us."

Ryder gave a laugh, surrounded by a groan so that the sound came out strangled. "I really want to get to those glow-in-the-dark and mint flavored ones," he said with a lecherous grin.

Yeah, because—as he'd informed her when he first brought them home—she was going to be the one enjoying the tangy fresh flavor while he enjoyed her oral ministrations. Personally, she wanted to turn out all the lights and try the glow-in-the-dark ones to see what she could see.

"But I thought we'd use the ribbed ones first—for your pleasure, of course."

Although she didn't know how it was possible, his comical leer turned even more wicked. Sparks of desire and amusement danced in the depths of his ocean blue eyes.

"I've got news for you, cowboy," she informed him, trying to affect a cocky, hands-on-hips stance while his warm breath blew on the nape of her neck. "Your hands and mouth do a heck of a lot more for me than those tiny little grooves do."

A groan was his only response. He pressed a hard kiss to her mouth, then straightened and took a conscious step away from her. His eyes darted to the mirror behind them, and the corners of his eyes crinkled in amusement.

"As if the toenails aren't enough, you're going to give my parents a heart attack when they see that pink streak in your hair, you know." He didn't seem overly concerned, just cautioning.

"It's magenta, not pink." Monica touched the back of her head self-consciously, but didn't move to take out the hairband. Shocking his parents was the idea, after all. Not to the point of causing actual cardiac arrest, but just enough to have them questioning Ryder's choice of bride.

From the moment she realized she'd have to face his parents, as well as half the town, at a party in honor of what they thought was a bona fide marriage, Monica had been working on a plan to keep everyone at arm's length. She liked Ryder's folks, truly she did, but the fact remained that marriage to their son was only temporary. As soon as she got her money back from Matt, they would be getting a divorce, and she would be on her way back to Chicago. It wasn't right to let Jordan and Ruth Ann or anyone else think her relationship with Ryder was more than that.

And if it took shocking them, letting them think she was some chippy from the big city who didn't have enough stuffing between her ears to fill a pin cushion, then all the better. This way, they would be less heartbroken when she and Ryder split up. They could even save face by saying they'd known all along she wasn't Ryder's type, was too strange and flighty, didn't have what it takes to be a rancher's wife.

The bright green toenails and magenta hair were a start. What could only be seen beneath the hem of her shirt when she raised her arms ought to do the rest.

Ryder brushed a finger over a stray strand of hair at her temple. "Ready?"

She wasn't. Her stomach clenched in protest, but she forced herself to take his hand and follow him through the house.

A cacophony of voices reached them long before they stepped onto the porch. Picnic tables, along with other stray tables and chairs, had been brought into the yard for guests. Sawhorses with boards across them had been arranged as banquet tables, which bowed with the weight of a hundred covered dishes. Only the dining tables had been set up the last time Monica had been out here, then Ruth Ann had insisted she and Ryder go inside to get ready while she took care of the rest. Judging from the amount of food and the number of guests, Ryder's mother was a one-woman wonder.

Off to the far side of the barn, a fire blazed. And over that fire was a pig on a spit. The sight made Monica want to cry, so she averted her gaze and focused on the crowd milling about in front of the house. As soon as they spotted Ryder and herself, they began clapping. Before long, all eyes were on them and the applause was almost deafening.

Ryder pulled her against him, grinned from ear to ear, and waved to his longtime friends. Monica blushed, all but burying her face in his shoulder. She'd known this would be difficult, but lord! Any hopes she'd had of getting through the evening with a minimum of effort and agony were shot straight to hell. The night was going to be a disaster.

And not one person seemed to notice her toes.

Chapter Twenty-One

It don't take a genius to spot a goat in a flock of sheep.

"Monica, darling, I want you to meet some of our friends." Taking her arm, Ruth Ann led her away from Ryder and down the porch steps into the waiting crowd. Monica curled and uncurled her fingers, wondering if she could pull an *I Dream of Jeannie* and blink herself into a wine bottle somewhere. Spotting a man with a bottle of beer, she actually gave it a shot. When it didn't work, she lamely swatted at an imaginary fly to explain her squinting and strangely wrinkled nose to anyone who'd been looking.

Fine, so blinking didn't work. She doubted a nose wiggle a la *Bewitched* would do her any good, either. So she was stuck. Thrust into the welcoming arms of Ryder's friends and family. What could be worse?

With a motherly arm around her shoulders, Ruth Ann introduced her to a bridge partner, a town councilman, two of Ryder's old school teachers—one from elementary, one from high school—and about three of his old girlfriends. The myriad names jumbled in her mind, leaving her smiling like an idiot and praying she wouldn't have to remember them all later like the unfortunate contestant in some nightmare of a game show.

Ryder's old girlfriends seemed nice. And judging from their natural, down-home appearances, she wondered what commandment Ryder had broken to end up with *her*. The three women—*all* the women in the crowd for that matter— wore either demure sundresses or jeans and comfortable tops. The younger ones seemed to prefer low-cut tees with lots of glitter or rhinestones, but none of them were flashing too much boob or thigh. Their makeup, if any, was applied out of necessity and not necessarily to doll themselves up, and hairstyles ranged from short, nondescript pixie-like cuts to long, curly, and *big*, as in teased and sprayed to stay that way. And they all seemed very sweet and earthy and Midwest proper.

Monica felt like the polar opposite of every single one of the women Ryder used to date—not just on the outside, but inside, too. Getting his parents to hate her was *not* going to be a problem if these were the types of girls they liked their son to hook up with.

She was just thinking what a breeze this alienation bit was going to be when a tall woman with a too-many-hours-in-a-tanning-bed complexion and hair so blonde it could only come out of a peroxide bottle sauntered up to them on the arm of a boy about Ned's age. Half the blonde's age, that was for sure. Although Monica was still using the spray-on lotion to give herself a bit more color than usual, she was glad she'd taken it down a few notches since returning from Hawaii. She wanted to keep Josie from recognizing her as the much paler woman who'd crashed her wedding reception, not walk around looking like an old sweet potato.

The woman's white suede dress had fringe at the arms

and hem, and was eons flashier than anyone else's attire. It put Monica in mind of something Dolly Parton would wear. But then, Dolly could pull it off; this lady couldn't. That didn't keep her from reveling in her supposed superiority, however, and Monica disliked her on sight. Slaughtered creature carcass aside, the unnatural blonde was sending off vibes of hostility wide enough to wipe out half of Wrigley Field.

The Coppertone Queen smiled and her bleached white teeth were almost fluorescent against her pumpkin-brown skin. Monica resisted the urge to throw a hand up to protect her eyes from the glare.

"This must be Ryder's new little wife," she preened, and Monica nearly looked down to see if the woman's snipe had put a hole in her shirt.

Ruth Ann's hold on her shoulders tensed a fraction. "That's right. Monica, this is an old friend of Ryder's, Stephanie Phillips."

Score one for Ryder's mom, Monica thought as Ruth Ann's double entendre about Stephanie's age hit home, and the blonde bombshell-wannabe's mouth tightened. Monica was pleased to note the crevices that lined her lips as she frowned. Miss Snotty Pants ought to spend less time in tanning beds and more time suctioning cellulite from her ass to be put into those crater-like wrinkles.

A moment later, Stephanie pulled herself together and tugged her May–December date closer to her side as she pasted on another fake smile.

"Poor Ryder. No one in town ever thought he'd get himself hitched," she drawled in a bad *Gone with the Wind* imitation.

Stephanie's accent didn't sound like that of anyone else Monica had met from this area so far, and she'd bet dollars to donuts the woman had picked it up from binge-watching too many episodes of *Nashville*.

If she was trying to impress Monica, however, she'd missed her mark.

"Stephanie and Ryder used to date," Ruth Ann supplied nervously, apparently trying to protect Monica without making a public scene.

Ahh. It all made sense now. Monica laughed inwardly. Cattiness was nothing new to her. She was more than used to dealing with uptight anorexic bitches—or as the world liked to call them, models. Stephanie was inconsequential compared to some of the spoiled ice princesses Monica handled on a regular basis.

In answer to Stephanie's jealousy-laced statement, Monica grinned and hitched her hips to the side just enough to show Stephanie that she wasn't impressed. "I guess he just had to meet the right woman," she said with a definite inflection of ownership.

"And you're the right woman, hmm?" Stephanie's brows raised as she fixed Monica with a dubious, challenging glare.

"Well, I don't know," Monica said softly, not the least intimidated. "You'd have to ask him, but considering that he hasn't let me out of his sight—or out of his bed—since he carried me off to Vegas to elope, I'd say I suit him pretty well."

"Damn straight."

Ryder's voice came from behind her a moment before his arms wrapped around her waist. Ruth Ann's hold dropped from her shoulders as Ryder pulled her back against his body. His fingers slipped under the loose hem of her shirt and lifted it until her belly button ring was visible. Then he began toying with it in a slightly distracted, totally possessive gesture.

"I hate to break it to you, Stephanie, but I really did get married."

Monica almost giggled at the look of disgust and pure hatred that crossed the jilted woman's features. Leaning into the cradle of Ryder's body, she put her hands over his forearms and let him dally with her stomach decoration.

"It won't last," Stephanie hissed, pitching her voice low to avoid attention from the other guests. "She's just some freak show oddity that you want to play around with for a while," she said, casting a glance at Monica's hair—which she'd obviously noticed had a streak of color running up the back—to her pierced abdomen, bare legs, and green-tipped toes. "As soon as the novelty wears off, you'll wish you'd stuck to your own kind, Ryder. Mark my words."

Ryder's grip on her waist tightened and Monica swallowed. Not because this Dolly Parton knock-off intimidated her, but because what she said was most likely true. Even if Ryder didn't tire of her off-key personality, the marriage *would* be over. She wanted to smack Stephanie for being so right for all the wrong reasons.

"I wouldn't count on it, Steph," Ryder replied easily, though Monica could feel the tension in the corded muscles of his arms and chest. With a nod to the young man on his ex-girlfriend's arm, he said, "Why don't you take your Flavor of the Month home and tell him about the birds and the bees."

Stephanie's hackles rose visibly. Her padded shoulders went back, her chin rose in defiance. "Well, I never!" she huffed, the fringe of her dead animal dress waving like a flag on a windy day.

Monica chuckled. "Yeah, it shows," she muttered under her breath.

And Ryder let out a loud guffaw that had the guests' beer vibrating in their bottles.

Stephanie stomped a high heel-clad foot, then turned and stormed away.

"That was rather distasteful," Ruth Ann said with a sniff.

"But right up Stephanie's alley," Ryder added. "It was a mistake to ever date her at all."

Then he turned Monica until she stood staring up at him. "You okay?"

Genuine concern shone on his face, and she smiled reassuringly. "With the exception of probably making an enemy for life, I think I came out of it relatively unscathed."

Ruth Ann patted her arm. "Count yourself fortunate, dear. That woman makes no better a friend than she does an enemy. You're better off without her around." She looked pointedly at her son. "Both of you," she stressed.

"Yes, Mother." One side of Ryder's mouth twitched up in a grin.

"Sorry about that little fib I told about how quickly Ryder and I got married after we met," Monica made a point of saying to Ruth Ann. Just because it was the truth didn't mean his mother needed to know that. It had just sort of slipped out, because she'd wanted so badly to put Stephanie in her place.

"No worries, dear. It's about time someone wiped the smirk off her face."

For a moment, they all stood there, not speaking, but sharing their small victory over the Wicked Witch of the Leather Dress.

"If you're finished introducing my wife around," Ryder said to his mom, "I think I'll take her over and get her started on dinner."

As they walked away, Monica heard someone behind her comment on the stripe of pink hair running up the back of her head. For a minute, her heart slowed in trepidation. Was this the moment everything would hit the fan?

Then she heard Ruth Ann's calm reply, as though the few simple words explained everything: "She's from Chicago, dear."

Monica didn't know whether to be impressed by Ruth Ann's easy acceptance or upset that no one other than

Stephanie seemed to disapprove of her yet, so she let Ryder lead her toward the trestle tables and hand her a plate to fill from the buffet. A real plate and real silverware; apparently Ruth Ann and every other adult female in town would have no part of disposable party supplies. Being slightly fanatic about non-recyclable waste, Monica had to commend the women on their environmentalism. There were no fewer than six mismatched sets of dishes put out for the guests. She would have to remember to offer her services when it came time to clean up and wash all the assorted dinnerware.

"You won't be able to eat all of this, even if you were a sideshow freak," Ryder said as he guided her slowly past all of the delicious-looking foods.

"She said 'freak show oddity,'" Monica corrected. "Not 'sideshow freak.'"

He chuckled. "My mistake." Then he leaned down close to her ear and whispered, "What's the difference?"

She shot him a withering glance over her shoulder as they stopped in front of a pan of baked beans. "One implies that I'm the Bearded Lady. The other merely suggests that I have a few too many body piercings."

"You mean like this?" he asked, giving her navel ring a little flick while he wiggled his brows suggestively.

"Exactly like that."

He dug a serving spoon into the baked beans and dropped a good-sized dollop on her plate. "Good thing she didn't know about the tattoo."

Ryder was lucky *he* knew about it, and she still didn't think he'd figured out what it said yet. He'd looked close, but not close enough. She smothered a laugh. Wait until the lights were on and he happened to have a magnifying glass in his hand.

Ryder moved to shovel out more beans and Monica looked closely at the serving on her plate. "What are those little brown specks?" she asked.

He put down the spoon and studied the beans. Then he picked out a piece of the questionable food with his fingers and popped it in his mouth. "Bacon," he answered. "Why?"

Her nose wrinkled, and she pressed her plate into his abdomen. "I don't eat bacon. Here, trade with me."

He took her dish and handed her his empty one. "Why don't you eat bacon?"

"Because it's an animal."

For the first time since she'd known him, he was struck speechless.

"You're not a vegetarian," he said, as though the word "vegetarian" was akin to "axe murderer."

"Sorry to disappoint you, but, yep, I'm a vegetarian."

He stared at her, totally flummoxed.

"Sweetheart," he whispered almost conspiratorially, "you do realize that I'm a cattle rancher. That means I raise cows and butcher them for meat. That's a pig over there, raised by one of our neighbors. You're not likely to find many meatless meals in these parts."

She crinkled her nose in distaste. Although she knew it was there, she couldn't bring herself to even look in that poor pig's direction. And while she'd heard several people comment on how good it smelled, she tried not to breathe too deeply because the scent of roasting pork made her nauseous.

"Yes, I understand that. But you're not a hopeless case. We'll work on it," she said with a pat to his stubbled cheek before moving on to closely study the rest of the dishes on the table.

While Ryder went right on eating anything and everything that had even the slightest relation to meat—just to vex her, she suspected, given the looks he tossed her way every time he took a bite of chicken pot pie or sawed on a big chunk of roast pig—she stuck with the three-bean casserole, peach cobbler, and anything else that wasn't created by way of animal suffering. And just to show him she hadn't given up on the idea of talking him into vegetarianism, she sat across the table from him, *mmming* and *aaahing* over every bite.

As soon as the plates were cleared and all the guests were groaning, practically unbuckling their belts, a band set up on a small platform near the old barn. Several guests moved closer to the band, turning the bare ground in front of the raised dais into a makeshift dance floor. Others remained seated, tapping their feet to the beat.

The music was blatantly country, which she wasn't all that familiar with. She knew some of the more popular country artists and songs that got airtime on Sirius XM's "The Blend" or whatever other Pop/Rock station she might end up listening to, but a lot of the more "down home" tunes were new to her. Even so, the band wasn't terrible, and her ears didn't bleed.

She thought it was especially sweet that they started out playing love—or at least romantic-sounding—songs, in honor of her and Ryder's newlywed status. The lyrics of the first song were about some guys having fame and fortune, but this guy having love, which made him luckiest of all. It was a lovely sentiment, even if it didn't suit Ryder's circumstances as much as everyone assumed.

Having eaten more than was wise, and feeling a little claustrophobic crushed between two guests on the picnic table's bench seat, Monica loosened the knot at the front of her borrowed shirt and smoothed aside the wrinkled material to hang open over the sleeveless crop top she wore underneath. It was one of the short tops Brooke had thrown in with her camera—as well as a few pairs of boy shorts for Monica to sleep in, not realizing she'd end up spending most nights wrapped around Ryder, both of them naked as jaybirds— and happened to be the perfect addition to her outfit. Not because it matched, but because it was her last-ditch effort to shock Ryder's friends and family. So far, nothing else had, at least not noticeably.

The band rolled into what she actually recognized as Keith Urban's "Blue Ain't Your Color," and she gave herself a mental pat on the back for that one. Then they started playing "Friends in Low Places"—an all-time favorite, judging by the cheers that rang out after only a few beginning notes. She might not know much about country music, but she didn't live in a cave, so even she knew who Garth Brooks was and was familiar with a handful of his songs.

She began tapping her foot in rhythm as more people got up to dance. The idea of crashing an ex's bash and telling him—Matt, of course—over a glass of bubbly to kiss her ass had its merits.

The thought of Matt brought her head around to briefly study the crowd. He and Josie had been due in on a late afternoon flight, and Ruth Ann had mentioned last-minute complications to their trip home, but it was almost seven o'clock and Monica had expected them to be here by now. Then again, maybe it was good that they hadn't shown up. Now that she'd contacted Simon and decided to keep her distance from Matt so he wouldn't get suspicious and try to move her money, the less time she spent around him and Josie, the better.

• • •

Ryder studied Monica across the picnic table as she watched the band. A slight smile lit her face as she fiddled with the front of the shirt she was wearing—his shirt—and he wanted to drag her away from this group of neighbors and let her strip for him. Maybe make love to her while she was wearing nothing more than one of his soft, cotton shirts. They had all those condoms to try out, after all.

Old Yancy Ingram and some of his friends, with Yancy's son singing vocals, rolled from a fast-paced Hank Williams Jr. song into Shania Twain's much slower "From This Moment."

Ryder reached across the picnic table and took Monica's hand from where it was busy fiddling with one of the small, round mother-of-pearl buttons on the front of the open shirt. "Come on," he said quietly. "Let's dance."

"To this?" she asked, glancing at him in surprise. But she stood before he'd even had a chance to answer.

"Unless you'd care to go inside and make a little music of our own." He waggled his brows suggestively.

She rolled her eyes and moved a step closer to keep their conversation private. "Number one: how do you manage to function on a daily basis with that sex drive of yours?" she asked loftily. "And number two: keep your voice down. We want these people to think we're madly in love, not that you married me just so you could legally jump my bones every five minutes."

He grinned and yanked her against his chest, letting his hands drift to the curve of her buttocks. "Number one: I function just fine—as I think you well know, given this afternoon's demonstration. Number two: married or unmarried, every inch of your body is a felony. And I don't give a baboon's ass who knows it." With that, he delivered a pinch to *her* ass. "Now let's dance."

He backed up enough to begin pulling her toward the dance area, but she pulled away for a second and quickly shrugged out of her shirt, leaving her in a short-waisted top with no sleeves and a scooped neckline that molded to her breasts like cellophane.

The fact that the top was scarcely more than a thin cotton undershirt raised Ryder's blood pressure enough. But it was the writing on the front that sent it skyrocketing.

There, in bold rainbow lettering that his neighbors could probably spot from a hundred yards, were four words that would kill his parents and have everyone else wondering if he'd married one of those "lipstick lesbians."

Chapter Twenty-Two

If women are foolish, it's because the good Lord made 'em a match for men.

GAY FOR A DAY.

Gay for a freakin' day. What the hell did that mean?

"You're trying to give me a seizure, aren't you?" he snapped, his eyes riveted on her bustline.

She looked startled and pulled her head back a fraction. "What?"

"First leaving the hair for my parents to see, then the announcement that you're one of those tofu-eating animal rights zealots. And now this." He ran a hand through his hair with impatience. "The belly button thing was my doing, I admit. You were keeping it pretty well covered, and I was the one who had to make that little power play in front of Stephanie. Okay, I'll take the blame for that one. But Gay for a Day?" His voice lowered so no one would hear. At least not those who hadn't already noticed the catch phrase emblazoned on the most eye-catching part of his wife's physique.

"You can't tell me you couldn't find another damn thing to wear tonight." Granted, she didn't have that many clothes with her—just what she'd stuffed in that equally ridiculous bag on the way to Hawaii and the things he'd bought her this afternoon. But she'd been wearing his shirts like she owned them. Why the hell couldn't she keep one on while his friends were around? If his father got a gander at this, he'd jump out of his wheelchair so fast he'd break his other leg.

She crossed her arms over her chest, which only managed to lift her breasts higher and frame the blazing motto. "Would you have rather I wore the one that says 'Meat Is Murder'?" she asked pointedly.

Her question momentarily stopped the rise of his anger. "You city folk just don't believe in wearing plain old plaid, do you?"

She lifted her chin and glared at him in defiance. "Nope. But they're having another gay rights marathon next year, if you want to come and get one of these for yourself. You'd probably be better off with the T-shirt version, though. I'm not sure you could pull this off." She flicked a wrist in front of her chest in reference to the much-too-appealing crop top.

His lips thinned as he watched her, running his tongue over his teeth while he mulled over her words. Then he burst out laughing, grabbing her up and kissing her hard on the mouth. In front of God, Mom and Pop, and every neighbor for ten kilometers. To hell with what they thought. Monica was one for the record books. And he was beginning to feel a fondness for dyed hair, navel rings, frog tattoos, and left-wing slogans that would have most people in town reaching for their shotguns.

He lifted his head, still grinning. "Meat is murder, huh?"

Her hands rested on his shoulders, and he was pleased to

note a slight dilation to her pupils, glad his kiss had put that glassy, absent-minded look in her eyes.

"Absolutely," she said with a nod.

With his arms wrapped around her waist and his lips at her temple, he asked, "So just how gay were you that day, Rapunzel?"

He felt her body shake as a laugh moved all the way up from her diaphragm. She leaned back to look in his eyes. "Wouldn't you like to know," she teased.

"Yeah, I would."

She gave a toss of her head, grinning at him wickedly. "Break open those glow-in-the-dark condoms and I might just tell you."

A bolt of desire chased down his spine, and he pressed close so she could feel how much he wanted to do just that. Right now. "Hot damn," he whispered.

He was about to suggest they ditch the barbecue when his mother strolled up to them. "Your father sent me over here to tell you that if you two don't break it up soon, we're going to have to hose you down." She smiled with motherly delight.

Ryder cast a glance over his shoulder and sent a knowing nod in his father's direction. Jordan was keeping a shrewd eye on them from his wheelchaired post near the buffet tables.

"We were just about to dance," he told his mother. "Care to join us?"

She laughed with amusement. "I don't think so. It's not safe to get between the two of you. You're sending off sparks."

Ryder chuckled and led Monica toward the crowd of dancers. As they moved away, he heard someone ask his mom in a low whisper, "Did her shirt say what I think it said?"

And Ruth Ann's unruffled reply: "She's from Chicago, dear. You have to expect these things."

• • •

Ryder and Monica stood on the porch, arms casually wrapped around each other like a long-married couple, waving goodbye to his parents. The party had finally wound to a close around midnight, but it had taken another hour to clean up all of the food and put away the tables, benches, and chairs. Luckily all of the townsfolk had stuck around to help out, and Ryder's kitchen was littered with every covered dish imaginable. Where his refrigerator had before contained only the bare minimum of milk and lunch meat, it now overflowed with half a roast pig, beans, cobbler, pies, chocolate-covered Rice Krispy squares, and some strange pink concoction that could have been a casserole or a dessert. They honestly didn't know. Monica suspected that, whatever it was, it would still be in there a month from now.

Josie and Matt never had shown up, but no one seemed concerned about their absence. They'd been on stand-by for a flight out of Honolulu, apparently, and couldn't be certain when they'd arrive home.

Monica and Ryder waved to his parents as they drove away, Jordan's wheelchair strapped in the back of the truck while he leaned against the passenger-side door with his casted leg stretched across the seat, his foot resting on Ruth Ann's lap. Monica turned her face into Ryder's chest to stifle a yawn as the truck's taillights drifted out of sight.

"So what did you think of your first full-blown barbecue?" he asked, stroking the back of her head.

"I think you people eat entirely too much meat."

"Yeah, well, you try roasting tofu over an open pit." He pinched her behind playfully.

She jumped slightly at the intimate tweak, but didn't move away. She was getting more and more used to Ryder touching her—everywhere and *all the time*. She kind of liked it.

"The music left a lot to be desired."

"You don't like country-western, I take it?"

She didn't dislike it, exactly, she just wasn't used to it. And some of the songs they'd played as the night wore on… well, they ranged from being hard to grasp or a little too twangy for her tastes, making her more fully understand the term "redneck."

"I liked your neighbors, though. They seemed really nice."

"They are. They didn't seem to mind that you were from the big city, either."

She scowled at him, even though her eyes were turning gritty with exhaustion.

"Your little plan didn't work, did it?" he asked quietly.

Her heart skipped a beat, and she had to swallow before she could speak. "What plan?"

"The plan to alienate yourself from my friends and family."

Her mouth fell open in shock. And then she managed a small gasp of indignation. "I don't know what you're talking about."

"Sure you do. If you'd wanted to endear yourself to them, you would have put on the jeans I brought back from town for you, left my shirt on over your gay rights statement, and worn your hair down to hide the pink streak. Since you made a point of wearing your hair up, repainting your nails that grassy color, and drawing attention to your political views, I figure you wanted them to take note of how different you are from the folks around here."

He turned her toward the house and guided her through the front door, closing it behind them. "I didn't catch on right away, mind you. I had a couple close calls about the hair and tank top before it all clicked." With a hand at the small of her back, he led her down the hall toward the bedroom. "But once I realized what you were trying to do, I also realized it wouldn't make one damn bit of difference. My folks are totally enamored of you. They think you're Betty Crocker and Marilyn Monroe all rolled into one."

Monica snorted in disbelief. "Yeah, right." The Marilyn Monroe thing she could understand. But Betty Crocker? No way.

"Doesn't matter," he said in answer to her silent thought. "I married you, and that's good enough for them. It also doesn't hurt that I can't keep my hands off of you, and they saw that, too." He slipped his hands down to cup her bottom and emphasize his point. "Face it, sweetheart, you could have a third head and they'd still adore you."

"A third head?" she shot over her shoulder with a frown. "Is there a second one somewhere that I don't know about?"

He swatted her behind. "Don't be a smart-ass—you know what I mean. Like it or not, you're stuck with us."

Only until we get my money back, she thought, but didn't put voice to the words. It surprised her how much the idea hurt. And how much the notion of being stuck with the Nash family *didn't* scare her the way it should.

The plan had always been to simply fake being married until she could get her money back from Matt and pay Ryder the amount she'd promised him. But could she help it that she was beginning to get kind of attached to Ryder? The man had hands that could make a statue blush. And he'd been entirely too sweet to her since they'd gotten back from Hawaii.

And his family...they seemed to accept her unconditionally, welcoming her with open arms. Regardless of her belly button ring and magenta hair and liberal views.

It made her feel like a fraud, and she wondered what she would have to pierce or tattoo to truly turn them off. She didn't even want to think about what would happen when she and Ryder announced that their entire marriage had been a sham. If people from this area still lynched, she'd be swinging from the nearest tree, that was for sure.

Two steps into the bedroom, Ryder darted past her and moved toward the nightstand. Straight for the condoms, she suspected. He'd made no secret of his raging libido. Monica suspected that if they hadn't been surrounded by a hundred people this evening, he'd have laid her down on one of the picnic tables beneath the moon and stars and given his new condom collection something to glow about.

Her heart sped up at the mental image. She'd have let him, too.

Even now, after hours of making pleasantries with virtual strangers and being so tired she could barely keep her eyes open, she wanted to feel his hands and lips on her skin. She wanted to be wanted the way Ryder wanted her—always.

It didn't bode well for her future. But Monica refused to think about that now. She kicked off her sandals and lifted the crop top over her head.

Ryder turned just as she was shrugging out of her skirt and tossing it into a corner. He cocked his head and shot her an appreciative grin. "I love a woman who can read my mind."

"It wasn't too difficult," she told him, walking across the carpeted floor and slipping her fingers into the waistband of his jeans. "You've been pressing your *mind* into my hip all night." Her hand grazed the bulge at his groin while she crushed her breasts to his shirt-clad chest. His mouth twisted in a lopsided grin. He was absolutely adorable when he knew he was gonna get some.

She took the packs of condoms from his hand and tossed them on the bed, then began releasing the fastening of his jeans.

"Ah-ah-ah," he *tsked* and caught her hands to halt their progress. "You are entirely too dictatorial in the bedroom, darlin'. How about you let me drive this time?"

"You drove last time," she grumbled. But a flutter of anticipation swept through her belly at his suggestion.

"No." His hands eased up her arms in a light caress. "I sat in the front seat, but you definitely drove."

She lifted her eyes to his face and stuck out her tongue. He leaned forward in a lightning-quick motion and caught her tongue between his teeth. She felt the pressure of his nip, but it didn't hurt.

Then he let go and said, "You'll put that to use later. For now..." He shuffled her against the bed until her knees hit the edge and she toppled backward.

He was still fully clothed. She was entirely naked. The scuff of his well-worn jeans rubbing the insides of her thighs caused an involuntarily shiver to course through her veins. Leaning into her, he brought her calves higher, toward his waist, and she locked her ankles behind his back.

"So which do you want to try first?" he asked, reaching behind her for the boxes of protection. Holding one in each hand, he shook them until the contents rattled, and waggled his brows at her suggestively.

She studied her options, then tilted her head to the side and met his gaze. "Which do you think?" she said, leaving him in no doubt that she had a definite preference.

He grinned and threw the mint ones over his shoulder. Then he handed her the condoms and began to strip. By the time he'd discarded his shirt, boots, and pants, she'd opened one of the small plastic packets and sat on the edge of the bed, patiently waiting to suit him up.

But when he finished, he took the condom from her and quickly rolled it over his rigid arousal. Grabbing her legs, he put them back around his waist and lifted her off the bed so that she rested above him, his arms and abdomen taking her weight. Her fingers drifted through his short hair, her breasts pressed against his firm pectorals.

He lifted his face, and she kissed him. His lips were warm and soft and tasted of the beer he'd finished just before they'd come in for the night. Loosening his hold a fraction, he let her slide an inch down his body. His penis pressed at the hot opening of her thighs. She moaned low in her throat, kissing him harder, grinding her tingling, sensitive breasts against his chest. With his palms on her buttocks, he moved her again, letting her glide onto his waiting erection. The sensation was so fierce, so carnal that she couldn't hold back a gasp of pleasure. Her mouth parted over his, finally letting air between them.

"The lights," she whispered.

Her whole being raced with building passion, electric shocks of need darting over her skin and through her very bone structure. But as much as she wanted to stay like this, to fall down on the bed and let Ryder begin moving inside her, she really did want to experience the full effects of his extra special condoms. She wanted to *see* them coming together.

Gripping her bottom more tightly, he walked across the room to the light switch. Every step, every motion of his body shifting against hers, had her panting in agonized pleasure. The movement forced him more fully into her damp heat until she couldn't bear it another moment.

And then he reached the doorway and flipped off the lights. The room went pitch black, and Monica had to blink several times to get her eyes to adjust to the sudden darkness. The flesh of her back, damp with perspiration, touched the wall as Ryder adjusted his stance, bracing them both.

His lips traced the line of her throat, his tongue darting out to touch her pulse points. He moved, drawing out of her slightly. She sucked in a breath. "Oh my God," she rushed on an exhalation of breath. Her cry echoed through the unlit room.

He thrust into her and then slid back out. Her nails curled

into his shoulders.

"Look," he commanded, and his voice sounded none too steady, either.

She glanced down and saw the greenish-yellow luminescence of the latex surrounding his penis. Her stomach clenched, she watched him move in and out, each stroke highlighted by the glow-in-the dark condom.

Finally, she couldn't take it anymore. She couldn't keep her eyes open, staring at the sight of their bodies coming together, of his piercing invasion as he drove inside her over and over and over. Squeezing her eyes closed, she let her head fall back against the wall and clutched at his biceps, tightening her legs high around his waist and tilting her hips to meet his thrusts.

Ryder's fingers gripped her ass, watching as his own hips surged against her, as they worked to reach the peak of ecstasy awaiting them.

"Now," he bit out in a rough whisper, and she felt herself building toward a shattering climax.

She gasped, her muscles tightening. He brought his mouth down to hers in a bruising kiss while the friction of their bodies rocking together heightened every emotion. He was plunging in a short, fast rhythm now, and she held him even closer as she stiffened.

A rush of sensation unlike anything she'd ever felt before exploded in her belly and she screamed. With one last driving thrust, Ryder shouted, too, and let himself hurl over the edge right along with her.

Some way—and Monica wasn't really sure how, nor did she care—Ryder managed to get them both back to the bed. He relaxed against the headboard while her cheek rested below his collarbone and her fingers drew lazy circles through the crisp blond hair on his chest. Under the sheets, her left leg was draped over one of his, and she honestly didn't care if she never moved again. She'd never felt so content, so absolutely boneless and comfortable.

Ryder wound one finger in her hair. "I'd say those things were worth the extra money," he commented softly. He let the curl fall loose before beginning to twist another strand. "I'll have to tell Walter they work real good."

She lifted her head slightly, making at least a partial effort to look into his eyes. "Who's Walter?"

"Owns the store in town. You met him earlier; he's a friend of Pop's. That was the first box of glow-in-the-dark condoms he'd ever sold, and he wanted to know how they turned out."

"Oh no," she moaned in mortification. "You mean someone at the party knew *exactly* what we'd be doing tonight?" She shook her head and buried her face in the crook of his shoulder.

"I'm pretty sure everybody had a clear idea of what we'd be doing tonight." His palm slipped from her waist to the curve of her hip and buttock. "We weren't exactly subtle."

She groaned and slipped farther under the covers. "I'm going to sleep now. Wake me when I won't be embarrassed to ever look another human being in the eye."

He chuckled. "I don't think I can wait that long," he said. Then he whipped the covers to the side and jumped out of bed.

Monica sat up, her spine straight, her lips pursed as she glowered at him. "What are you doing?" she all but snapped as he flipped on the overhead light.

"Exploring," he said, coming back to tower over her. "I want to take a closer look at this tattoo of yours."

Then he grabbed her ankles and gently yanked her to

the bottom of the mattress. She gave a yip at the sudden movement as she fell back and slid across the cool sheets.

"I know it says something," he told her as he knelt on the floor and spread her legs. "But frankly, I was just too damn preoccupied to care the last couple times I visited the area."

"Are you sure you're ready for this?" Monica asked, lifting her head slightly and feeling somewhat awkward at her position on the bed. She was far from shy, but it did feel kind of odd to have Ryder fixed on studying a decidedly private area of her anatomy as something other than straightforward foreplay.

That's what she got for having a tattoo put *there*.

"Let's see." He leaned forward, propping an elbow on either side of her body, his face so close that his warm breath ruffled the springy curls at the apex of her thighs.

"It's a little green frog with some kind of hat on, I can see that."

Her stomach clenched at his close observation, the heat from his breath sending shivers of excitement over her suddenly cool skin. "A crown. It's a frog prince. The hat is a golden crown."

"Ah, a frog prince with a golden crown. I'm beginning to suspect your obsession with fairy tales is rooted deeper in your psyche than I thought." The tip of one finger ran back and forth very lightly over the tinted skin. "First the hair climber thing, and now I discover my little Rapunzel has her very own frog prince painted in a very intimate place. Hmmm. I wonder what would happen if I kissed this little amphibian."

Monica all but groaned as his head lowered and he placed a soft kiss on her tattoo. So much for his inspection not being foreplay. She watched as he lifted his head, a superficial frown curving his lips.

"Nothing. Turning a frog into a prince with a single kiss

must only work when a princess does it."

He placed his palms on her waist and brought her lax body into a sitting position, his mouth pressed to the flesh around the ring in her belly button, his tongue flicking the little piece of silver back and forth erotically. She shuddered—literally shuddered—at his touch.

"Luckily," he continued in a low, somber tone, "I have my very own princess right here."

If he only knew what his words did to her. Her blood tingled beneath the skin, and her heart wept for his utter gallantry. She'd tripped over enough frogs in her lifetime; Matt was only one in the long line of slimy pond-dwellers she'd hooked up with. Ryder, on the other hand, was every hero she'd ever read or dreamed about, all rolled into one magnificent creature. If only he realized what he was doing to her very soul.

Ryder continued, his words bathing her in the warm glow of complete and utter pleasure. "And the only frog she's going to be kissing in the near future is me. I may not be a prince, but I am a pretty good hair climber. I've got the right boots for the job and everything."

She tried to smile, but the effort got lost in the feel of his rough palms on her sensitive skin. He put his hands on her torso and she leaned back, arching her spine as he slowly returned her to sprawl on the bed.

"But I'm getting sidetracked," he said. "I want to know what this little piece of paper in the frog's hands says."

He leaned close once again and began to read. Although her eyes were closed as she rested against the mattress, she could picture him squinting, trying to read the tiny print the tattoo artist had actually done a fair job of squeezing into the small space.

"If you can read this," he began slowly, reading off one word at a time. "There'd better be a ring on my finger."

Chapter Twenty-Three

Most everything you hear about cowboys is true. But the important thing is—they take care of the cows.

Ryder laughed. A big, gut-deep hoot, totally out of place in the subdued, sexually charged atmosphere surrounding them. Monica lifted her head and shot him a dirty look, which only made him laugh harder.

"You really were drunk when you had this done, weren't you?" he asked between chuckles.

She scowled at him over the inviting curves of her nudity. "My best friend and I had discussed the idea at length," she explained. "So even though I *was* intoxicated at the time, she was there to vouch for my wishes. And I was only drunk because I'd heard it helped to dull the pain."

He didn't see a hint of betrayal in her eyes, but he knew she was trying to feed him soup in stew's clothing. "Liar."

At that, she pushed up on her elbows, brows knit in affront. "I am not lying."

"The first time you mentioned your tattoo, you were

asking me if you'd gotten *another* one because that's what you'd done the last time you got drunk."

She looked thoroughly chastised. "Okay, so I was already drunk. But Brooke and I *had* discussed the idea beforehand. I just don't think I'd have gone through with such a... *comprehensive* design if I'd been sober."

Ryder chuckled at her choice of words. Comprehensive was right. He didn't know how the tattoo artist had managed to get so much in such a small space, but he guessed Monica was lucky she hadn't gone in asking for something like the Emancipation Proclamation. She'd have probably gotten it.

"So what gave you the idea to post a warning *here*?" He pressed his palm to her bikini line.

"You're a guy," she said simply, shrugging a bare shoulder as best she could with both elbows flat on the mattress. "You know what your gender will do to get into a woman's pants."

"So you figured posting your land—so to speak—would cut down on the number of poachers?"

Her lips pinched together. "Something like that."

"I hate to break it to you, darlin'," he said, still smiling, "but once one of my gender gets to this point, they're not much in the mood for reading material—or following instructions." The smile that had turned up his lips since he first read her tattoo slipped a bit. "You haven't had much luck with men, have you?" he asked bluntly.

She shot him a withering glare. "Not much, no."

"So did you have this little caution sign before you started dating Matt?"

She nodded, still propped on her arms and craning her neck to meet his eyes. "He wasn't amused."

No, he didn't suppose Matt would be. He, however, got a mule-sized kick out of it. And he didn't want to think any more about Matt and Monica's sex life, so he refused to voice the other questions popping into his head about if and how often Matt had trespassed on her property.

Monica sat up then, apparently tired of arching her back to maintain eye contact. She draped her arms around his neck and ran her fingers through the hair at his nape. He moaned low in his throat at her light, erotic touch.

"Are you going to give me the third degree about my tattoo all night, or are you going to kiss me?" She closed her eyes and lifted her mouth to his, stopping only a fraction of an inch from his lips.

He smiled and wished she could see the wicked glint in his eyes. With the thoughts he was thinking, wickedness had to be shooting out of his every pore. "Oh, I'm going to kiss you, all right."

And then he broke her hold on his neck, pushed her down to the mattress, and threw her legs over his shoulders. She gave a squeal of surprise at his abrupt movements and her eyes shot open.

Now she could see the wickedness. And he didn't apologize for it. He merely smiled and lowered his head.

His mouth was a fraction of an inch from heaven when the phone rang, tearing through the hazy sexiness that had enveloped them from the moment they'd entered the house together.

"Son of a bitch!" he swore, and had never meant it more in his life. "I hate that damn phone. Don't move," he ordered brusquely as he slid her legs from his neck and moved to the nightstand.

"What?" he barked, not the least bit concerned about who was on the other line. God help the man, woman, or child who called at two in the morning, when he was just about to make his wife scream in octaves even dogs wouldn't hear.

As soon as the person on the other end of the line began to speak, he knew exactly who it was and why they were phoning so late.

"I'll be right there," he said, the last of his words cut off as he hung up. "That was Ned," he told Monica, barely sparing her a glance as he moved across the room. "Chynna's in labor."

Monica sat up, dazed, confused, and more than a little offended by the fact her husband's attention had been so easily sidetracked. It was one thing for a phone call to distract him while they were eating dinner; another thing entirely for him to be distracted during...what he was about to do.

And he just left her there. She could hear his footsteps moving down the hall toward the front door, and she was still lying naked in the middle of the bed.

A man and his horse.

Of course, she couldn't blame him. Chynna was obviously one of his favorites, and he'd been awaiting this moment for months. Rolling off the mattress, she began grabbing up her discarded clothes.

She yelped and nearly had a heart attack when Ryder poked his head back into the room. "If you're coming out, wear your boots and those new jeans I got you today. This'll be messy." And then his heels clicked their way back out of the house.

"Messy" didn't sound terribly inviting, but she did want to see this. She'd been absolutely enamored of the mare and her baby ever since she'd felt the foal moving around inside Chynna's belly.

Rushing around the room, she found the jeans and boots Ryder had bought for her and shrugged into the first shirt she found, which just happened to be the *Meat Is Murder* one she'd threatened Ryder with.

She felt like Annie Oakley, but ignored the awkwardness of the new boots (without socks) as she raced out of the house and into the horse stables. Ned was standing outside Chynna's stall, leaning on the door. As she approached, she saw that Ryder was inside, one hand on the horse's halter, another running over and under her belly.

"How's she doing?" Monica asked.

"Real good," Ned answered. "She just started, but Ryder likes to be with the mares the whole time."

That sounded like Ryder.

"What are you doing here, by the way?" she asked the young man, leaning against the swinging door and mimicking his stance.

"I stay in the back room whenever a mare's time is coming up." He shrugged. "I just live with my brother, anyway, and the back room is at least as nice as his trailer. Besides, if I didn't volunteer to do it, Ryder would be out here every night, probably sleeping in the straw next to the horses."

Watching Ryder, she believed that, too.

"I'd keep the rest of my opinions to myself, if I were you," Ryder warned Ned, never taking his eyes or hands off of the horse in front of him. "Otherwise, you might find yourself out riding fence for the next month."

Ned frowned at Ryder's back, then tilted his head and made a comical face at Monica.

She smiled. "He *is* a tad overprotective," she defended on Ned's behalf.

This time, Ryder did look at them—just long enough to scowl at her.

"You, too, Mrs. Nash," he warned. "I can come up with a much better punishment for your disloyalty." Then he winked and turned his attention back to Chynna.

They spent the next few hours in and out of the mare's stall. Ryder would leave the horse alone and stand with Ned and Monica, occasionally going back in to check her progress. He kept up his end of the conversation, but was obviously distracted, and Monica was simply entranced.

She'd never experienced anything like this before.

Her heart was beating so fast, she felt like her system was overloaded with caffeine. At one point, she raced into the house for her camera and began snapping pictures. Of Chynna, of Chynna and Ryder, of Ned (who was fooling around just to keep the mood light and to get Monica to focus her lens on him).

Monica was about to snap a picture of Ned walking on his hands down the middle of the stable's runway when Ryder came out of Chynna's stall and moved intently toward the back room. She peeked over the edge of the stall door and saw the mare lying on her side on the straw-covered floor. Alarm shot through Monica.

"Is she all right?" she asked Ryder as he returned, drying his freshly washed hands on a clean towel.

"She's fine," he answered briefly. "The foal's coming."

"*Now?*" Monica asked, her eyes widening partly in excitement, partly in trepidation as she leaned over the stall door to get a better look.

Ryder knelt on the ground behind Chynna and pushed the long strands of her tail out of the way.

Monica made a face. That wasn't exactly anywhere she'd be wanting to touch with her bare hands. Of course, Ryder didn't even blink as he set to looking and feeling around the area.

"Want to help?" he asked, shooting her a quick glance.

"Really?" she asked, already opening the door and stepping inside. At the last minute, she remembered the camera around her neck and turned to hand it to Ned, who was behind her on the other side of the wooden partition. "Here."

He lifted it to his eye and looked through the lens, his finger moving toward the button that triggered the shutter. She thought of warning him not to mess around with such an expensive piece of equipment, and then realized that for the first time in her life, she didn't care if a stranger was feeling up her best Nikon D5. She even hoped he got some nice shots of her and Ryder helping to birth a foal.

She turned to Ryder. "What should I do?"

"Just kneel by her head and talk to her. It'll keep her calm."

Monica shot him a disappointed look.

"Trust me, darlin'," he said with a slight tip of his lips. "You don't want to be on this end."

Watching where his hands were going, she decided to take his word for it. She went to her knees beside Chynna's head and whispered soft reassurances in the mare's ear while stroking her neck and face. Most of what she said didn't make much sense, but then, she didn't think Chynna would notice. Neither would Ryder, as focused as he was on his end of the situation.

Chynna's abdomen was contracting, visibly working to bring her foal into the world, and her body was twitching, though she didn't kick or twist hard enough to hurt anyone. Ryder kept flicking her tail out of the way as the baby began to appear; even Monica could see something emerging from her position at Chynna's head.

"That's it, baby. That's it, girl." Ryder was muttering nonsense words the same as she was, and little by little, the foal appeared. Although they were hard to make out, Monica thought she saw a hoof and then a tiny nose as Ryder pulled the sack away from the animal's face.

When the baby had been pushed out to its belly, Ryder got to his feet and hunkered down, wrapping his hands around the softball-size hooves.

"Stand back," he said, and Monica hurried out of the way, waiting and watching from the far wall of the stall. With a grunt, Ryder pulled the baby free.

And it was a good thing Monica had moved, because

only moments later, Chynna rolled to her feet and turned to examine her new baby, sniffing and licking the wet bundle still huddled in the straw.

Ryder checked the foal's nose and mouth one last time, then moved to the doorway. Ned handed him the same towel he'd dried his clean hands with earlier, and he began wiping away the blood and fluids that reached to his elbows.

"Oh my gosh," Monica sighed. "That was *amazing.*" She threw both hands over her heart and absolutely melted at the sight of mama and baby. "He is *so* adorable!" she gushed. "Slimy, but adorable."

Ryder chuckled, and she finally raised her head to look at him. She was crying and she didn't care.

"Give them a couple minutes and you can pet him if she'll let you."

"Is it really a him?" she asked. "Or is it a her?"

"It's a colt." And then, probably thinking she might not recognize the term, he added, "A boy."

Monica bounced on the balls of her feet, overrun with excitement. She moved toward Ryder, wrapping her arms around his waist.

He raised his arms high and took a step back, away from her. "You don't want to do that, sweetheart. I'm a mess."

"I don't care," she said emphatically and took the last step necessary to press herself to his solid form. She rested her head on his chest and when Ryder refused to lower his arm, she reached up to do it for him, draping it over her shoulder.

Everything they were wearing could be washed. She didn't care if their clothes had to be burned, she wasn't going to let a single thing ruin this moment. This was even worth putting a halt to what they'd been doing in the bedroom.

When Ryder pressed a kiss to the top of her head, she started crying even harder. Thankfully, they stood there long enough, gazes riveted on the newest addition to Ryder's stable, that her tears dried before he could see them.

Almost immediately, the foal started to get up, rocking back and forth, trying to get to his feet. It looked so sweet, Monica grabbed her camera back from Ned and began clicking shots left and right. She had plenty of extra memory cards stuffed in the tiny Velcro pockets on the camera strap, too, so she could keep at this all night.

Once mama had licked the baby clean and he'd gained his footing, he began to feed. Ryder moved slowly toward Chynna's head and let her nuzzle at his shirt before trying to pet her. She didn't seem at all inclined to snap, so he motioned for Monica to come closer. They didn't make a move toward the baby, but continued to stroke Chynna's neck and face.

"What are you going to name him?" Monica asked, watching in complete fascination as the colt suckled.

"I don't have a clue. What do you want to call him?"

She turned to him, surprised. "Me?"

"Yeah." He gave her a lopsided grin, then turned back to face the horse whose muzzle he was stroking. "You've been here all night, I figure you have as much stake in his name as anyone. What do you want to call him?"

"I have no idea," she muttered. Then she shot him her most brazen smile. "But you know I'll think of something fabulous!"

Chapter Twenty-Four

*Once her broken heart mends, a woman usually feels like a
brand new man.*

From that moment on, Monica spent all of her spare time
in the barn, playing with Chynna and the colt, and taking
pictures of everything in sight. She kept a slip of paper and
the stub of an old pencil in her pocket to keep track of any
horse baby names she thought of. The small dappled gray
foal was two days old now, and she had yet to settle on a name
for him. Ryder teased her about how seriously she was taking
this endeavor, but Monica knew that the perfect name would
come to her eventually. And she wasn't about to settle for less
than the best for her baby.

Chynna may be his birth mother, and Ryder may have
done more than she had to bring him into the world, but this
little guy was the first thing she'd ever seen born, and she was
staking her claim. And if her newest plan worked out, Ryder
would be more than happy about her possessiveness. He'd
probably wrap the colt in a big red ribbon and give him to her

as an early Christmas present. Monica was almost giddy at the prospect.

Being with the animals so much, watching Ryder and his hands at work, she had begun to think of what a great backdrop the ranch would be for a photo shoot. She'd already used several memory cards and downloaded thousands of pictures for herself, but she could easily see Calvin Kline, Tommy Hilfiger, or a magazine like *Mademoiselle* or *Glamour*—even *GQ*—sending models out and setting up an extensive layout.

She planned to call Brooke during her friend's lunch hour and see if she could get the ball rolling, toss the idea out to a few of her contacts. With Monica already here and offering to work the shoot gratis, at least one designer or magazine ought to jump at the concept.

"Thought of a name yet, Rumpelstiltskin?" Ryder came in the side door of the stable, marching toward her purposefully, and smiling.

She rolled her eyes at him and lowered the camera. "Rumpelstiltskin was the one demanding the queen come up with *his* name; he didn't actually have to think of any himself."

Ryder's hand settled on her hip. "Whoops. Guess I mixed my fairy tales again," he said before swooping in for a kiss. A long, hot, wet kiss that left her clutching the front of his shirt.

He was apparently making up for lost time. They hadn't made love since the night of little Nameless's birth, but not for lack of trying. Monica just hadn't been able to concentrate. They could be in the middle of some very pleasurable foreplay and all of a sudden her mind would flash to the colt, and she'd begin asking Ryder all kinds of questions. What breed is he? Who's the father? Where's the father? How did he get up and start walking so quickly? Why did you pull him the rest of the way out, was Chynna having trouble? Are any of your other horses expecting? When? Can I watch?

Finally, Ryder had simply given up on her and any hope of ever again getting lucky. He'd heaved a great sigh of resignation, rolled away, and snuggled up to his pillow instead. And Monica had curled herself around his back, falling asleep with images of her new foal in her head. Evidently, Ryder now thought that if he could just get her to settle on a name, she'd be less preoccupied in the bedroom.

When he lifted his head, she took a deep breath to fill her lungs with much-needed air and brushed the corner of her mouth with a fingertip, where she could still feel his touch.

"Rumpelstiltskin isn't a bad name, you know," she offered, thinking it might give him a bit of hope for the future of his condom collection.

One eyebrow quirked as he studied her. "You can't tell me you'd shackle such a small boy with such a big name."

She thought about that, and then lifted a shoulder. "We could call him Rumpy."

Ryder started laughing and soon she joined him. But the truth was, she kind of liked it.

"I was thinking of going over to Mom and Pop's for a bit. See if Josie and Matt have gotten home yet. Wanna come?"

A part of her did, just to put the screws to Matt again, but she'd promised not to do or say anything to put him on the alert, so she should probably keep her distance. She really needed to call Brooke, anyway, and if Ryder was at his parents' house, she wouldn't have to worry about him walking in on the middle of the conversation. If things went well, it would make a nice surprise. If they didn't, it would be less disappointing for Ryder not to know she'd tried to set up a shoot on his property in the first place.

"I don't think so. You can tell everyone I said hi, but I'd rather stay here."

"You just can't bear to be away from that colt, can you?"

"Nope," she said with a grin. Her fingers toyed with one of the buttons on his shirt while they talked. "See if you can get Matt to sign that card, as long as you're there."

Ryder had picked up a get-well card for his dad on his trip to town, and they both wanted to get a copy of Matt's signature, just in case it came in handy down the road.

"Will do." He wrapped his hand around the one she had on his chest, leaning in for another kiss. "I'll be back soon."

With a coy grin, she said, "I'll look forward to it."

He shot her a lascivious grin and patted her behind. "You should, provided you can get your mind off that damn horse long enough to do anything about it."

She stuck out her tongue, then said, "I'll work on it."

He disappeared through the open door while she remained in the barn, looking for more picture-perfect things to freeze-frame. After a few minutes, she made her way to the house for a snack and to put in a call to Chicago without getting distracted.

Brooke answered her private line on the second ring, and after assuring her friend that she was alive, well, still married, and still not sure what she was going to do about it, Monica launched into her brilliant plan to use Ryder's ranch as a backdrop for a fashion shoot. At first, Brooke acted as though Monica was suggesting they feed the already anorexic models diuretics. But as Monica described the layout of the property, the horses, and the cowboys—real, honest-to-goodness cowboys—Brooke began to warm to the notion and promised to make a few calls.

When Brooke began giving her a rundown of messages and vital information she'd missed so far during her absence, Monica had to scrounge around in a kitchen drawer for something to write on. She found some sort of thick pamphlet stuffed toward the back and began writing around the label with Ryder's address on it with the broken stub of pencil from the back pocket of her blue jeans.

After she hung up, she read her notes more carefully. Two weeks ago, she'd have jumped on them, returning calls posthaste and setting up appointments for the next few weeks. Now, they all seemed like things that could be pushed to the backburner. She wasn't in Chicago, and as long as no fires cropped up that she absolutely had to be there to put out, she didn't plan to rush back anytime soon. Everyone would just have to deal with that.

And she would just have to deal with the fact that her reluctance to return home had more to do with wanting to stay at the ranch—with Ryder—than it did with having to go back to her job of directing prima donna models and appeasing uptight designers.

But not now. She would think about that later. Now, she wanted to look through this newsletter addressed to Ryder. It was a Nevada Breeders' Association newsletter, filled with all kinds of interesting facts about horses.

Meandering out of the kitchen, she folded her legs beneath her on the wide wooden swing at the far side of the front porch, and settled down to read while enjoying the view and the slight breeze on an otherwise warm day. She found the information on the light blue pages in front of her enthralling, teaching her the difference between a stud horse and a brood mare; the best times, seasons, and temperatures for breeding; and the proper feed and bedding to use during pregnancy and birth.

It was fascinating. Before meeting Ryder, she'd never seen a horse close-up, never given much thought to the species one way or another. But suddenly, she couldn't get enough. She'd fallen in love with little Rumpy and Chynna and even found herself spending time with the other horses in the stable.

Her nose no longer wrinkled at the smell of Ryder when he finished working. She no longer minded her own ranch clothes, especially now that they fit half decently. And as much as she'd despised the chores when Ryder first tried to make her work off her debt, she now looked forward to helping him feed and water the livestock. She even enjoyed helping him clean the stables.

She still felt like Eva Gabor on *Green Acres*, except that she'd stopped longing for city life. Her head fell to her knees for a minute and she left it there, wondering when she'd fallen so very far from grace. If anyone had told her a year ago that she would end up on a horse and cattle farm and actually *like* it, she'd have probably had them arrested for slander. Brooke would die of laughter when she heard.

Monica closed the newsletter and had begun to stand when a caption on the last page caught her attention. *NBA, Inc.'s Eighth Annual "Best of Breed" Competition*, the header announced. *Win $25,000!* And below were three pictures of "sample" foals and a list of instructions for entering the contest.

Ryder would kill her. The entry fee was a thousand dollars. He didn't have a thousand dollars. *She* didn't have an extra thousand dollars to play around with. At least not yet.

But, oh, Rumpy could win. She just knew it. He was the most beautiful foal ever—how could he not win?

She scanned the rules anyway, the whole time thinking, *Yes. Yes. Yes.* Rumpy qualified on every count. There were a few things she wasn't sure about, but she could easily wheedle the answers from Ryder under the guise of a normal conversation.

They required photos from several different angles. No problem, she had that covered. So all she needed were a few vital statistics and the entry fee.

The entry fee was the hard part. But then, that's why she stayed such close friends with Brooke. Brooke was not only a barracuda in the business arena, but she had a heart of gold and backed up Monica's wild schemes on a regular basis.

Digging her cell phone from the pocket of her jeans, she tapped Brooke's contact for a redial and immediately launched into her reasons for wanting to enter this competition and why she would be such a good candidate for an advance against her salary. Truthfully, she just needed to make sure she didn't incur finance or late fees on her credit card after charging the fee to PayPal, if her checking account was getting a little low. And since she didn't know how long she'd be on the ranch or how any of this—Matt having her money, entering this contest, her relationship with Ryder— was going to turn out, it was better to be safe than sorry.

Laughing, Brooke agreed to make an early deposit to Monica's account to cover the Nevada Breeders' Association fee, but only after Monica acquiesced to doing a shoot that coming winter with a particularly hard-to-work-with designer who everyone else avoided like the plague.

That taken care of, Monica began filling out the paper entry form in the newsletter so she'd know which spaces she needed Ned's or Ryder's help to complete, and so she'd have all the correct information to copy when she filled out the entry online. And she would go to the barn next to take the necessary photos—because even though she had a million and one pictures of Rumpy already, she wanted to have lots and lots to choose from and make sure she had the perfect one to enter in the contest.

She chuckled as she filled in the space for the Foal's Full Name: *Ryder's Royal Rumpelstiltskin.*

Wait until Ryder heard about this—of course, she had no intention of telling him, unless she was holding a check for $25,000 at the time…

"I've got some bad news."

Ryder entered the stable behind her, and Monica jumped guiltily, letting her camera whap against her chest. It occurred to her a moment later that she was always taking pictures out here; Ryder wouldn't think it the least bit odd for her to be doing so now.

She really wasn't too good at this secrecy business, was she?

The frown on his face and his determined stride told her something was wrong.

"Matt skipped out on us."

She pulled back, surprised by his words, not fully comprehending. "What?"

His brow furrowed as he jammed his hands into his front pockets. "The jerk jumped ship. Josie is back at Mom and Pop's, bawling her eyes out. I guess they had a huge blowout about coming back from Hawaii so soon. Matt didn't want to cut the honeymoon short just to visit 'an old man with a broken leg.' His exact words, according to Josie."

Monica was frowning now, too. "I told you he was an ass." Quietly, she added, "Maybe it's best for Josie to find out now, instead of ten years down the road."

She raised her eyes, expecting Ryder to shoot her a withering glare. Instead—and even though he didn't look happy about it—he nodded.

"Maybe I should talk to her," Monica offered, straightening her shoulders. "One dumpee to another."

"Mom's taking care of her. I couldn't stand all that weeping and blubbering," he said with a small shudder. And then his eyes narrowed. "Aren't you the least concerned about our money? With Matt still in Hawaii—or Hong Kong, or Paris, or wherever the hell they were planning to go next— there's no chance of us being able to forge his signature if we need to in order to get your money back."

Monica almost laughed but instead stood there in stunned silence. Until he mentioned it, she hadn't even thought about the money. All that she'd gone through, all that *they'd* gone through, and the money had been the last thing on her mind when she heard about Matt's alienation of Ryder's sister.

She would have laughed if she didn't feel so much like crying. Because she was a total goner. She'd fallen in love—with Ryder, his parents, his ranch, his horses, his house... And he hadn't fallen back in love with her.

Oh, she thought he probably liked her well enough. He'd stopped scowling every time she said something he found perplexing and actually chuckled over her quirks now.

He lusted after her, definitely. But then, that was mutual. The two of them together...whew, they were lucky they didn't set off the smoke alarms in the middle of the night.

Love was something else entirely, though, wasn't it? As much fun as they were having, as much as he may have given up being angry with her for not having the money she'd promised, their relationship was still just a business agreement. He still wanted his money—*needed* it to keep this place running. And after spending so much time here, seeing how a ranch was and getting attached to some of the animals herself, she thought he darn well deserved it.

But that didn't mean she was foolish enough to believe that any of that translated to deep, genuine, or lasting emotions. She was a good way to pass the time until he got paid—not that she was complaining. As soon as that happened, though, she'd be headed back to Chicago and he'd stay right where he was, doing what he loved best...without giving her too much of a second thought.

Carpe diem and c'est la vie, she thought. She'd done plenty of seizing the day lately; now she just had to deal with the "such is life" part that often followed.

Fingering the lens of the camera around her neck, she

thought about the contest she was entering for him. Even if they won—and beyond her maternal faith in Ryder's Royal Rumpelstiltskin, she realized their actual chances were minimal with the number of ranchers likely to enter—it was only twenty-five thousand dollars, half of the fifty thousand he'd been expecting from her. And the winner wouldn't be announced for months, she didn't think. She hadn't actually checked, but she knew it would take the panel of judges quite a while to go through all the entries.

"We'll think of something," she said in a low monotone. "Maybe Matt will show up after he's had time to cool down. Maybe he really loves Josie and will come back to apologize."

She almost hoped she was right. Matt was a rat, no doubt about it, but she wanted Josie to be happy. Even with the man who'd proposed to *her*, left her practically at the altar, and run off with her money.

Ryder snorted, leaving Monica in no doubt of his opinion of the situation.

"In the meantime, I think I should talk to Josie." She started out of the stables, then noticed he wasn't following. She turned back to face him. "Are you coming?"

He hunched his shoulders and started after her reluctantly. "Fine. Just...try to keep her from blubbering all over me again. My shirt is still damp," he complained, pulling at the offending material.

"If you'd ever been dumped by a husband or boyfriend, you'd know sobbing is about all you can do for the first few days." Then she added ruefully, "Better bring a lifejacket."

Chapter Twenty-Five

Avoid becoming emotional over a jackass.

Josie did indeed blubber all over Ryder. And Monica. And Ruth Ann. And Jordan, who pulled her into his lap and held her as best he could over his hip-to-toe cast. She cried until her eyes all but swelled shut and her chest heaved with hiccupping sobs. She went through a full box of tissues just trying to stop her runny nose. They all tried to comfort her, but Josie was well and truly inconsolable. Her moods swung from being heartbroken by Matt's betrayal, to furious over his ungentlemanly behavior, and back again.

When they began taking turns out on the porch to get away from her distress, Monica decided something had to be done. She gently pried Josie away from Ryder's now sopping-wet shirtfront, tipping her head in a sign for him to go out on the porch with his parents—which he wasted no time in doing—and leading Josie back to the bathroom.

Closing the door behind them, she sat Josie on the closed lid of the toilet and soaked a washcloth with cold water.

Perched on the edge of the tub, she bathed Josie's face, wiping away tears and trying to cool the skin turned puffy by her misery.

"Can I talk to you for a minute?" she asked softly, handing Josie the cloth and sitting back on the tub ledge.

Josie quieted for a second and fixed her watery gaze on Monica. Then she nodded.

This wasn't easy, and she didn't know exactly where to begin. Or how much to tell her. But enough was enough, and at the very least, Josie deserved honesty.

"There are some things you don't know about me. About Ryder and me, and how we met."

Josie's tears subsided even more as she listened intently.

"I told you that I knew Matt in Chicago. That we'd worked together."

Josie nodded.

Monica took a deep breath, then pressed on. "That's not exactly the whole truth. I *did* know Matt in Chicago, and we *did* work together, but we were also engaged."

Josie gasped, nearly inhaling the washcloth over her mouth.

Closing her eyes briefly, Monica continued in a resigned, almost narrative tone, as though it was no longer her life she was talking about, but some other person's. It all seemed so long ago. BR—Before Ryder.

"Matt and I dated for quite a while. Then he came up with this idea for us to start our own magazine. He asked me to marry him around the same time, and I agreed—to both. He borrowed fifty thousand dollars from me as start-up collateral for the magazine, and I was going to be the head photographer. But the next thing I knew, I opened the *Chicago Tribune* and saw a picture of Matt on the Weddings and Engagements page. He was with another woman." She met Josie's eyes. "You."

Josie still looked stunned, and Monica didn't know if she could stop pouring out her heart now that she'd started.

"Needless to say, I was not a happy camper," she announced bluntly. "I was pretty much devastated. And furious. I ranted and raved and cried just about as hard as you've been crying all day. And then I grabbed my wedding dress and headed for the airport."

Josie's eyes widened. Monica licked her lips, realizing that in retrospect, her actions could be interpreted as just a tad over-the-top.

"I caught the next flight to Nevada and crashed your wedding reception."

"That was *you*?" Josie asked, her face paling as her mouth dropped open.

Monica cleared her throat before answering. "Yes, that was me. I apologize, by the way." Her fingers dug into the cool enamel of the bathtub. "I knew I'd be too late to stop the wedding or anything like that. I just wanted him to know that he hadn't gotten away with it. He hadn't run off to marry another woman with his clueless fiancée sitting at home with her fingers up her…nose. I was also a little tipsy at the time, I admit. I'd brought a bottle of champagne, and I think I drank it in the cab." She scratched the side of her head with chagrin. "I may have also consumed the contents of a rather large number of those miniature bottles of airline alcohol."

"I can't believe this," Josie muttered in stunned disbelief.

"I know. I'm sorry," Monica commiserated, covering one of Josie's trembling hands with her own. "But I wanted you to know what kind of man Matt is. I'd hoped he'd changed for you, I really did. Then when I heard he refused to come back with you… I thought you should know."

She gave Josie's cold fingers a squeeze. "Don't spend your life crying over him, Josie. He doesn't deserve your tears."

He deserves a good, swift kick in the butt, she thought, but refrained from saying so. Maybe in a few weeks, when Josie wasn't quite so distraught over her husband's abandonment.

"You mean…" Josie began quietly, her voice cracking. "You mean you and Ryder aren't really married?"

Monica sat back in surprise. That was the last thing she'd expected Josie to focus on. Matt's betrayal, yes. Her betrayal, yes. Her and Ryder's marriage, no.

"Actually," she answered, "we are."

Her eyes narrowing, Josie fixed Monica with a stern gaze. "What do you mean? If you were engaged to Matt before coming here, then you hadn't been dating Ryder. Had you?" Her voice rose on those last words, and her eyes widened with a look that told Monica her supposed infidelity put her one step lower than mule dung.

"No," she said slowly. "I hadn't been dating Ryder." And then she averted her eyes. "I hadn't even met Ryder before your reception."

"I don't understand," Josie whined in frustration, throwing her arms in the air. "If you didn't know Ryder, how did you end up getting married to him on the same day Matt and I married?"

Monica winced. "Did I mention that I was slightly tipsy?"

That caught Josie's attention for a moment. "Ryder wasn't," she pointed out.

Monica released a pent-up breath. "No, Ryder wasn't. It's a long story, Josie. Can we just say that Ryder and I made a deal, and that the marriage was part of it?" Her tone begged to be let off the hook.

"What kind of deal?" she wanted to know. And she didn't look like she'd let Monica escape until she'd heard the whole story.

"When Matt left, he took some money from me," she said. "The fifty thousand dollars I'd lent him for the new magazine, except there *is* no magazine."

Josie's gasp portrayed Monica's feelings perfectly.

"Somehow," she stretched out the word, making it sound like aliens had come down from Saturn and invaded her body, "while I was still inebriated, I offered to pay Ryder if he married me to help make Matt jealous."

"And my brother went along with it? That doesn't sound like Ryder."

"Apparently, I was very convincing." She rolled her eyes. "And even though he probably wouldn't agree to anything quite so crazy under normal circumstances, I think he saw my offer as sort of an answer to his prayers. He insisted we make it a business agreement—I invest in the ranch, and he pays me back once it starts turning a profit. You know how much he needs the money to repair the ranch after that tornado and to get the ball rolling on his equine therapy program.

"Anyway, when I woke up the next morning, I didn't give a fig if Matt was jealous or not, I wanted nothing to do with him. Unfortunately, Ryder and I had already been married and he expected his money. The same fifty thousand dollars Matt had run off with. So we've remained married, hoping to get the money back."

"How?"

"I don't have a clue. We got into Matt's laptop in Hawaii and got some account information, but unless Matt authorizes it, we don't think there's any way to access the account or transfer the money out. Since we know Matt would never willingly sign over fifty thousand dollars—or fifty dollars, for that matter—we were hoping to get him to sign a get-well card for your father so I could forge his name if we figured out a way to fake the authorization, but even that's out the window now."

Monica stood and began pacing the small confines of the bathroom. "I know it's stupid. From the very beginning, everything I've done has been ridiculous. My head should be hung in the Great Idiots of the World Hall of Fame. I wish I could click my heels together and have it all go away, but Ryder expects his money, and Matt is your new husband, and your parents think we're really married…" She shot Josie a pointed glance. "The never-break-up kind of married."

"So you don't really love Ryder," Josie said softly. Her eyes held the same pain as when she'd been sobbing over Matt.

Monica's spine straightened, and she folded her arms over her chest defensively. "I didn't say that."

"So you *do* love him."

Monica averted her gaze, looking over Josie's head, at the shower wall, into the mirror over the sink…anywhere but at Ryder's sister, whose scrutiny seemed to be drilling into the depths of her psyche.

"I didn't say that, either." But her tone softened and creaked the tiniest bit, and she doubted she was fooling anyone, least of all Josie. She just prayed her sister-in-law wouldn't press the issue.

"Matt's not coming back, is he?" she asked instead.

Returning Josie's frank stare, she answered honestly, "I don't know. But past experience doesn't lean in his favor."

"Why did he bother to marry me if he was just going to run off after our honeymoon?"

Monica knelt at her side, stroking a hand over her hair. She had her own suspicions about that, but wasn't sure she wanted to share them just yet. Ryder had told her that his parents planned to give Josie the cash equivalent of what her share of property was worth when she was ready to settle down or strike out on her own. Most likely, Matt had found out about Josie's fair-sized nest egg and decided to woo it out from under her.

Who knew why he'd gone ahead with marriage to Josie, but not to Monica? Given enough time, perhaps he would have married them both just to get to their bank accounts. Or maybe Josie hadn't been as gullible as Monica and he'd had to marry her to attain his goal. Either way, they'd both been used, and she could only shake her head at her own stupidity.

"Why didn't someone tell me he was such a jerk?" Josie cried, burying her face once again in the washcloth.

This question, Monica could answer. "Because they didn't know. Matt is a con man, a master manipulator. You don't know he's lying to you until it's too late. And then you're left feeling like the dumbest human being on Earth. That's why no one can stop him," she continued. "He moves so fast, you don't know what hit you, and he doesn't leave any proof of his deceit."

Josie mumbled something beneath the damp washcloth.

"What?"

She lifted her head and faced Monica with red-rimmed eyes, but no more tears on her cheeks. "I have his signature."

Monica blinked, not quite comprehending her words. "What?" she asked again, feeling like a definite runner-up for that Idiots Hall of Fame.

"I have his signature. You said there might be a way to get your money back from his account if you have his signature." She stood, tossing the wet cloth into the sink as she opened the bathroom door and marched down the hall. When they reached the front room, she began digging through the suitcases someone had deposited near the front door. Pulling something out of the pocket of a carry-on, she straightened.

"He'd already checked us out of the hotel when we got into the fight about cutting our honeymoon short. He signed the room receipt." She handed the paper to Monica with a flourish and the hint of a smile at the edges of her formerly turned down mouth. "Will it help?"

Monica stared at the page, seeing Matt's signature at the bottom, but still not quite believing Josie had solved her and

Ryder's problem so easily. "Yeah. I mean, it should." She looked at Josie. "Thank you."

A flash of pain crossed Josie's features before she quelled it and forced a smile. "I'm sorry about what Matt did to you. The money and the engagement. I'm not real happy about what he did to me, either," she said with a forced laugh. "I figure the least I can do is help you get your money back. That ought to tick him off well and good, don't you think?"

Monica returned her grin. "I should hope so."

Josie held her hand in the air for a high five. "Score one for the jilted brides."

They slapped palms and then wrapped their arms around each other, as much to celebrate their plan as to support each other's heartache.

The front door opened and Ryder peeked his head in. "I don't hear any crying," he shot over his shoulder to Jordan and Ruth Ann.

Josie sniffed and straightened away from Monica. "Women don't spend their entire lives crying over men, you know," she informed her brother tartly.

Ryder opened the door all the way and stepped inside, eyeing them—especially Monica—with trepidation. "What were you guys doing in the bathroom for so long?"

"Powdering our noses," Josie replied. "And discussing how much better off the world would be without *men*." She said the word like she'd meant to say "rotting dung beetle larvae."

"You don't mean me?" Ryder asked, feigning offense and putting a hand over his heart while one side of his mouth lifted. But he looked relieved that Josie was no longer beside herself with grief.

He moved next to Monica and put an arm around her waist, pulling her snuggly against him. "I'm your Prince Charming, right, darlin'?"

She rolled her eyes at Josie and fought a smile as she returned his dubious gaze. "I'm beginning to believe there's no such thing as Prince Charmings," she taunted. "Just evil witches and frogs that need a lot of kissing."

At that, his lips turned up in a full-blown grin to reveal his straight, white teeth.

"My thoughts exactly, darlin'." His eyebrows wiggled dangerously. "Frogs. And lots and lots of kissin'."

Chapter Twenty-Six

You know you're in love when there are only two places in the world—where she is and where she ain't.

"I can't believe you told Josie that our marriage is only temporary," Ryder huffed for what had to be the fifteenth time.

"Hush, I'm trying to work here." Scowling, Monica hunched even farther over the papers in front of her, continuing to trace, carefully trying to perfect her version of Matt's signature. Over and over again, she'd been practicing ever since they'd gotten home with the hotel bill Josie had given her. She still didn't know if they'd even need his signature for anything, but it felt like the only proactive thing she could do about getting her money back until some other brilliant alternative fell into her lap.

She'd even printed out a sample authorization form from the offshore bank's website so she'd know what they required for a transfer. And thanks to another conversation with Simon Farraday, she had a little more information than before. Still not enough to take any bold steps, but enough that she wanted to be ready if being able to forge Matt's signature came in handy.

"But now she knows." Ryder did an about-face and stomped back across the room, following the same path he'd been pacing since she first mentioned her small bathroom tête-à-tête with his sister. "She knows it's a fake marriage, and that you were engaged to Matt, and that you'll be heading back to Chicago as soon as we get this blasted money back from that bloodsucker."

Her fingers tensed when he mentioned Chicago, jerking the pen in the wrong direction.

"Dammit," she cursed. She pushed aside the empty sensation his words caused and focused on his antsy behavior instead. "Will you please sit down, you're driving me bonkers."

Shoving his hands into his front pockets, he dropped onto the nearest chair with a thump. "There," he said in a clipped tone. "Happy?"

"Ecstatic," she agreed, without lifting her head.

"What are we going to do about Josie?"

She tossed him a questioning glance.

"She *knows*," he emphasized again. "She'll tell Mom and Pop we're not really married—not planning to stay married, anyway—and then the shit will really hit the fan."

With a sigh, Monica threw down her pen and faced Ryder. "She knows the circumstances of our wedding, Ryder. It's not like we're mass murderers and she's going to turn us in to the FBI. And if she'd told your mom and dad, don't you think they'd have run the phone off the hook or kicked down the door by now? It took them all of three minutes to get here when they found out you were married…I'm guessing it wouldn't take them half that long if they found out you weren't."

Taking a deep breath, she picked up the pen again and bent back to her task. "Josie's husband just refused to come home with her from their honeymoon. I think she has a few more important things on her mind than how genuine a relationship we're involved in." Her hand shook as she spoke, and she held her breath to try to stop the tremors.

Ryder crossed his arms over his chest and leaned back in the chair. "She did give us the hotel bill so we could copy Matt's handwriting," he said. The first sensible thing out of his mouth since they'd arrived home.

"Exactly. She wants us to get our money back, even though she's wrestling with some pretty nasty demons herself right now. And to be completely honest, she didn't seem all that shocked when I told her how we came to be married." She shifted her shoulders in discomfort. "She just wanted to know how we felt about each other now."

She finished copying the signature just as she said the last and had no choice but to look up. Ryder sat studying her, a fierce expression on his face.

"And what did you tell her?" he asked in a low voice.

Monica swallowed and then quickly stood and moved to the refrigerator to grab herself a beer and pop the top with the magnetic opener he kept on the fridge. Yet another change she'd noticed since staying with him—she'd always opted for wine or a cocktail before, but now she found herself actually enjoying a cold brew once in a while. She'd also discovered that beer went well with the kinds of food Ryder kept on hand. Not meat, though; just because she wore blue jeans and drank Michelob Light didn't mean she was anywhere close to abandoning her vegetarian convictions.

After taking a nice, long swallow straight from the bottle, she answered his question in a low voice. "I didn't tell her anything."

Ryder was hot on her heels, following her to the fridge

for his own beer, then boxing her in against the counter so she was forced to continue when she might have otherwise let the subject drop. "I told her about Matt, and crashing her reception, and bribing you to marry me with a promise of large sums of cash…I didn't think the rest was any of her business."

"The rest?" he asked softly, standing so close she could feel the warmth of his body and the light exhalation of his breath on her neck.

Choosing to ignore him, she took another sip of beer and stared at the intricate pattern on his plaid button-down shirt instead. Her heart was beating too fast, her lungs so tight, she could barely breathe. How easy it would be to admit she had feelings for him, that while she hadn't told Josie she loved him, his sister had concluded as much, and Monica hadn't corrected her.

But what if he didn't share her affections? What if the only feelings he had for her were about the money she'd promised and the passion they shared in the bedroom? She'd never considered herself a coward, but where Ryder was concerned, she was terrified of finding out she meant absolutely nothing to him while he'd come to mean…so very much to her.

When his arm snaked around her waist to pull her flush against his chest, she tensed. Not because she didn't want him to touch her, but because she wanted it *too* much…and if he started to kiss her, stroke her, rev her up, she was afraid she'd open her mouth and confess everything.

"I asked you a question," he whispered above her ear. "What's the rest?"

She swallowed, still not meeting his eyes, and fought the urge to bare her soul. "What do you want me to say, Ryder? I'm doing everything I can to get your money for you. That's what you want, right? We get the fifty thousand dollars from

Matt's account, and you let me go back to Chicago. That was the deal."

She stopped talking before her voice cracked and bit her lip to keep the tears that were stinging behind her eyes at bay.

Dropping his arms, he stepped away from her. "Right. That was the deal. Thanks for reminding me," he said, turning on his heel and marching out of the house.

• • •

Ryder pitched hay with a fury that left Ned and another hand eating his dust. Literally. The air around them turned hazy and almost unbreathable as he forked pile after pile through the hole in the barn floor, into the barred cattle grate below.

That was the deal, huh? What if he didn't give a good goddamn about the deal anymore? How could she turn to molten lava in his arms and still talk about going back to Chicago with such cold indifference?

He dug into the pile of hay with such force that the tines of the pitchfork imbedded themselves in the wood of the barn floor. The jolt rippled up his arms and rattled his teeth. With a curse, he dropped the handle—which remained standing upright in the floorboards—and stormed out of the barn, leaving the rest of the job to the other two hands. They didn't say a word, correctly reading his black mood.

Yeah, he needed the money. He'd just gotten another notice from the bank, warning him about missing payments and threatening foreclosure. Another couple of months, and he could lose the entire ranch. Fifty thousand dollars would save his ass. And when Monica had been a stranger newly escaped from the local loony bin, letting her invest in the Rolling Rock in exchange for a fraudulent marriage hadn't seemed like such a bad idea; he'd needed the money, she'd thought she needed a husband, and no one was supposed to get hurt.

But now the idea of that damned money left a sour taste in his mouth. Sure, it would go a long way toward setting up the equine therapy barn, buying equipment, and repairing the damage caused by last summer's tornado. The back wall of the old barn still wasn't finished, and what was done leaned outward precariously. Sections of fence around his property were still weak and demanded replacement, adding the worry of losing stray cattle or horses to his already long list of major concerns. The entire equine-assisted therapy thing was up in the air, and until he built up his herd and purchased a couple studs—which cost a pretty penny, unfortunately—he couldn't even get his breeding operation off the ground. There was no money coming in, and no money to expand. He was stuck between a rock and a freakin' hard place.

But, dammit, he didn't want money to be the only significant thing between him and Monica. He didn't want her to think she meant nothing to him unless she could find a way to get the fifty thousand back from her ex...or nothing more than a walking ATM and a warm place to park his dick.

He cursed again, loud enough and foul enough that the mare on the other side of the fence laid her ears back. "Sorry, Lady," he apologized, giving her forelock a gentle pat before continuing his trek around the corral.

Although he couldn't remember his folks ever being in quite as deep a hole as he was at the moment, his parents' ranch hadn't always been as successful as it was now. He remembered how strapped they'd been a few times when he was a kid...a couple of disappointing Christmases and years when he and Josie both had to wear clothes until they were little more than threads and shoes with holes in the soles.

Yet they'd survived. More than survived—they'd triumphed. Together.

And if they could, then he could. Somehow. He'd make

do with a dilapidated barn, small herd of cattle, and only the already-pregnant mares in his stable. He'd sell off a couple pieces of equipment or saddles. He'd start giving riding lessons to kids and trail rides on the weekends. Hell, he could even sell one of the foals.

Not Chynna's colt, though. At least not until Monica wasn't looking. She'd have his hide if he sold the little man out from under her.

Half a smile tugged at his lips. She sure loved that foal. In fact, she didn't seem to mind ranch life nearly as much as she had when she'd first arrived. Her jeans and boots and the shirts from his closet that she adapted to her size fit like a second skin now. She didn't even bother wearing those strappy little sandals outside anymore, or the cropped tank tops that had every man in a five-mile radius thinking he was suffering heat stroke. And he caught her in the barn about eight hours a day, playing with the horses and snapping pictures on that damn camera that was always around her neck. He even thought he'd heard her call it Nikki once, but refused to ask if she'd actually named her camera for fear she'd admit she had.

So why was she in such a damn hurry to get back to Chicago?

She has a life, you dolt. The thought came out of nowhere and hit him in the gut like a two-ton dump truck. Of course she had a life. She was a big-time fashion photographer; her whole life was back in Chicago. And New York. And L.A. And probably any number of big cities and foreign countries. What could she possibly find appealing about his piddly little financially challenged ranch?

He tried not to be hurt, but the fact that she didn't find *him* reason enough to stay stung like whiskey over an open wound. He had nothing to offer her, yet he wanted her to stay. More than he wanted that cursed money. More than he wanted a thriving stud business or to fix the floundering ranch.

Monica was in the house right now, working at getting that money for him, and he didn't even want it anymore. Wasn't sure he'd be able to use it once he had it, not without getting physically ill. He would rather swallow his pride and ask his parents for help, even though he'd promised himself nothing would ever push him to that point.

So he wasn't going take Monica's money, no matter what. He'd rip up that damn "contract" he'd insisted on scratching on the back of an envelope outside the Chapel o' Love, and if Monica actually managed to get her money out of Matt's account, he'd just let her have it. Let her take it and go back to Chicago.

Dammit. He hadn't used one penny of that blasted money, and he already felt sick to his stomach.

• • •

Ryder stayed away from the house until dinnertime, and after practicing Matt's signature until her hand cramped, Monica kept herself occupied by going through every single photo she'd taken of Rumpy with an eagle eye for the "Best of Breed" competition. There were so many, she felt like Sophie's choice or Solomon deciding to split the baby. He was just too wonderfully adorable—how could she choose only one? Finally, though, she did. Praying it was the right one to enter, she uploaded it to the entry form, along with all the other information they asked for, and charged the thousand-dollar fee to her PayPal account.

She was giddy over the fact that she'd gotten everything done without Ryder's knowledge or even rousing his suspicions. And the whole time, she actually managed not to think too much about what had occurred in the kitchen before he'd stormed out of the house. She'd yearned to tell him how she really felt, but considering his obsession with getting enough money to keep his ranch in the black, she didn't think he'd appreciate her suddenly breaking into song and declaring her undying love.

Playing house while they waited for the payoff to come through was one thing. Keeping house after the check arrived was a different matter. One she didn't think Ryder would be too fond of. So she would bite her tongue and do her part to get the money for him. And if at all possible, she would help him even more by getting Rumpy to win the "Best of Breed" competition. After all, the grand prize would be another nice chunk of cash for Ryder to put into his beloved Rolling Rock. As much as it hurt to realize that was more important to him than she could ever be, she still wanted him to have the money and make a success of his dream to breed beautiful horses and run a successful ranch.

When Ryder came through the door and slapped his dirty leather gloves and hat down on the countertop, Monica darted around in the guise of fixing supper, wanting to look busier than she'd actually been. For most meals, they just dug into the covered dishes people had left after the barbecue. He finished off the meat-based fare while she picked at the few meatless courses. And once in a while she'd make rice or pasta to go along with the leftovers.

Ryder paused behind her at the entrance of the kitchen. Her lungs hitched, but she didn't turn. And he didn't say anything. After a moment, he continued down the hall to the bedroom, and she heard the water turn on in the shower.

She released a breath and paused with her hand on two plates in the cupboard. Oh, this was fun. A few hours ago, they'd been *this close* to locking themselves in the stable's tack room for a little slap and tickle. Now they were treating each other like strangers, using silence and avoidance to keep from talking about what was really going on.

But Monica didn't want to be the first person—the only person—to blurt out her feelings, when Ryder might not be thinking the same thing at all. What if he was worried about his sister's marriage, and getting the money back, and keeping his ranch running? What if she was the only one wishing their marriage was for real?

The shower shut off and Monica's lungs went back to giving her only a fraction of the oxygen she needed to function. No wonder her brain felt like oatmeal.

Setting the plates on the countertop, she began doling out portions of the food she knew Ryder liked. She didn't think she could swallow a bite, so she didn't bother putting anything on a plate for herself.

A minute later, Ryder came back from the bedroom, his clothes changed, his hair wet and curling at the ends. Their eyes met and her heart leaped. This was ridiculous. They were both adults, and adults did not go around walking on eggshells when a single conversation could clear the air.

What's the worst that could happen if I tell Ryder I love him?

Well, that was a no-brainer. He could tell her he didn't love her in return and was looking forward to the moment when she finally headed back to Chicago.

Okay, fine. It would hurt like another body piercing in a very sensitive place, but it wouldn't kill her. Matt dumping her for another woman hadn't killed her. Finding out that Ryder didn't have any feelings for her beyond enjoying her body wouldn't kill her, either.

Except that it might. Her stomach clenched at the thought. It sure as hell would feel like she was dying. But she opened her mouth anyway and started to speak.

"We need to talk," they both said at the same time.

The air stalled in her chest.

"You first," Ryder offered, making a considerate gesture with his shoulder.

"No, go ahead."

"You go first. Really."

"I'd really rather—"

Her phone rang from the rear pocket of her jeans, interrupting their argument about who should go first in a conversation they obviously didn't want to have. She thought about letting it go to voicemail, but what if it was important? And what if *not* sharing a moment of pure candor was best for everyone involved?

Pulling the phone from her pocket, she checked the Caller ID and sucked in a breath. "It's Simon," she told him. "I should probably answer."

Ryder nodded, crossing his arms over his chest and leaning back against the counter to wait.

"Hello," she answered.

• • •

Ryder studied her while she listened, noting every nuance of her face, every tiny change in her expression. She shot him a panicked glance, but even before that, he knew something was wrong. Whatever this Simon guy was telling her, it wasn't good.

"Okay. Yes, I understand. I know, thank you. All right. Thank you for trying, Simon. I'll talk to you soon."

Monica ended the call, setting her phone screen-down on the counter in a slow, almost dazed motion. She looked on the verge of tears, and all Ryder wanted to do was reach out and pull her into his arms. But since that hadn't gone well when he'd done it earlier, he resisted the impulse.

"What's wrong?" he asked. Only when it looked as though she might faint did he place a hand around her upper arm to make sure she stayed upright.

"It's gone," she murmured, moving toward the kitchen table with stiff movements until she could fall into the nearest chair.

He dragged another chair directly across from hers, sitting down and trapping her knees between his spread legs. Bringing her hands to his thighs, he covered them with his own. Her skin felt cool and dry, not at all like her normal warmth and vitality. He rubbed his palms back and forth gently, trying to speed up the circulation to her fingers.

"What's gone?" he asked softly.

She blinked a couple of times like she hadn't even realized he was there, then looked him straight in the face. "The money. The money is gone. Simon was keeping an eye on things, but there was nothing he could do. Matt cleaned out the account yesterday...or this morning, I'm not sure which." Her brow wrinkled, head shaking back and forth. She sounded dumbfounded and looked as heartbroken as though she had just foreseen the demise of the *Titanic* and then witnessed her prediction coming true. "It's all gone—every penny. There's no way we can get the fifty thousand dollars back now."

A part of Ryder was disappointed. It was her money, and no one had the right to steal it from her. Another part of him—the bigger part—was just kind of relieved. Yeah, it was a hell of a lot of money to lose, and the idea of Matt jetting off to Singapore or West Africa on Monica's dime didn't set well. But that money had started to give him an ulcer. He rubbed his stomach at the thought.

He opened his mouth to console Monica when she stood and mechanically moved toward the back of the house. For a minute he sat there, then he rose to his feet and followed her down the hall.

He found her in the bedroom, gathering panties and bras

and other assorted female apparel. Arms full, she brushed past him and walked across the hall into the guest room, where she hadn't spent a single night, despite the fact that her "luggage" from their trip to Hawaii still took up space on the mattress. She began stuffing the garments into that bag he'd hated when she insisted on buying it, but now he thought it kind of suited her, then picked it up and carried it back across the hall to his room. Moving into the bathroom, she began dumping toiletries on top of the clothes she'd just jammed in there.

Ryder watched all this, feeling as confused as he ever had in a woman's presence. He knew she was upset, so he didn't want to agitate her further, but he really wanted to know what in blue blazes she was doing. If he didn't know better, he'd think she was packing to go somewhere.

"What are you doing?" he asked as she exited the bathroom and moved back across the hall to the spare room.

She didn't answer him at first, and when she did speak, it was to say, "I left my camera equipment in the dining room."

What that had to do with anything, he didn't know, but he followed her anyway. She stalked down the hall, into the dining room, and over to the desk he used to take care of ranch business, where she must have left her camera after downloading more pictures of her favorite subject—the new colt she insisted upon calling Rumpy, even though he'd hoped she would come up with another name for him.

Brushing past him, she hustled back down the hall to the guest room, but when she tried to cross over to his bedroom again, he stepped into the doorway, blocking her exit with his spread legs, crossed arms, and what he hoped was a determined scowl. She was going to stand still for five seconds if he had to get his lasso from the barn and hog-tie her.

"What are you doing?" he asked again, more slowly and in what he hoped was a firmer, brook-no-arguments timbre.

Rather than fight him, she returned to her things on the bed, struggling to get her camera paraphernalia to fit in its bag.

"I'm packing," she said, and he could have sworn her voice shook.

So it looked like exactly what it was. What he didn't understand was *why*.

"Why?" he asked dumbly.

She stopped what she was doing and turned to face him. Tears glittered on her lashes and he was more confused than ever.

"You heard what I said. The money is gone, Ryder. Matt ran off with it—*again*—and we're not likely to track him down this time."

He gave a brusque nod. Yeah, he got that. "So? Why are you packing?"

Her eyes widened and she gave him a look that clearly implied he wasn't the sharpest tool in the shed.

"The money is *gone*, Ryder." She spoke slowly and enunciated each word clearly. He half expected her to hold up her hands and begin signing, in case he was both dumb and deaf.

"I understand that," he said with an edge to his voice. "What I don't understand is why you're packing. And stop looking at me like I'm the village idiot," he snapped, his glower deepening.

"I'm *packing*," she stressed, "because there's no money left to collect." She turned back to the bed and began punching things to make them fit, forcing zippers closed. "And our agreement was that I would remain here until I got the money back for you."

Swinging the strap of her camera case over her shoulder, she held the remaining bag in her other hand and moved forward a step. He didn't move from his sentry position in the doorway. If anything, he stance became even more rigid.

"I'm sorry I can't get the money I promised you," she said, then added belligerently, "but you can't keep me here."

Ryder clenched his jaw and pretended she hadn't just driven a redwood-size stake through his heart. He let his arms fall to his sides and took a step back, into the hall, out of her way. "I have no intention of keeping you here," he said quietly, the words like broken glass in his throat.

Monica wasted no time darting past him, and all he could do was stand there, watching her go.

Chapter Twenty-Seven

There's only two things you need to be afraid of: a decent woman and bein' left afoot.

Tears streamed down Monica's face as the screen door slammed behind her and she staggered off the porch toward the dirt drive leading to the main road. She didn't know where she was going or how she'd get there, she only knew she had to leave. *Now.* Before she completely lost it.

Already her vision blurred so badly she couldn't see the screen of her phone well enough do anything with it, and she needed to call...somebody. A cab or Lyft...or at least look online for the nearest bus station and schedule. She could walk that far, if she needed to. Especially since she was wearing the really comfortable cowboy boots Ryder had bought her and that she'd spent the past week breaking in.

Memories of her short time at Rolling Rock Ranch and how happy she'd been fewer than twenty-four hours before made her cry even harder, this time with a deep, shuddering sob that wracked her entire body and sent her stumbling on the gravel-strewn path. Taking a deep breath, she quickly regained her balance, determined to pull herself together before she twisted an ankle and got stuck here. Wouldn't that be lovely, to end up collapsed in the middle of the road, a quivering, blubbering mess.

She shouldn't be acting this way, not when she'd known it was coming. Just this morning, she'd stifled the need to tell Ryder she'd fallen in love with him. Why? Because she'd known this was how things were going to turn out! Even if she or Simon had somehow managed to get the fifty thousand back from Matt, this is still how it would have ended.

But, God, she wasn't ready!

She'd started to feel so at home here, to be so comfortable in these new clothes, around the animals and the ranch hands, even around Ryder's family and friends.

She wasn't ready to leave her little Rumpy—she wanted to stick around and watch him grow, find out if he won First Place in the "Best of Breed" contest. She wanted to learn to ride a horse and maybe watch another foal be born.

But most of all, she wasn't ready to leave Ryder. Not today, not tomorrow, maybe not a decade from now. Love suddenly seemed like such a paltry word for how she felt about him. She wasn't just *in love* with him, she realized; she was very much afraid she'd come to need him. Like she needed air, water, sunshine... He was strong and warm and dependable. She loved the little lines around his eyes when he smiled and the way his chest rumbled when he laughed. She loved the way he looked at her, like he truly *saw* her and wasn't the least bit disappointed in the view.

And the way he made her feel in bed... Funny that sex was the last thing to come to mind, considering it had come first and—she'd thought at the time—was the strongest tie she had to him and the only thing they had in common. They were positively combustible together, and she didn't think that would change if they made love every minute of every hour for the rest of their lives. A shiver of longing rolled through her and almost caused her to stumble again.

Wiping a sleeve across her face, she sniffed loudly and readjusted the camera bag on her shoulder so she could try again to use her phone. She was tempted to call Brooke just to have a shoulder to cry on while she walked all the way to town, but that didn't seem like the most expedient plan for getting away from this place and back to Chicago. And the sooner she did that, the better. She needed to be able to fold her arms and blink herself somewhere else now more than ever before.

She'd almost reached the mailbox at the end of the drive and had finally managed to look up the number for the cab company that had dropped them off after their return from Hawaii when a low rumble registered in her brain. Was it a sound or a feeling or both? Whatever it was reverberated slightly beneath her booted feet and sent her spinning around, afraid she was about to be trampled by a herd of runaway horses.

Instead, she saw Ryder's truck barreling toward her, throwing up a cloud of dust large enough to make her think he was being chased by a tornado. With a yip of surprise, certain he was about to run her over, she jumped to the side, arms wheeling as she dropped her camera and bag and fought to stay on her feet. But at the last minute, he stepped on the brakes and brought the pickup to a screeching, shuddering halt.

Climbing out of the truck, he slammed the door and rounded the hood, marching straight for her. "Where the hell do you think you're going?" he barked, stopping only a couple of feet away.

Not this again, she thought with a groan. Not when she'd finally managed to calm down enough to breathe through her nose and maintain a semblance of dignity. Picking up her camera and tote, she climbed back onto the driveway and tried not to let her voice quaver when she spoke. "I told you— home."

"So that's it," he said, shoulders lifting as he parked his hands on his hips and gave her an irritated look of outrage.

"What do you want from me, Ryder?" The words came out a lot more watery than she'd have liked, tears once again brimming her eyes. "I'm sorry about the money. I tried, really tried, to get it back for you. And if you want, I'll find a way to send you something to follow through on my promise to invest—payments, maybe. Or I can move to a cheaper condo, take on more work to build up the amount faster."

"Is that all you care about?" he demanded. "What about Chynna and the colt you claimed to care so much about? What about what we've shared these past few weeks?"

. . .

Ryder hadn't meant to sound so angry, but dammit, he was. Angry and hurt and so blasted scared to lose her, he was shaking with it.

Her gaze snapped to his and he saw the confusion in her eyes.

"I don't... I'm not..." Monica started, then stopped, shaking her head and letting both her camera and tote drop to the ground. "I don't understand. I thought you wanted the money. That's the only reason I was staying here. Now that I can't get it for you, I thought you'd want me to leave as soon as possible."

"Yeah, well...maybe I don't," he told her.

Her breath hitched. He saw her chest freeze, her mouth drop open a fraction. The muscles of her throat convulsed as she swallowed before she asked softly, "What does that mean, exactly?"

She sounded more fragile than he'd ever known her to be, like the wrong answer might break her. His heart pinched in his chest, because he knew how she felt, even if he'd never meant to be the cause of that pain or defenselessness for her.

Refusing to give in to the trepidation that filled his gut with broken glass and tightened like barbwire around his throat, he forced himself to tell her what he needed her to know, what he should have told her sooner. "It means you don't have to leave. I can't stop you if you want to go, I know that, but I wouldn't turn you away if you wanted to stay."

Ryder held his breath, half hoping she would launch herself into his arms so they could go back to the way things were. No more talk, no more uncertainties, just teasing and laughter and lots of long, wet, bone-melting kisses. If she wanted to return to Chicago, he shouldn't try to stop her—and he wouldn't. But damned if he could stomach the idea of a single night alone in his bed without at least trying to keep her with him—not after sharing it with the most beautiful, passionate woman he'd ever had the dumb luck to stumble across.

He was her hair climber, by God. He'd rescued her from the tower, and now she at least owed him a fairy tale or two of his own.

A long, tension-filled minute ticked past while she stared at him, not moving so much as an eyelash. Finally, her lips moved enough to ask, "What about the money?"

"Screw the money," he half growled. "You don't have to take off just because there's no fifty thousand dollars left to keep us together." Then, in a voice rough with emotion, he said, "Stay. Please."

She blinked a few times, as though she wasn't sure she'd heard him right. "Stay," she repeated, her own words sounding strangled.

He nodded, one quick, harsh motion of his head.

"Why?" she asked softly.

Dammit! Why did she have to talk so much? Why did she have to have an explanation for everything? Why couldn't she just hear him say "stay" and stay, for chrissake?

"Why do I need a reason?" he snapped, frustrated. "Why can't you just stay because I asked you to?" Shoving his fisted hands into the front pockets of his jeans, he hunched his shoulders and rocked back on his heels. "We were doing just fine before that blasted money came between us again. We were getting along okay." He raised his eyes. "Weren't we?"

Monica nodded, wiping her palms up and down along her outer thighs.

"So why can't we go back to the way things were? Why does having the money or not having the money make a damn bit of difference?"

Licking her lips, she tried to get a grasp on what Ryder was saying, what she was feeling, and what he might mean. She couldn't stay just because he asked her to, no matter how much she might want to. She had to know that their relationship was about more than money, more than sex, more than jumping into an ill-planned marriage and deciding to stick it out.

"It makes a difference because..." Taking a deep breath, she steeled herself for what she was about to say. "Because while we were waiting to get the money back, I could tell myself we were just having a fun little fling. Enjoying each other's company until the check cleared, so to speak. I was taking a vacation from my regular life to play at being a rancher's wife. And having a good time, too," she added with a wobbly smile. She toyed nervously with the stitching at the side of her jeans and forced herself to go on. "But without the money...what do I tell myself?"

He studied her for several long seconds, until she wanted

to squirm under his close scrutiny.

"You could tell yourself that you really are a rancher's wife," he said at last, his voice harsh and gravelly, like sandpaper on concrete. The hands came out of his front pockets, and he began to clench and unclench his fingers. "That—money or no money—you belong here more than you belong back there."

He inclined his head to the side and she assumed he meant Chicago.

"There are people here who love you, dammit," he gritted out. "How can you just pack up and walk away from that?"

Tears stung behind her eyes and her heart skipped a beat. "I'm not worried about 'people,'" she almost whispered. "I'm only worried about you."

In a low voice, he asked, "What if I told you *I* love you?"

She squeezed her eyes shut, trying to block out the pain that she was surely opening herself up for. "Would you mean it? Really mean it, not just I-want-you-for-your-money or you're-a-great-lay love. Real, *real* love." Opening her eyes, she fixed them on Ryder's strong, handsome, beard-stubbled face. "The kind your parents have. The kind I have never known in my entire life. The kind that gets you through tough times and tornadoes and lousy ex-fiancés who run off with your life savings."

Damp trails trickled down her face now, but she didn't care, didn't bother brushing them away. This was a double-or-nothing situation. She was baring her soul, and she would either win the jackpot, or walk away with nothing but a broken heart.

She looked at Ryder and thought she saw a sparkle of moisture in his eyes, as well.

"It's the real McCoy," he said, and his voice cracked. "The kind that convinces you to climb castle walls and rescue a drunken princess because there's just *something* about her that you can't ignore. The kind that doesn't give a rat's ass if she has fifty thousand dollars to rebuild a broken-down barn or not. The kind that has you thinking it might not be so bad to leave the ranch once in a while and spend a couple months in Chicago."

His lip curled with derision on the word Chicago, and Monica laughed. She sniffed, wiped her nose on the sleeve of his shirt, which she hadn't bothered to take off before racing out of the house, then launched herself across the expanse of dirt road separating them, straight into his open arms. He hugged her to his chest in a vise grip, squeezing the air from her lungs.

"You have got to curb this impulsive streak running through your blood," he chastised, holding her close. "Crashing your fiancé's wedding and marrying the first man you meet to get back at him is one thing. Planning to run off and leave me just because you lost fifty thousand dollars is completely unacceptable."

She buried her face against his neck. "I'd have stayed if I knew you wanted me to," she told him. "Why didn't you say something sooner?"

"Because I didn't know if you'd want to hear it."

She pulled back, staring into his deep blue eyes, so open and vulnerable with his confession. "Why wouldn't I want to hear that you'd fallen in love with me?" she asked, completely incredulous. Only a man could think that was something a woman wouldn't want to hear.

"I'm not exactly a prime catch, sweetheart. The creditors are only about half a step behind me, with no windfall in sight. And I know you have a life back in Chicago. A very important life, with a very important career. I didn't know if you'd want to spend any more time here than absolutely necessary. But I meant what I said," he declared solemnly. "I'm willing to spend time with you in Chicago, or travel wherever your job takes you, whenever I can get away from the ranch."

She smiled and kissed him full on the mouth, her arms wrapping even more tightly around his neck. When she lifted her head, she said simply, "I love you, Ryder Nash. And it just so happens that I *like* living on your ranch. I like your barns and your horses and your family. I even like the smell of leather and cows on your clothes when you come in at night. And I most especially love my little Rumpy."

When he snorted at the name she was working hard to make stick to her favorite little foal, she tipped her head back and gave him a warning glare. "And for your information, I've come up with a way to blend your ranch with my auspicious photography career."

"Oh, yeah, what's that?" he asked, his lips quirking in a grin as he lifted her to dangle an inch or two off the ground.

"I invited a couple of magazines to do shoots here."

His smile fell, amusement replaced by concerned bewilderment. "You did what?"

"Cheer up," she said, flipping a little piece of hair away from his face. "They'll pay at least five thousand dollars per day, probably more, depending on how large a spread they have planned."

She continued to toy with his sandy blond hair, soft between her fingertips. "This is a good, good thing," she assured him. "And since I'll be the on-sight photographer, I won't have to go back to Chicago or anywhere else to continue my work. Not very often, at least. Besides, I've discovered quite a fondness for livestock photography."

Ryder threw his head back and laughed. Then he kissed the tip of her nose before moving on to her cheekbones and mouth. "I love you, my ever-resourceful Mrs. Nash."

He molded his mouth to hers, his tongue deftly sweeping away any doubts that might have lingered in her mind. Ryder loved her as no other man ever had. As no other man ever would. And after traveling from city to city for most of her adult life, she was finally, truly home.

"Rapunzel, darlin'," he said, raising his head and sweeping a hand behind her knees to lift her into his arms, hero-style. Leaving the truck right where it was, he started toward the house, his long strides eating up the length of the driveway much faster than hers had. "What do you say we explore some of those fairy tale fantasies you seem so fond of?"

She crossed her wrists behind his neck and swung her legs while he made her feel exactly like the princess he professed her to be. "Which one?"

"Start at the top of the list and name 'em off."

"The Emperor and His New and Quickly Discarded Clothes?"

"Uh-huh."

"The Princess and the Penis?"

"Uh-huh."

"Snow White and the Seven Erogenous Zones?" she suggested as they reached the porch.

He gave a snort of amusement, opening the screen and carrying her across the threshold. "Uh-huh."

Without missing a beat, he kicked the door closed with his booted foot and continued down the hall to the bedroom.

"Little Red Riding Him?"

He shot her a devilish grin and winked. "Yep, that's the one. We'll start there and work our way through the rest." Tossing her onto the bed, he followed her down, covering her with his weight and masculine warmth while his fingers went to work removing her clothes. "Then we'll pick a favorite and start again from the top."

Epilogue

Life isn't bearable with the opposite sex until it's unbearable without them.

This time, they were doing it right.

They'd set a date—exactly one year from their first wedding day—booked a reception hall, hired a DJ, and let his parents throw them an engagement party.

Ryder was in a tux and dress shoes—no cowboy boots this time around, at Monica's insistence. According to his bride, he looked good enough to eat, and not at all like a penguin.

He decided not to ask about the penguin remark and only hoped she remembered the "good enough to eat" part when it was time to leave for the honeymoon.

Monica was decked out in a brand new wedding gown. A simple, straight-cut, beaded dress that left her shoulders bare and fell a little too far above her knees for Ryder's peace of mind. It suited her personality better than the full-length, frilly dress she'd been wearing the first time they met, though, he had to admit.

And if anyone thought it odd that the couple they had known as Mr. and Mrs. Nash for the past year were back in church, not just renewing their vows, but getting full-out, no-holds-barred remarried, they refrained from comment.

Shania Twain's "You're Still the One" filled the crowded room while the bride and groom swayed back and forth on the hardwood floor in their first dance. Cheek to cheek, Ryder held Monica close and thanked the good Lord again for bringing this woman into his life.

Tilting her head toward the raised platform where his parents and sister sat at the bridal table, she asked, "Do you think Josie's having a good time?"

Her divorce from Matt had been final for only two weeks, and though she was doing an admirable job of keeping her spirits up in front of everyone, his bride seemed to think his sister was still heartbroken over Matt's betrayal and her short-lived marriage. And though Josie and Monica got along like twins separated at birth, it probably didn't help that he was very publicly remarrying the woman who had crashed her wedding all those months ago.

He glanced over her shoulder. "She's smiling. I think she's okay."

"I think she'll be better when they find Matt and prosecute him for embezzlement."

Monica, as well as several other people Matt fleeced over the years, had gone to the authorities to press charges. The police were now looking for him, but so far he had escaped their clutches by remaining safely out of the country.

Catching a glimpse of something in his peripheral vision, he touched his wife's shoulder and said, "Turn around for a minute."

Monica swiveled around and he lifted her loose hair over the backs of his hands, careful not to jar the pastel pink miniature roses and baby's breath that crowned her head.

"Just as I thought," he mumbled with amusement.

She turned back, her eyes sparkling with mischief. "I thought it suited the occasion," she said simply.

"Let me guess—something blue, right?"

"Your mother insisted."

"I don't think a stripe of blue hair up the back of your head was quite what she had in mind."

Monica shrugged and then once again leaned into their dance. "She just said I had to have all four things. She didn't give me specifics."

"So what are the rest?" he asked, his hand resting at the small of her back.

She held up her left hand, which now boasted four rings that together looked rather gaudy. But when he'd insisted on buying her new rings this time around—because, frankly, he wasn't overly confident in the quality of the first set—Monica had decided to wear them all at once. At least for today.

"Something old," she said, pointing to her original wedding band and diamond below the more recent set.

She placed a hand low on her abdomen and whispered conspiratorially, "Something new."

She touched Josie's strand of pearls at her neck. "Something borrowed."

"And something blue," Ryder concluded of her newly dyed hair.

Eighteen months ago, he wouldn't have willingly gone anywhere near a woman who drew wild stripes of color in her hair. Now, nothing about Monica shocked him. Not her hair or tattoo or navel ring. He loved her distinct personality, her touch of wildness.

At her urging, he was even considering an earring. He hadn't decided for sure yet, and if he went through with it, it would be only a small stud or hoop, nothing extravagant. And nothing as painful or low on his anatomy as she'd first suggested. The idea of putting a needle through his nipple, belly button, or...*lower* still sent shivers down his spine.

"Do you think we should tell your parents about the baby?" Monica asked quietly.

He shook his head. "Not yet. Mom can only handle so much excitement in one day, and I think she's reached her quota." He flashed a glance to just below the dais, where his mother was talking exuberantly with several guests. "We'll tell them later."

She nodded.

They separated a fraction when Ned approached them, an eager expression on his face. "Sorry to interrupt," he said, still dressed in the clothes he'd worn to work this morning. "This was delivered to the ranch a couple hours ago, and I thought it looked kinda important."

Ryder took the official-looking envelope and Ned turned toward the buffet table. Reading the return address, Ryder muttered, "How important could something from the Nevada Breeders' Association be?"

Monica gave a small squeak and grabbed the document out of his hands. Tearing it open, she scanned its contents and squealed again, throwing her arms around his neck.

"We won! We won!" she cried, bouncing up and down.

More confused than he thought a groom deserved to be on his wedding day, Ryder took the paper and read for himself. "Ryder's Royal Rumpelstiltskin?" he asked, arching a brow.

Monica stepped back, her face awash with delight. "That's Rumpy," she explained. "I thought it sounded regal."

And then she flattened the page and pointed to a specific line. "This is the important part. Twenty-five thousand dollars. That little horse you keep calling Stumpy instead of Rumpy just won you *twenty-five thousand dollars*!"

Ryder stared at her in patented disbelief. And then his eyes narrowed. He'd seen the entry form in his Association newsletter every year, but had never thought of entering, always lacking the steep entry fee, a suitable foal, or both. "And when, exactly, did your precious Rumpy enter this contest?"

"When he was only a few days old. He's a very advanced colt," she said with an air of maternal smugness.

Ryder chuckled, pulling her close for a hug as other couples flooded the dance floor and a faster-paced song began to play.

If he'd learned anything in the past year and a half, it was that his wife was an amazing woman. She'd brought in thousands of dollars by using the ranch for photo shoots, which had pretty much single-handedly kept them afloat. She helped pick out new livestock at auction, delivered foals and calves in the dead of night, steered the wheels of justice toward her swindler of an ex-fiancé just so no one else would be cheated by him, and in her free time scoured the internet for deals on quality equine therapy equipment. They weren't able to build the new barn just yet, but she'd wheeled-and-dealed her way into enough of the necessary trappings that when the time came, they'd be well ahead of the game.

Ryder thought he'd better watch his back or she'd oust him out of a job.

"I guess that just goes to show you," he said, swaying side to side with her to the low bass beat of the music. "We fairy tale folk don't need anything but a tower and a little bit of pixie dust. Right, Rapunzel?"

She laughed, letting him spin her in a circle in the middle of the dance floor. "I think you're mixing your fairy tales again," she told him. "Peter Pan is the one with Tinkerbell and pixie dust. Rapunzel just had the tower."

Ryder gave a deliberate, sensual smile. One he hoped got his point across loud and clear, because he planned to drag her out of here in another two seconds.

"Well, then…Rapunzel, Rapunzel, let down your hair." And he kissed her, long and slow like every good Prince Charming should.

Acknowledgments

An additional tip of my Stetson is owed to reader @MSmeowsie for the suggestion of "Nash" as the last name for Ryder and his family when I realized they needed a new one...

And to Rebecca Andrews for the Las Vegas maps and information, and for answering all my questions. Any mistakes or fudging of details are my own, because your help was invaluable.

Thanks a bunch, ladies!

About the Author

USA Today bestselling author Heidi Betts loves to laugh and bring a smile to others' faces whenever possible—which is why she writes fun and flirty romance. Often described as "delightful," "sizzling," and "wonderfully witty," Heidi's books mix sassy heroines with sensational heroes to create smexy tales of love and laughter. When she's not writing, Heidi is usually busy wrangling furbabies, encouraging readers to *Save a Horse, Ride a Cowboy!* or poking around online in the name of "research."

The next time *you're* online, take a minute to visit Heidi's hangouts and learn more about all of her fabulously sexy titles:

HeidiBetts.com (the website)
HeidiBetts.com/WIPSandChains (the blog)
HeidiBetts.com/newsletter (the mailing list)
Twitter.com/HeidiBetts (the tweets)
Facebook.com/FansofHeidiBetts (the posts)
Pinterest.com/TheHeidiBetts (the boards)

HANDLE WITH CARE
a *Saddler Cove* novel by Nina Croft

First grade teacher Emily Towson always does the right thing. But in her dreams, she does bad, bad things with the town's baddest boy: Tanner O'Connor. But when he sells her grandmother a Harley, fantasy is about to meet a dose of reality. Tanner spent two hard years in prison, with only the thought of this "good girl" to keep him sane. Before either one thinks though, they're naked and making memories on his tool bench. Now Tanner's managed to knock-up the town's "good girl" and she's going to lose her job over some stupid "morality clause" if he doesn't step up.

SCREWED
a novel by Kelly Jamieson

Cash has been in love with his best friend's wife forever. Now Callie and Beau are divorced, but guy code says she's still way off-limits. Cash won't betray his friendship by moving in. Not to mention it could destroy the thriving business he and Beau have worked years to create. But this new Callie isn't taking no for an answer. He's screwed…